Veronica Stallwood was born in London, educated abroad and now lives near Oxford. In the past she has worked at the Bodleian Library and more recently in Lincoln College library. *Deathspell*, her first novel, was published to great critical acclaim and became a local bestseller, as did the novels featuring sleuth Kate Ivory which follow: *Death and the Oxford Box*, *Oxford Exit*, *Oxford Mourning* and *Oxford Fall*.

When she is not writing, Veronica Stallwood enjoys going for long walks, talking and eating with friends, and gazing out at the peaceful Oxfordshire countryside from the windows of her cottage.

Praise for Veronica Stallwood's novels:

'Novelist Kate Ivory snoops with intelligence, wit and some nice insights' Marcel Berlins, *The Times*

'One of the cleverest of the year's crop [with] a flesh-and-brains heroine . . .' *Observer*

'Ruby rich on local colour . . . darker whiffs, some from corpses, soon arise' *Oxford Times*

'Kate Ivory is an appealing sleuth, the writing is literate and amusing and there's a nice stylistic touch . . .' *Scotland on*

Deathspell

Veronica Stallwood

HEADLINE

First published in 1992
by Macmillan General Books

First published in paperback in 1997
by HEADLINE BOOK PUBLISHING

10 9 8 7 6 5 4 3 2 1

ISBN 0 7472 5750 7

Typeset by
Letterpart Limited, Reigate, Surrey

Printed and bound in Great Britain by
Caledonian International Book Manufacturing Ltd, Glasgow

HEADLINE BOOK PUBLISHING
A division of Hodder Headline PLC
338 Euston Road
London NW1 3BH

For Annabel and Giles
with love

ACKNOWLEDGEMENTS

With thanks for their expert assistance to Emily Beacham, Sandra Dwek, Robert McNeil, Richard Thompson at Mahogany, and Peter Ward Jones.

Chapter One

Tess Farrell slipped out before the others were awake, stepping out of the warmth of the house into air like damp cobwebs. Below her the river mist drifted waist-high and the tops of the trees floated above it like disembodied heads, as she took the footpath up towards Bennett's Farm.

In the field to the left of her path they had harvested the wheat and baled the straw into cylinders, so that Tess imagined some huge beast rambling over the fields during the night, leaving its giant droppings behind it on the stubble before sinking beneath the skin of the earth to slumber during the day.

In the field on her right the wheat was turning from gold to a pale biscuit colour as the early sunlight burned through the haze, and from this field rose a ticking and rasping and clicking from the dry stems: he is stirring his limbs and twitching like a sleeping dog beneath his blanket of growing corn, she thought. On the headland the poppies were still blooming but fading from vermilion to a soft, deep pink, and there, climbing widdershins up a discarded chestnut stake, was the bindweed, its flowers twisting open as the sun touched their white petals. Tess dropped down on her knees to press her hands against the earth.

'I have to get rid of them, Dad. I have to make them disappear.' She stretched forward to pick four of the flowers. Surely it would happen if only she wanted it hard enough? 'Deasil for them, you said, but widder-shins for you and me.' The petals felt thick as silk as she put them in her pocket.

But now the August sun was growing warm on her hair and the magic was flying out of the morning with the dissolving mist and she knew it was time to return to Martenswood.

At six twenty-five the alarm went off and Malcolm Benson announced, '. . . meeting at the Bicester office at nine o'clock, and remind me to speak to the ferret,' as though dictating a memo he had begun the previous night.

'Ferret? What ferret?' Hanna's voice was blurred by sleep, her head still full of a dream of sunlit fields, larksong and the lovemaking of a faceless, but definitely exciting, man.

'Aren't you listening to me, Hanna?'

The satin skin and hyacinthine curls of her dream-lover slipped away as she swam up through watery layers of consciousness into a weekday morning. 'Yes, of course, Malcolm,' she said. Memory prodded a warning at the word 'ferret' as it paddled through the dark pond of her mind, but Malcolm's next words sent it sculling off into oblivion.

'And hurry up with my breakfast, will you?'

Nagging mode this morning, thought Hanna, as she

groped for the knob on top of the alarm clock and dutifully answered, 'Yes, Malcolm.' Her gummy eyelids parted on sunlight rippling through the bedroom curtains, skimming the layer of dust on her walnut dressing-table and revealing the fingerprints on the wardrobe mirror. As Malcolm returned to the even breathing of sleep, she slid from the bed, pulling the duvet up round his back. The clock was set to sound again in fifteen minutes when it was his turn to get up.

Three loads of washing this morning, she thought, as she crossed to the wardrobe and lifted a shirt from the small pile of clean, ironed ones, hung it on the wardrobe door, chose a blue and red paisley-patterned silk tie, draped it over the shoulder of the shirt, and stood back to gauge the effect. Five children, five problems; and she exchanged the tie for a green one with blue spots. She put out a white percale vest and boxer shorts and black woollen socks on the chair at his side of the bed. Well, maybe Harry and Aurora weren't so bad, but the other three were like a shrill background noise, she thought, finding a cleanish T-shirt, sniffing at yesterday's jeans and sweatshirt in the dirty linen basket and pulling them on.

In the kitchen, Hanna found that her elder daughter, Tess, was already up and sitting at the table, sharpening a black-handled chef's knife. She was wearing a green cotton dress that had fitted her well enough last year but now was a couple of inches too high in the waist and tight around the armholes. She looked elfin and waif-like, with her reddish-gold hair and odd, pale eyes. But what is going on inside her head? wondered Hanna once again.

'Shall I set the table for you?'

'Super. Thanks.' Anything to stop the child from sharpening knives. 'Have you been out already?' she asked, noticing Tess's scuffed sandals, dark with moisture.

'Just to check on things.'

'Check on what?'

Tess dealt bowls, plates and mugs out on to the table. 'They've cut the wheat in one of the fields, but left the rough bits at the ends. They call those headlands,' she said.

'Oh yes? That's interesting, dear.' Hanna cut bread for toast.

'And you can hear it ticking in the field.'

'It? What? Who?' Hanna was listening out for the buzz of Malcolm's electric razor. She couldn't quite hear it from the kitchen, but from the moment he switched it off and came bounding down the stairs, exuding a cloud of Eau de Vétiver, he would expect his toast to be ready, warm and pale golden-brown.

'I don't know what it's called, but it lives underneath the field. And if you put your ear against the earth, you can hear its heart beating.'

'No wonder your knees are so muddy!' Malcolm's toast had to be made from the sort of fresh white bread that she could never manage to cut into even slices. Her hand on the bread-saw hovered uncertainly over the loaf.

'He's full of power,' said Tess. 'Are you listening to me, Mum?'

'Of course I am, but I thought the spirit of the fields was female,' said Hanna, visualising a marble statue with overstuffed thighs and a heavy cornucopia. 'Demeter, is she? Gaia?'

Tess shook her head impatiently. 'Not that lot. It's different. Dad showed it to me. When I really want something, and I can't get it any other way, then I . . .'

But Hanna was hurrying out of the kitchen, alerted by masculine footsteps on the upstairs landing.

'I can't find my blue shirt.'

'I put your grey one on the wardrobe door.'

'But I wanted to wear my blue one with the white stripes and the white collar.'

Why did Malcolm look so funny in underpants and socks? Was it all the curly black hairs that clambered over his legs and chest and sprouted even on his shoulders?

'I'm sure it's in the cupboard,' and Hanna went up to look it out for him, relieved to find that it was clean, dry and ironed, although half-a-dozen others still crouched grubbily in the linen basket.

Downstairs again, she said, 'I think you should wear your boots if you go out in the wet grass, Tess. And what are you and Aurora going to do today?'

'Dunno.' Then she added, imcomprehensibly, 'I have to keep practising, you see.'

Hanna cut more jagged slices from the mutilated loaf, showering crumbs over the board and on to the floor, wondering whether to bake a batch of bread this morning: the smell was wonderful even when the bread itself was not.

'Mum?'

'Yes, dear?' Hanna was again listening out for Malcolm.

'Joe says Malcolm doesn't want us to go to the convent any longer. He says—'

Hanna sensed a change in the background noises of

VERONICA STALLWOOD

the house, and a creaking like a foot stepping on a loose floorboard.

'Just a minute, dear, while I concentrate on this.' She placed the blade of the bread-saw as precisely parallel as she could to the vertical surface of the bread and steadied the large white loaf on the wooden block with her left hand.

'But, Mum, Joe says—'

'Not right at this moment, please, Tess. You can see I'm busy. And anyway, Malcolm deals with decisions about your education now, not me.'

Tess sat very still and watched her mother. The blade had see-sawed its way halfway down the slice and now it had twisted so that it was gouging out a great hillock on one side and was perilously close to the surface of the loaf on the other. Hanna looked up to find Tess's golden eyes watching her, and she had the feeling that her daughter longed to wrench the bread-saw out of her hand and wield it herself, producing neat, even slices. She sometimes sensed the same desire, barely held in check, in Malcolm.

'Well?' she challenged her daughter.

'I'll do it for you if you like. I know how to use a knife. Dad showed me.'

There was something so unchildlike in that yellow gaze, that for a moment Hanna felt compelled to hand the bread-saw over, but she took hold of herself, grabbed back her slipping control and carried on producing uneven wedges and ramming them into the unwilling maw of the toaster. Then she realised that she had forgotten to make the coffee so she put the kettle on to boil and threw a couple of coffee beans on to the

6

hotplate so that the kitchen was filled with a deceptive smell of brewing coffee. Behind her the first batch of toast smoked blackly in the toaster.

Tess, meanwhile, was opening a tin of cat food and forking it out on to a pottery dish. Her arms were fair-skinned and sprinkled with a million freckles, like grated nutmeg across the top of a glass of warm, creamy milk.

'Here you are, Vinegar,' said Tess. 'Breakfast.'

A large black cat, with yellow eyes that matched her own, appeared from his basket beside the stove and bumped his bony head against her ankles before settling down to eat.

'I can't think why you call that cat Vinegar. What's wrong with Finnegan?' Hanna had hidden the first batch of toast in the outside dustbin and now ran to rescue the kettle as it seethed and spat beads of water on to the hottest part of the hob.

'Sometimes he's Finnegan, but other times he's my cat, Vinegar. I've ground the coffee beans for you,' she added.

Hanna poured the ground coffee into the expensive foreign coffee-maker, wondered what to do with the plunger, and filled the glass container with boiling water as Malcolm breezed in.

'Breakfast not ready yet, dear?' he asked triumphantly as he sat down and picked up the newspaper that had been placed ready for him, turning straight to the financial pages. His dark hair was shiny and smooth except for the strand that sprouted from his double crown.

Wrong tie, thought Hanna. When he had finished his first cup of coffee he said, 'Prices up another two point three per cent in the south-east this month,' and put down the paper. He helped himself to toast and spread it with Flora margarine and Tiptree marmalade. Tess watched as he fished out the thickest bits of peel from the jar to balance on his toast. She watched as he parted full red lips and exposed healthy wide-spaced teeth, then her eyelids blinked down in time with the closing of his jaws. Hanna watched her daughter watching Malcolm and wished that she wouldn't stare at him like that. You couldn't blame him for getting irritated with the child.

'Toast's cold,' said Malcolm, and frowned. A lock of hair edged forwards over his forehead to join the dark eyebrows. It was the sort of face that, with a strong and jutting nose, would have resembled one of the more successful Roman emperors, but in some celestial workshop a mischievous deity had pressed her thumb into the soft clay of Malcolm's nose and broadened and flattened the bridge. His chin, in compensation, was square and cleft.

'Going to get the place tidied up a bit today, Han, love?'

She hated being called Han. 'It isn't easy when all the children are home for the holidays,' she said, hearing the defensive note in her voice and despising herself for it.

'It's not that I'm criticising,' he said, drawing breath to continue.

'It sounds like criticising,' interrupted Tess. 'It sounds just like Sister Patrick when she catches you with an untidy desk before she sends you off to the chapel to say an extra decade.'

'—not criticising,' he repeated, 'I'm just helping your mother to organise things better by learning to delegate.

And,' he said, turning back to Hanna, 'that's just the sort of thing I dislike about that convent of theirs.'

'The nuns care about their moral welfare,' said Hanna, wondering why she was standing up for them.

'What's that?' asked Tess. 'That moral thing?'

'How to be good,' said Malcolm.

'But they don't teach you how to be good,' said Tess unwisely. 'They just teach you to be afraid of doing anything at all in case something awful happens to you. That's not good for you, is it, Mum?'

'I'm sure that isn't true, Tess.'

'And then they teach you that if you do something wrong, it's best to hide it so that you don't get caught.'

'Tess—'

'They don't mind if you doss around, as long as you pretend to do what you're told and don't make trouble.'

'What's the point of sending the girls to St Fred's if that's what they're learning?' said Malcolm. 'But let's get back to the point, shall we? What we were talking about was running this house. Organisation. Time management. Delegation.'

'What does delegation mean?' asked Tess.

Hanna turned back to the coffee machine. She wondered if she could top it up with a bit of boiling water or whether she'd have to dismember it and clean it before making a fresh pot. She still wasn't sure what to do with the plunger.

Behind her, Malcolm confronted his stepdaughter. He had been about to say that Hanna could organise the children into doing all the chores, but the level golden eyes with their thick black lashes were staring straight at him and he changed his mind. No child should have eyes like that. Most brown eyes were opaque, but hers were as transparent and as richly amber-coloured as golden syrup. And then he told himself he was being ridiculous: how could golden syrup make anyone feel nervous? He lifted the blue and white coffee cup clear of the puddle of coffee in the saucer and opened his mouth to suck in a mouthful. Tess's eyes were still following his every movement. He put the cup back in the saucer without drinking.

'I've been telling your mother to get a woman to come in and do the housework,' he said. 'You can see she can't manage it on her own . . .' and he paused for a second or two so that they could all register Hanna's inadequacy.

Perhaps, thought Hanna, putting the second pot of coffee down on the table and making a dark brown ring on the white surface, this was what Malcolm had been talking about at half-past six.

Malcolm went on, 'Old Dishpot used to—'

'Old *who*?' Tess's voice rose high on a note of joyful disbelief.

'Um, Dishpot. Sorry. It's the name I had for . . . Anyway, you've got to do something about the mess the place is in, Han. This is Fox Hill, not your Hampstead *Guardian* suburb.'

'But,' said Hanna, ignoring the joke, 'no one wants to cycle all the way up here to do housework.'

'Professionals, that's what you need. And, as a matter of fact, I got Janet to give an outfit called Technicleen a ring yesterday. They'll be in to see you about it this afternoon.'

'But you can't just ask someone in at short notice like that. I need time to give the house a good clean first—'

She broke off, for Malcolm was no longer listening, but staring instead at something on the other side of the kitchen.

'Just tell me,' he said, 'what that *thing* is, Hanna.'

'It's a mouse,' replied Tess.

'I can see it's a mouse. I want to know what it's doing in my kitchen.'

'We did mice last term at school,' Tess went on, helpfully. 'I'm sure it's a mouse because of its long tail and its large ears. Voles have much shorter tails and shrews have ears that are hidden in their fur. Whereas rats—'

'No, not a rat,' put in Hanna. 'A mouse. A *small* domestic mouse.'

'Right. Well, when you've all finished the natural history lesson, perhaps someone would explain to me what the hell it's doing here.'

'I thought it was women who were afraid of mice,' said Tess, watching Malcolm with interest.

'Who said anything about afraid?' replied Malcolm, too quickly and just half an octave too high. He aimed at a note somewhere below Middle C and tried again. 'And look at that lazy great cat eating his head off over there. Why isn't he chasing it?'

'Finnegan doesn't eat that much, really,' said Hanna, who rather liked small furry animals. 'His food only costs about two pounds a week.'

The loose skin on Malcolm's forehead fell into puzzled lines. We shouldn't be arguing with him, thought Hanna: it confuses him.

'Actually,' said Tess, 'I don't believe that is a house mouse at all. It looks more like a fieldmouse to me, which means that—'

'Shut up, Tess! I don't care what particular type of mouse this is, neither do I wish to know its name, nor its life history. I merely wish for it, and all its relations, to be removed from my house.'

'Oh, don't be so pompous, Malcolm,' said Hanna. 'It's only one small mouse, after all.'

'Just get rid of the thing, will you? Preferably before I get back from work this evening.'

Tess went over to where the mouse crouched, then gently picked it up, hiding it in her folded hand.

'I'll take her outside, if she's worrying you,' she said, and opened the back door before Malcolm could argue. He glared at the black droppings that were all that was left behind on the kitchen floor, then glared again at Finnegan who, having finished his breakfast, was now busy with his morning toilet, one leg lifted ceilingwards, his third eye staring anally at Malcolm.

'Well, let's hope these Technicleen people can get you organised. And look up someone in the Yellow Pages to come and clear the place of mice, OK? Don't worry yourself about how much it costs, just get rid of them.' He drained his coffee cup. 'I must get off; I've a report to go through before the meeting.'

Hanna jogged out to give him a farewell kiss. He would be cross, later, if he left without it: he had read somewhere that being kissed goodbye in the morning by your wife added five years to your lifespan.

'Goodbye, dear,' said Hanna, pecking at his left cheek, touching for a moment the springy hair at the back of his neck that awakened faint memories of desire. Then, as Malcolm threw raincoat and briefcase into the passenger seat and buckled himself into the seatbelt, she said bravely, 'Should I do anything about the ferret?'

Malcolm's brows drew together, and for a moment she was afraid that she had said something particularly stupid, but then they relaxed again. 'That's all right, I'm dealing with it this afternoon. I'll give you all the news when I get back.'

She turned the uninformative phrases over in her mind, but could extract no more sense from them than before. She would have to wait until the evening, she thought, as she watched the Volvo back impatiently out of the garage, spattering gravel against the door as it disappeared up the drive.

'What did he mean about seeing the Ferret?' Tess was at her elbow, pulling at her sleeve, her face screwed up with worry, and this time Hanna heard the capital F. 'It's not true what Joe says, is it, Mum?'

'Take no notice of Joe,' said Hanna, briskly. 'And I haven't a clue what Malcolm meant about ferrets.' She turned back into the kitchen to ruin another batch of food for the children's breakfast. Get the laundry sorted out into loads, she thought. Ring Anne Sutton about taking the children swimming. We're running out of cat food and toothpaste, but the Persil will probably last till the next trip to Tesco's. Tell the kids to tidy their rooms before they go outside to play. And the stairs need hoovering. Malcolm was right: she must organise, delegate. She would start by making a list. There was plenty of scrap paper lying around, but she couldn't find a usable pencil anywhere.

Upstairs, Joe was working on a large drawing that he had brought back from school at the end of last term.

He was good at art – the best in his form, in fact – and resented the way Mr Timms, the art master, criticised his pictures.

Joe worked in pen and ink, his drawings full of nervous details and swirling, looping lines like the tendrils of some hungry plant.

'Yes,' Mr Timms would say, standing behind Joe's shoulder, speaking slowly, as though he grudged the words of praise, 'very accurate. A nice, firm line there. A positive statement. Very mature style for an eleven-year-old, you could say.' But when Joe turned to look at him, he saw his shaggy head moving slowly backwards and forwards as though trying unsuccessfully to understand what he saw. And when he had finished studying the picture that Joe was working on now, he had reached out a stained forefinger and traced out the intricate pattern, saying, 'The subject I gave you was "A day at the seaside". So why have you drawn this . . . this thing?'

'But I have done what you said,' said Joe, reasonably. 'We went to the seaside at Easter. It was too cold to go in the sea, so we went for a long walk with Dad. And I've drawn the dead dog we found on the beach.'

He hadn't been able to understand the distaste on Mr Timms' face: it was good, this piece of work – he knew it. He turned up the volume on his Sony Walkman – Ozzy Osbourne sounded best good and loud – and picked up his pencil again. It needed just a little more cross-hatching to bring out the details before he took it in to show Aurora and waited for her to start screaming.

Hanna was eating cold blackened toast spread thickly with marmalade when she heard Aurora.

DEATHSPELL

'Stop that silly noise,' she shouted up the stairs. 'It's time to get up now, children. And don't leave a mess in the bathrooms,' she added, thinking of the coming inspection by the Technicleen person.

There came the sounds of opening and closing bedroom doors and the hissing of water in elderly plumbing, and ten minutes later the three boys and Aurora entered the kitchen.

Chapter Two

Martenswood broods in its leafy island, waiting for Miss Technicleen. No human sounds disturb its silence, just the humming of drowsy insects in the summer air and the occasional roo-rooing of doves. Its cream-coloured rendering is speckled with lichen and the weathered red tiles of its roof are cushioned with moss, but Martenswood was built in the first decade of this century and underneath its shabby exterior it is a solid and well-built house. Upstairs it still has its original sash-framed windows, but downstairs these have been replaced by modern units cunningly designed to look like the old ones. All the paintwork is a sun-softened ivory, except for the front and back doors, which are painted the colour of oxblood.

A paved terrace extends behind the French windows of the hall, and there are bicycle sheds and a greenhouse beyond the kitchen, and a garden shed beyond that. On this side of the house there is a paved area with room for a large rotary frame to dry Hanna's laundry, and there is a patch that the Bensons call their kitchen garden, and a loose pile of leaves, grass cuttings and rotting weeds which make do for a compost heap.

To one side of the gravel drive and extending around the sitting-room end of the house is a lawn, bordered by a rough shrubbery. This lawn is not, as you might expect up here on Fox Hill, lushly green and trimly edged, but long and unkempt, standing up golden in the sunlight like ripe barley, for this is 1987, the property market is booming, and Malcolm has been too busy so far to control his garden.

Malcolm feels obscurely cheated when Hanna fails to provide the right setting for his ambitions. She looked so right when he first met her, walking into the interview wearing something slim and black and classy. Her fair hair was brushed back from her face and pinned up in a knot, and she was wearing make-up. She had wonderful references, too (the result, he now realised, of her employers' eagerness to be rid of her), so he had expected her to be shit-hot at running the house. And then she had turned those dreamy blue eyes on him, and he had been lost. Now that he knew her, he realised that once the interview was over, her hair would have scattered its unfamiliar pins over the gravel drive and she'd have slipped off her high-heeled shoes and pushed her feet into something flat and disreputable to walk back to the bus-stop. But for the half-hour of the interview he had imagined his house looking like one he'd seen in a glossy magazine, and Hanna posed against it, with the cool stare and immaculate grooming of a fashion model. But, in spite of the copies of *Country Living* and *House and Garden* that he brings home every month, the interior of Martenswood still has the battered look of a house that harbours five children.

And what of Hanna? For her part, she just wants to

lie in the long grass with her eyes half-closed against the sunlight and watch the children playing some gentle game, while the smell of baking bread drifts out from the kitchen and envelops them all. She has yet to experience such an idyll – and where on earth, she wonders, are the children on this particular afternoon, anyway?

She stands in one of the bedrooms at the top of the house, looking out across the garden towards Oxford. In spite of her early start, the sunlight holds up veils of dust in every room, and discarded grey socks creep slug-like from under rumpled bed covers. She steps back from the window in case she is caught by Miss Technicleen twitching at the curtain like some suburban busybody.

Hanna longs to run away from the coming interview, through the meadows and up through Ruskin Wood to the sunny heath at the top of the hill, where she and Malcolm – a very different Malcolm, this, from the man who sulks if he can't have his clean blue shirt when he wants it – passed warm afternoons, with the white clouds drifting through blue skies behind Malcolm's head, and the air sharp with the scent of crushed bracken. Butterflies spiralled past like autumn leaves, and somewhere high above them a skylark sang its heart out. Malcolm's solid head and shoulders had blotted out everything else from her sight and, while the careless wind gushed through the trees, she had gladly succumbed to his unsubtle, but convincingly masculine, love-making. She had felt then, with a certainty that she now sees as naïve, that Malcolm would sweep away all her problems and stand foursquare in her life like a large friendly rock, hiding the past from view. She yearns to recapture that certainty. (She would like to recapture the satisfactory lovemaking, but hasn't admitted to herself that Malcolm's performance has been less scintillating since they were married, while her own enthusiasm has been flattened by exhaustion.)

And now, from the Oxford road, down the Gothic tunnel of the drive, comes the hiss and crunch of gravel heralding the arrival of a bright van – secondhand, perhaps? Refurbished and resprayed? TECHNICLEEN it says along its side in navy-blue letters.

Miss Technicleen cuts the engine and gets out. She presses the brass button in its white porcelain surround and waits. It is one of those unnerving bells that rings (if, indeed, it does ring at all) so far away in the depths of the house that it is inaudible to the visitor. The perspiration trickles down her back under the crisp whiteness of her blouse. Perhaps the bell has been disconnected and regular visitors to Martenswood know that you have to knock rather than ring. There is no knocker. She bends down, pushes at the tarnished brass letterbox, applies her eyes to the aperture, sees a creased pink skirt approaching and hastily lets the flap drop back into place.

Somewhere beyond the house, out behind the beech trees, shrills a cry as from some small animal being torn to pieces by a predator: a rabbit or a cat, perhaps, caught by one of the many foxes that roam the suburban woods. It is an eerily human-sounding cry, and Miss Technicleen holds her breath, half-expecting to hear it repeated, as the door opens.

'Are you Technicleen?'

'Jean Rainbird.' She put out a hand for Hanna to

shake. 'From Technicleen, that's right.'

'Oh, do come in. I'm Hanna Benson, by the way. My husband telephoned you. Or perhaps it was his secretary, Janet. But of course, you know that, don't you? I mean, that's why you're here. Oh, and I must apologise for the mess.'

'There's really no need to apologise for that,' said Miss Technicleen. 'You could say that other people's mess is my bread and butter. In a manner of speaking, that is.'

Hanna led her through the entrance tumbled with skateboards and cricket bats, across the wide hallway littered with discarded anoraks and the scattered pieces of a jigsaw puzzle. 'I just don't seem able to cope when all the children are at home from school at the same time,' she said. 'And do mind out for those roller skates. I've told Joe to put them in the playroom but he never does what he's told. Do you like children?'

'Umm,' said Miss Technicleen.

They were standing in the centre of the sitting room. Although Hanna had spent all morning picking things up and moving them out of sight, the children had covered all the empty spaces with a new layer of clutter. 'Do sit down,' she said, scooping up a heap of belongings and holding them like a large and misshapen infant in her arms before dropping them out of sight behind the sofa.

'Tea? Coffee?' she asked, hoping to distract the professional eye from the large stain – something liquid and sticky and recently applied – on the arm of her chair.

'No, really, I've only just finished lunch.'

From behind the skirting board came a scrabbling of small rodent paws pattering from one end of the room to the other, and a faint, high-pitched squeaking. Hanna ignored the sounds, as she would have ignored those of a guest's rumbling stomach at a dinner party. Miss Technicleen made a comment in her Filofax and prompted, 'Perhaps you could tell me something about the job you want me to do.'

'The job? Oh, yes. Well, there are rather a lot of us, you see. I try to get the girls to help me, but they're not very big and when the boys refuse to do anything in the house it's very difficult to insist that the girls should do it, isn't it? So they don't really do their share at all, I'm afraid. I mean, you don't want to bring them up to believe that girls have to do all the housework and boys don't have to do anything.' Hanna wrapped a strand of hair around her finger like a golden corkscrew, then tucked it behind her left ear and captured her left hand in her right and anchored it securely in her lap while it dawned on her that the children did nothing and she did it all.

'How many children are there?'

'Five,' said Hanna. 'Not all mine, of course. The two girls, Tess and Aurora, belong to me. And the boys – Joe is the eldest, then there's Harry, who's the easiest of the lot, and Tom, who's the littlest one and a lot like Joe, really – they're my husband's.'

'They're very quiet, aren't they?' said Miss Technicleen.

Well, yes, it was unnaturally silent. 'I can't think where they've got to this afternoon. But at least we can talk in peace. They'll be home soon enough when they get hungry. And Joe is a big boy for eleven. He'll keep an eye on the little ones. I'm sure they're quite safe.'

'Perhaps,' said Miss Technicleen, sneaking a swift

glance at her large and masculine watch, 'you could show me round the house now.'

Hanna stood up. 'Well, this is the sitting room. I expect you can see that everything needs a good polish.' And a good dust, and a good hoover, and a good going over with a damp cloth; and all the books would have to be taken out of the bookcases and cleaned and dusted and put back again.

'Hmm,' said Miss Technicleen. Her chestnut-coloured pumps with their one-inch heels tapped along after Hanna's spongy rubber-soled sandals into the next room. 'We bring our own cleaning equipment, of course.'

She probably thinks I don't even own a Hoover, thought Hanna. 'And through here we have my husband's study. He likes a view over the garden when he's working, you see.'

As they looked out of the window, they saw three small figures emerge from the trees and advance towards the house, fanning out into the shape of an arrow-head, with the tallest figure slightly ahead of the other two, moving steadily towards Martenswood.

'I expect he likes you to do a lot of entertaining for him,' said Miss Rainbird.

Hanna watched the three figures for a moment more, fingers coiling and uncoiling the much-abused strand of hair, before turning back to Miss Rainbird. 'What? Oh, yes, of course. Entertaining. Business friends, neighbours, people like that. Malcolm would like to entertain more, I think.' What had happened to the other two children? 'I expect that puts us up to Level Five on your scale, doesn't it?'

'Level . . . Five?' Miss Rainbird queried. 'Oh, I see.' She smiled suddenly, so that her eyes looked very green in her pale face and her long silver earrings swung against the sharp angles of her jaw. 'The house redolent with the smell of beeswax, you mean? Silver forks gleaming, table napkins starched and folded, a couple of bottles of claret chambréing on the sideboard, the *filet du boeuf en croûte*—'

'No,' said Hanna. 'Definitely not beef in any sort of fancy packaging. I suppose I can cook a casserole: beef casserole with a glass of red wine, or chicken casserole with two glasses of red wine. And trifle.'

'Have you tried using a cookery book?' asked Miss Rainbird.

'Oh, come on,' said Hanna, leading the way into the kitchen. 'I think there's half a bottle left over from yesterday's casserole in here somewhere.'

They sat at the table with cloudy glasses of cold red wine, while around them heaps of Benson belongings sprouted like weeds from the floor and furniture.

'Over there,' said Hanna, gesturing grandly, 'are my cookery books. Have you ever tried reading the things? Can you understand them at all? Have you' – and her voice was reaching the outer fringes of hysteria at this point – 'ever tracked down a preserved goose or attempted to remove all the bones from a dead, but uncooked, chicken?'

'Have another glass of wine,' said Miss Rainbird sensibly, and laid her Filofax open on the table. 'I think I'm beginning to get the picture here.'

'It's a tip, now, isn't it?' said Hanna, who had eaten only one plain yoghurt (scorned by the children and well past its sell-by date) for her lunch. 'Just look at it all!'

'How many bedrooms?' asked Miss Rainbird.

'Seven,' said Hanna. 'Quite small, some of them, but tips, every one. Tips. And the bathrooms.'

'How many?' asked Miss Rainbird, writing neatly.

'Three, and the spare. That one,' she added, 'is less of a tip. But then, the downstairs cloakroom more than makes up for it. Three boys, and not one of them can aim properly. And that'll be another fiver on the bill, I suppose.'

'Plus VAT,' confirmed Miss Rainbird.

'More wine?' asked Hanna, deftly pulling the cork from a bottle which she extracted from under a heap of ironing on the window sill, and refilling her own glass.

'So, Miss umm . . .'

'Jean,' said Miss Rainbird economically.

'Jean,' said Hanna, who could still get her tongue round a name if it had only one syllable. 'So what can you do for us, then? Can you sweep in and wave a magic wand and turn this place into an immaculate home?' And can you, she asked silently, stop all this clutter from catching at my feet, tying me to the past?

Jean Rainbird tapped at her solar-powered calculator for a moment, added a couple of figures to the list in her Filofax, and said, 'I suggest that first of all we send in a team to do you a major spring clean – to bring the house up to our minimum standard.' She stared for a moment at the floor by the fridge. 'And can I make a suggestion about your other little problem?'

'Any of them,' said Hanna. 'All of them, if you like.'

'I was thinking about the mice,' said Jean. 'I couldn't help noticing the droppings. And I've got a phone number here of someone who'll come in and deal with them for you.'

'Hand it over,' said Hanna. 'I rather enjoy their company, but I suppose they'll have to go, one day. Just as long as you can beam me up to Level One.'

'Right. We'll wash paintwork and clean all work surfaces, as well as cleaning the floors, of course; we'll polish the outside of wooden furniture – beeswax polish, naturally – dust picture rails and skirting boards, move beds . . .' She must have caught the glazed expression on Hanna's face for she stopped at this point.

'How much?' asked Hanna.

'One hundred and sixty-eight pounds,' said Jean Rainbird, quickly and firmly. 'Plus VAT of course.'

'Of course.' If this wiry person would clear up the house for her, she could advance into a life decked with leaves and flowers.

'And sixty-four pounds a week,' to maintain the standard,' Jean Rainbird was saying. 'Plus VAT.'

'Level Five?'

'Well, not to begin with. Let's just aim for Level Three and see how we go, shall we?'

Hanna resisted the impulse to lay her head down on yet another pile of ironing. Somehow, strands of hair had found their way into her mouth and she chewed them absent-mindedly. 'I'll have to talk to my husband about it, but I think,' said Hanna in a rush of words, pushing the pile of cleanish but crumpled clothes on to the floor, 'that I can safely state that your proposal will be quite acceptable to us.'

Jean Rainbird picked up her glass of wine. 'Good,' she said.

'How soon can you start?' asked Hanna.

'Next Monday?'

'Oh, wonderful!' And they both emptied their glasses. Hanna noticed that Jean gave a slight shudder as she swallowed her wine and there were small beads of perspiration on her upper lip.

'I must be going,' said Jean Rainbird.

Hanna lurched to her feet and shuffled unsteadily through the hall behind her, opening the front door to see her out to the van.

'Please call me Hanna,' she said as Jean seated herself behind the steering wheel. Jean's reply was drowned by the staccato drilling of a woodpecker on a nearby tree, and the van retreated down the drive.

As she went to clear away the wine glasses and the bottles, Hanna did hope that Malcolm would think that she had made the right decision. Oh, to hell with it! She poured another half glass of wine, drank it and waltzed twice round the table before noticing that her three stepsons were standing at the open back door, watching her.

In Ruskin Wood it had been Aurora who screamed. Tess took her hand. 'It's all right, Rory, he can't hurt you while I'm here.'

'But look at what he's done to the sparrow!'

Better not to look. Instead, Tess pulled a clean handkerchief out of her sleeve and passed it to her sister. 'Blow!' she said, so that Aurora stopped crying and blew her nose loudly and messily. And then Tess walked towards Joe, staring straight into his eyes. Joe stood his ground for a moment, but took a step backwards as she got close to him, and he didn't interfere when she picked up a heavy stone and brought it down on to the head of the thing that bled stickily into the turf by his feet. When she had done her best to cover it up with twigs and dry leaves she returned to Aurora and helped her to clean up her face. Behind her, she heard Joe's angry voice.

'You can't stay with her all the time, though, can you? You won't be able to protect her every day. I'll get her! You just wait! That's our father's house, not yours, and you've got to do what we tell you.'

'It's Mum's house as well, now, and you'd better remember it, or—'

'Or what? What are you and your whining little sister going to do to us, then?'

'I'm going to destroy you. And your father.' She went on staring at him, and there was a moment's hesitation before he returned to his attack.

'And how're you going to do that? You can't fight us. And there's no way you can stop me killing what I want in these woods. You don't own them.'

'She's got the magic,' shouted Aurora.

Her sister's loyalty was embarrassing and Tess wished she would shut up.

'Magic! That's girls' crap!' Joe laughed, and Tom joined in.

'I can get power from the earth and the trees and that. And when I've got enough of it, here in my hands, I'll use it.'

Joe made a noise in his throat as though he was about to spit and held up the length of wire, rusty with bloodstains, that he had used to trap the sparrow. Tess tried to grab it from him, but he held it beyond her reach.

'Just wait till you leave that convent of yours and come to Gryphons with us.' And without bothering to say more, he turned and set off through the woodland. Harry and Tom followed him. Harry looked worried, but then, Harry often did.

Tess kept firm hold of Aurora's hand and watched them go. Harry's long, thin white legs, like sticks of half-cooked spaghetti, twisted from his pinhead knees at every step and his feet slapped against the ground at unpredictable angles, so that he seemed in danger of entangling them and losing his precarious balance. Joe stumped through the dark leaves ahead of him, his legs thick and sturdy, and one day to be furred with coarse black hair like Malcolm's. Tom pushed ahead of Harry so that he could catch up with Joe.

'Shouldn't we follow them, Tess?'

'No. Let them go. You're all right here with me.'

'They scare me, in spite of the magic.'

'It's only another eighteen days and they'll be going back to school.' She spoke as though the weeks stretching dangerously in front of them were nothing. 'They can't hurt us when they're back at Gryphons and we're at the convent.' Already she could smell the mixture of incense, furniture polish and yesterday's boiled cabbage that signified St Fred's. She would be safe at her desk with her name scratched inside the lid, opening a blue exercise book with a hand-drawn cross in the top left-hand corner of every page.

'But Joe said—'

'You don't listen to Joe, OK?' Sister Patrick would be waiting for them, with her scoured white fingernails and spiteful brown eyes.

'What can we do about them, Tess?'

'We can make them go away, so it's like it was before.'

'Can we go home now, Tess? Please, Tess. *Now*.'

'Right. No problem.'

But they were too far away to hear the comforting hum of the traffic on the bypass. Here in the woods, they were surrounded by the uneasy silence of the countryside, punctuated only by the crash of a pigeon erupting through the bushes like a clumsy child. Tess wished that she were back in London, with the familiar feel of concrete under her feet instead of soft, treacherous leaf-mould.

'But do you know the way?' Aurora was threatening tears again.

'Of course I do.' She was the spell-weaver, the maker of magic.

It was dark among the trees and with the sunlight flickering fitfully through the thick leaves, it wasn't easy to tell where Martenswood lay. She got down on her hands and knees and put her head against the ground. Beneath the surface, water moved and trickled with a gurgling sound, mustering its strength, seeping through the meadows, dripping secretly into the river. She could feel the faint movement of life below and she pictured the power travelling up the veins in her arms.

'Shut your eyes, hold my hand and think.'

'What about?'

'About Mum.'

'Will it work?'

'Yes.'

Tess closed her eyes and held tightly to her sister's hand, trying to call up her mother's face, the flowery smell of her skin, the soft feel of her old cotton dress.

Dad, she cried silently. Lead us back to her, will you? Help me find her.

'Come on, Rory,' she said after a few moments, 'it's over here.' Dad would show her, if she trusted him. She only had to listen hard and do what he told her. And she led the way through the beech trees until the sunlight dappled the undergrowth, the trees thinned out and they could see the house in front of them, still some way across the fields, but *there*, solid and within their reach.

Looking down at Aurora, she saw that she had lost her hair ribbon and her face was stained with recent tears. She had promised Dad that she would look after her and so she'd just have to do it. 'The four of us belong together,' he had said. 'There's no changing that.' The knowledge was like a heavy weight that she carried on her shoulders.

Chapter Three

Tess learned the trick of it one day when she was out for a walk with her father. She was nearly four years younger then, and she remembered how she had had to struggle to keep up with him as his long legs scythed through the grass ahead of her. He had vaulted the stile and turned to lift her over. Mud tugged at their boots as they waded through pink and yellow flowers towards the bridge where they could watch the minnows.

Bullocks were grazing in the long grass in the far corner of the field that afternoon, and as Tess and her father approached, they turned their faces as though pulled by a single invisible string and drifted across the field towards them. Tess clutched her father's hand in its green woollen glove.

'You're not nervous of the poor beasts, are you, Tess?'

But she was.

The bullocks had faces that were flat and white and their pale eyes were rimmed with paler lashes. Steam rose from their moist nostrils.

'They look very fierce,' said Tess.

Her father's voice murmured into the air above her head. 'Now, these are bullocks that you see here: soft,

33

gentle creatures that haven't a wild thought in their
stupid heads. So there's no need to be afraid of them.
Why, if we ran up and waved our arms and shouted, they
would turn round and go galloping away across the
field.'

'But supposing—'

'Yes? Supposing what, now?'

'Supposing there's a bull hiding in the middle there?'

Her father's laugh rang out across the meadow. 'And
why should the farmer have put a bull in among the
bullocks, do you think?'

She couldn't think of a reason, or not one that would
make sense if she put it into words. But that didn't mean
she was sure that no bull lurked among the black and
white herd. This bull might well be passing himself off as
a harmless bullock, but at any moment he would throw
off his disguise and emerge, snorting and roaring and
pawing the ground, huge in his blackness, with nameless,
unimaginable swinging appendages, ready to trample her
into the earth. And the ground would tremble under his
advancing hooves and she would be gobbled up in his—

'Here, Tess, I have a talisman for you. Will it keep us
safe from the man-eating bulls, do you think?' There was
bindweed threaded through the hedge and he held up
one of the white trumpets on its tough stem. Then he
pulled the bindweed away from the hedge and ripped the
white flower from its stem and handed it to her. 'Magic,'
he said.

What use was a flower? But she took it in her free
hand and tried not to show her fear of the ever-
approaching bullocks. 'Mother Philomena says we
mustn't believe in magic. Magic's wicked, she says, like

fortune-telling and witchcraft.'

'No magic? I shall have to speak to that Mother Philomena of yours. I can't have her telling my daughter there's no magic in the world when it's plain as perfidy all around us.'

'Is it real? Where is it?' In her excitement she forgot to ask him what perfidy was.

'You'll send it flittering back across the river if you dance around like that. Just look and listen.'

And then, as she stood there, with her white flower and her father's hand clasped in hers, she understood what he meant. She heard the magic in the water that hissed and stuttered beyond the willow trees. It raced through her father's fingers into her hand and up her arm. Gerard was conjuring it up out of its secret home beneath the fields and passing it to her across the barrier of their skin. They could do anything when they were together like this with the magic flowing through them like an electric current.

Above her the clouds wheeled, white and gold flecks pasted on to the far-off blue of the sky, while lower, nearer, the full-bellied pink and grey of rainclouds gusted past. She wanted to catch them and hug them to her like a bunch of fat feather pillows, until time itself stopped flying by and she could lock this day up so that it would be hers, with its magic, for ever.

'It's just for you and me, isn't it?' she whispered, as the magic tugged at her hand until she knew that if she didn't break free, her arms and legs would twitch and jerk and go flying off to do its dangerous bidding. She pulled her hand away from Gerard's and set off alone towards the far gate. But before she could reach it, the herd of bullocks turned towards her.

'Make them go away, Daddy!' she cried. 'I don't like them!'

'Why don't you magic them away?' said Gerard. 'You know you can do it.'

She shouted at the beasts, but her voice blew back in her face, as weak as the cry of a bird.

'Louder,' said Gerard. 'Shout at them some more.'

And then she looked at the white flower in her hand and she shouted out again. Magic, he had said. Power grew inside her like a fever as she waved her arms and stamped her feet, till at last the bullocks frisked and tossed their heads; rolling their eyes and turning their solid rumps towards her, they jostled their way to the far corner of the field. *I did it*, she thought. *I did it*. In her hand the convolvulus lay bruised and sour-smelling. She let it fall to the ground.

'Well now,' said Gerard, close beside her again, 'that's something you've learned today, isn't it?'

Later in the afternoon rain spilled out of the sagging clouds, falling in great splashing gouts on their arms and faces, washing the magic out of the sky and scouring it out of the earth, sending it spiralling off in brown rivulets down to the stream. And when it had quite gone, she was ordinary – her own seven-year-old self. But she knew how to call up the magic now. On the way home she held fast to Gerard's hand to remind herself how she had felt, alive and singing with its wild power.

Tess Farrell has kept the green glove that Gerard wore that day. It is fraying around the wrist now, and faded a little, but she has wrapped it in a paper bag and hidden it in the bottom drawer of her bedside chest, which is where she keeps all her treasures.

She had both the gloves once, but in the grief that followed Gerard's death, she cut one of them to pieces with her mother's embroidery scissors. She spent a lot of her time eaten up by anger in those early days, and now, more than three years later, she hasn't entirely forgiven Gerard for abandoning her, nor God for taking him away. But, even as she stabbed and sliced at the green wool, trying to release the hard ball of sorrow from inside her chest, the memory came filtering back: again she stood on the bridge to watch the minnows through the window of the stream; she walked across the water meadow and, over and over again, she waved the magic flower at the bullocks till they fled from her in fear. And then she dropped the scissors and held the poor, mutilated thing that had once been Gerard's against her cheek to try to catch a last breath of him.

They have left the London house and the old, safe life. For three years Tess and her sister have spent their terms at the convent and their holidays playing quietly and inconspicuously in the houses of their mother's various employers, until six months ago, when they were told that Hanna was marrying this large dark man, Malcolm Benson, and that from now on Martenswood was to be their home.

But from time to time Tess gets out the glove to remind herself of Gerard.

'He has dark red hair,' she recites to herself in her secret litany, 'straight and soft. And he has brown eyes the colour of the Irish Sedge Peat that Malcolm has bought to put on the garden. He is tall and his limbs are loose, like a puppet's, and he looks the way poets ought to look. His bones are very long and thin, and so are his hands and his feet.' Once, when they were all watching television, Hanna remarked on the artistic hands of some actress and later, when Tess saw Gerard's feet, white and damp and naked after a swim, with their straight toes and the indigo veins showing through the translucent skin, she said without thinking, 'You've got very artistic feet, Daddy, haven't you?' and then wondered why everyone laughed at her.

The green glove has long, thin fingers, like Gerard's. When she holds it, twisting its soft fingers around her own, and closes her eyes, she can feel again the magic seeping through the ground, passing through his hands and pricking her skin until it beats in her veins and she knows that she is as powerful as Gerard.

'Hello, darling. Have you had a good day?'

'Bloody awful. Here, hang this up and pour me a drink, will you?'

'Whisky?'

'Yes. Not like that. For God's sake, Han, make it a decent one. I could use a proper drink.'

Malcolm unfastened a button to release his captive paunch. 'That's better,' he said, swallowing a drink the colour of strong milkless tea. 'Why don't you pour yourself one?'

She really shouldn't, not after the half-bottle of wine that had somehow slipped down while she was getting the supper ready, but she did as she was told. If she humoured Malcolm before his mood gelled for the evening, he might agree to the Technicleen contract without a fuss. On the other hand, he might start picking on one of the children, so that she spent the whole evening feeling guilty for their crimes as well as her own and wouldn't be able to ask him for anything. Sometimes she could judge by the first thrust of his key into the lock how amenable he was going to be, but this was one of the uncertain evenings.

In the light from the standard lamp, the room looked deceptively welcoming and cosy: bruised chairlegs were wrapped in shadow, the stains on the upholstery disguised by the chintz roses.

'Come and sit over here,' Malcolm said, and Hanna moved obediently to the sofa. 'Anything wrong? You're very quiet tonight.' It sounded like an accusation. 'I've been thinking about Tess, Han,' Malcolm went on. 'She's been on my mind all day. Did you hear her this morning? Did you see what she was doing? Look, I just want her to be normal, like the boys. I don't want any more of that staring at me and clocking every move I make. You've got to be firmer with her, Han. Firmer with the lot of them, if it comes to that.'

'No, Malcolm.' It felt as though the space between her ears was filled with porridge. Malcolm's voice came at her from the end of a long tunnel.

'What? I tell you, it's weird and it's got to stop.' The roll of fat above his collar was turning pink and Hanna knew she had said the wrong thing.

'Yes, Malcolm,' she corrected herself. After her third – or was it her fifth? – glass of wine, Hanna was finding it tricky to pick up her cues and deliver the correct line. She hung on to the fact that she mustn't upset Malcolm. She would sort out all the problems tomorrow: she'd be able to cope with them when she'd had a night's sleep. Meanwhile, Malcolm's voice droned on.

'. . . and Joe just turns up the volume of his Sony Walkman when I try to talk to him. That kid doesn't listen to a word I say.'

'No, Malcolm.' She'd got it right this time. If his mood didn't turn soon, she'd never be able to tell him about Miss Technicleen.

'. . . and did you do something about the mice?' He put out an arm to draw her shoulders closer to his.

'Mice? Oh, yes. Yes, I did.' She shifted herself into a more comfortable position. 'He'll be phoning back this evening to say when he'll be coming to have a look.' She wanted to escape to the kitchen to rescue their supper; she longed to put her feet up and disappear into a magazine in complete silence, but if she failed to respond to Malcolm's affectionate overtures he would stay in a foul mood until the next morning.

'Good old Han.' His thigh was pressed against hers and she could feel its heat through her skirt. She reached out an unwilling hand to caress his cheek, just as a small figure pushed open the door of the sitting room and entered, holding up a teddy-bear in a grey pullover.

'Hello there, Harry.' Malcolm was particularly fond of his middle son.

'Orly's thirsty,' said Harry.

'Well, I think we could find him a glass of water, don't you, Hanna?'

'Ribena,' said Harry. 'That's his favourite. Without too much water,' he added. And he climbed on to Malcolm's knee. 'Tess says she's going to destroy us all,' he told him. 'With magic.'

'Just her little joke, I expect,' said Malcolm in his ho-ho voice.

'They have to do what you tell them, don't they, Dad?'

'They certainly do,' said Malcolm. 'And they might show a bit of gratitude for all I'm doing for them, too.'

'Joe says that they'll have to do what they're told when he's got his gun. Otherwise he'll shoot them, he says.'

Malcolm's colour started to rise. 'And just where does Joe think he's getting this gun from?'

'He says you'll buy him one. And he says you're getting him a mountain bike, too. He says you always get him what he asks for.'

'I'll take a strap to that child,' said Malcolm.

'Not now, Malcolm,' said Hanna. 'It's too late to start an argument with Joe now.'

'I'm not talking about an argument, I'm talking about getting a bit of discipline into this house.' He ran a finger like a large beef sausage round between the collar of his shirt and the purple swell of his neck and breathed heavily through his nose while Harry sat looking nervous. Then, with an effort, Malcolm puckered his eyes and bared the top row of his teeth in his direction: Harry wouldn't defy him, he was a good kid. 'But right now, old chap,' he said when Harry at last raised his face from his comforting mug of Ribena, 'time for bed, don't you think? And we've got to have our supper.' He stood up, hoisting his son on to his shoulders, and the two of them disappeared out of the room. Harry's high voice informed his father, 'We had burned beans for supper,' as they went. 'Is that what you're having?'

'Now, you were telling me some news of yours,' Malcolm said when he returned, sitting down next to her and placing a heavy arm round her shoulders.

'I've managed to find someone to come in and do all the housework,' she said quickly.

'Wonderful!' Malcolm released his grip for a moment and held up his empty glass for Hanna to fill. As she did so she reflected that he sounded genuinely pleased that she had arranged for sixty pounds or so of his money to be spent every week on hoovering carpets and scrubbing tidemarks from baths.

'There! It wasn't so hard, once you got used to the idea, was it? I knew a professional outfit would sort you out.'

'Yes. You're right, of course.' She handed Malcolm the full glass. It was going to take a long time to tell him about Jean Rainbird and she hoped that the dinner wouldn't spoil if it was cooked for an extra quarter of an hour or so. She caught the smell of caramel floating out of the kitchen, which was odd, because the pudding was a trifle made with the cake that she had baked last week and that for some reason no one had eaten. She drank more wine to stop herself worrying about it, and concentrated on keeping her eyes open. 'Yes, Malcolm,' she said into the pause in the monologue going on next to her. Bull's-eye, she thought, as he smiled at her.

Upstairs, in her neat bedroom – the only neat room in the entire house – Tess lit the two candles in front of Gerard's photograph and knelt down.

'Hello, Dad,' she said. 'I'm trying to look after us all, like you wanted. But sometimes it gets a bit difficult, especially when Joe is horrible to Aurora. I'm working to find the magic, and I think it's getting stronger, but I'll need your help to destroy Malcolm.'

Gerard smiled down at her, his eyes moving with the dancing of the candle flame.

Sure, he said. *Didn't I help you find your way home this afternoon when you asked me? And didn't I tell you that I'd always be here, helping you and looking after you?* Since his death, Gerard's voice had taken on a strong Dublin accent, rather like Sister Patrick's.

'I want to make him disappear,' said Tess. 'Like the bullocks, but for ever, this time. I hate him, Dad. I hate his thick dark hair and the way the black stubble pushes through the pink skin of his face. I hate the bristles that grow in his ears, and the fold of flesh above his blue striped collar. We've got to get rid of him. Like we did—'

You're right. He must go away for ever.

'So go on, Han. What happened then?'

'A Miss Rainbird turned up.'

'Miss *who*?'

'Rainbird. She owns the company, apparently. She's small, with very short bright red hair and a suit with power shoulders.'

'A punk?'

But at this moment the telephone rang, and Hanna escaped from the room.

'That was Ratsaway,' she said when she came back a couple of minutes later. 'The mouse man. I left a message on his answering machine and now he's rung me back. He said he would. At least, I suppose his machine said it, really, though I didn't realise that it was a machine. Not at the time, that is. He can come and see what the problem is tomorrow afternoon.'

'Well, we know what the problem is, don't we?' said Malcolm. 'It's mice.' And his eyes scurried round the room as though searching for small rodents. 'Our problem's mice. His problem's getting rid of them. Simple.' Strong fingers pulled at her arm until she fell on the sofa, then urged her nearer to him. 'Sorry about what I said just now,' and Malcolm smiled at her in the way that used to make her knees go funny but which didn't seem to have been working so well lately. 'Why are you sitting right over there, Han?' The smell of caramelised dinner was growing stronger, but she felt it best to ignore it. 'I always said I'd look after you, didn't I? I told you I'd give you a comfortable life. By the time I've done the garden and this Technicleen woman has spring-cleaned the house, you won't recognise yourself.'

It sounded so restful when he described it, but somehow her head seemed as stuffed with anxiety as the chair with horsehair.

'And we'll do something about the furniture and the decoration, and why aren't you wearing one of your new dresses?' Then he stopped talking while his hands worked busily. Some time later he said, 'So where's this supper of yours?'

'I'll dish it up straight away.'

'Oh, and Hanna, before you disappear into the kitchen—'

'Yes?'

'I nearly forget to tell you—'

'Yes?' There was something in his tone that stopped her as she was walking out through the door. 'What's that?'

He lumbered after her so that when she turned she

found his face only a couple of inches from her own, huge and out of focus in its nearness.

'I've been in touch with Ferris again.'

'The Ferret?' she asked, light finally dawning, as she took a step backwards.'

'That's what Joe calls him, yes.'

'Why, Malcolm?'

'Because he's the headmaster of Gryphons, Han,' he explained patiently. 'And he's agreed to take the girls this term, instead of waiting till after Easter. He took some persuading, but I knew I could talk him round. I'll be buying him some new books for the library or something, in return. Bit of luck that, don't you think? We won't have to worry about them any more. They'll get all the corners knocked off them at Gryphons, and Tess'll soon forget that nonsense of hers.'

Red wine bubbled on the base of the dried-up casserole as Hanna recklessly splashed it in. Then she poured the rest of the bottle into her own glass and drank it quickly, standing in the kitchen where Malcolm couldn't see her, before carrying their dinner into the dining room.

'I don't suppose you'll let me smoke a ciggie?'

'No, Tracker.'

'You can be a hard woman, you know that, Jean?'

'That's not what you were saying ten minutes ago.'

'Ten minutes ago, I wasn't in need of a smoke.' He shifted to accommodate a friendly arm under a shoulder. 'Tell me about your day, then. What's this new contract of yours?'

'Tracker, my eyes are closed because I'm asleep.' She

sighed. 'Well, I went to see some silly cow up on Fox Hill. Second marriage, five kids, bully of a husband and no clue how to run a house. And overrun with mice.'

'I hope you gave her my number.'

'You don't deserve it, but yes, I did.'

'Tell me more.'

'The husband is in property—'

'An estate agent?'

'Yes. And into developments and Christ knows what else. Loaded, anyway, by the look of it and he wants his expensive house clean and shining, with matching kids and wife. All part of the image. He'll look around him and order new furniture and carpets in a week or two, I bet you.'

'I can hear there's a but.'

'But there was something about that house that I didn't like. Something in the atmosphere of the place. Anyway, I suppose I'd better go and sort out dear Hanna. Dreams, Tracker, that's what I sell, not just clean houses, for the Hanna Bensons. She sees her husband walking through the front door at the end of the day into a clean, tidy house, full of clean, tidy kids; a gourmet meal in the microwave and a gin and tonic on the patio before dinner. She'll never get there, but she can dream, and I can help her.'

'Mmm.'

'Goodnight, Tracker.'

'Jean?'

'Yes, Tracker?'

'Do you always have to call me by my surname?'

'Yes, Tracker.'

Chapter Four

There was another row the next morning when Malcolm, wishing to check something in his new *Economical Gardener's Guide to the Gardening Year*, found it with its navy-blue cloth covers still relatively intact but with its pages shredded into strips. A sudden scrabbling, a squeaking, and a silence in quick succession behind the wainscoting, gave him the clue and he came shouting into the kitchen. Hanna calmed him down by making rash promises, waved him off to work, fed the children, cleared the kitchen, made some phone calls and sent Tess to fetch Aurora and Joe.

Tess found Aurora with her mouth puckered like a walnut and her nose running.

'What's Joe done this time?' she demanded, but Aurora just hiccuped and pushed her fingers over her messy face and up into her hair. 'Well, Mum wants you,' she said, 'so you'd better put a flannel over your face and go downstairs.' She left her sister in the bathroom and went into Joe's room.

'Mum wants to see you, too,' she said.

'Tough shit,' said Joe, without looking up from a tangle of wire and string.

47

'And I've told you to leave my sister alone.'

'But they tell me she's my little sister as well as yours, now.' The face that Joe raised was blandly benign, but he jerked the two ends of his string until its loops disappeared into a small, tight knot. 'That should do it,' he said.

'Harry's the only sister you've got.'

'Leave Harry out of it.' Then, 'Not long now till we all go to Gryphons: seventeen days, I make it. And I mean to enjoy myself here before we go.'

'I'm going to destroy all this,' said Tess, looking around his room, 'and I'm going to get rid of you, too.' She held his gaze until he fidgeted and got up and left the room. 'And you'd better look out for those brothers of yours,' she shouted after him. 'We're going to get them!' And she slammed the door shut.

Well done, said the voice in her head. *But you know words aren't enough on their own.*

Joe kept Hanna waiting a few minutes longer, then wandered along the passage, past the other bedrooms. Harry's door was closed, so he opened it and walked in. He found Harry over by the window, holding up a one-eared grubby teddy-bear by both arms and singing to it. In a circle on the floor were another dozen bears of different sizes and mostly worn with age and loving. Joe listened for a moment, then said, 'Not another bloody dolls' tea party!'

Harry dropped the teddy-bear and turned round, his face scarlet. He picked up a couple of the oldest and shabbiest bears and held them close to his chest.

'They're not dolls. They're my teddy-bears. I'm just putting them away now, anyway.'

48

'You can go and play at fairies in the woods with the girls when you've done that then, can't you?' As he went on across the hall and down the stairs he could hear the long intake of breath that meant that Harry was getting upset. He needed to toughen up, did Harry, so that Tess couldn't accuse him of being a girl. Joe stood outside the kitchen for a few minutes, listening to Aurora's voice rising and wailing in protest.

'I don't want to go to that school. Don't make me, Mum!'

'Come on, Precious, Tess will be there with you, and Joe and the others, of course: they're your big brothers, now.'

'No, they're not – I hate them!' There were sobbing and gulping noises from Aurora. Joe smiled. Gryphons would soon sort Little Precious out – and Tess.

He pushed the door wide and walked into the kitchen without closing it behind him. Hanna was sitting on a chair by the table, with Aurora on her lap, stroking the child's tangled hair.

'I want to go *home*, Mum.' Aurora was crying in her usual boring way, rubbing her fists in her eyes.

'This is your home now,' said Joe, '*Precious*. And don't you forget it,' he added viciously.

Aurora snuffled into Hanna's shoulder.

Hanna said, 'Don't cry, darling, everything will be fine.' And, 'Don't be horrid to Aurora,' to Joe.

Tess had come in and was making a fuss of that bad-tempered cat, Vinegar or Finnegan or whatever his name was, and listening to their conversation without joining in.

Hanna smiled at him, still rocking Aurora in her arms.

Stupid cow, he thought. 'I phoned Mrs Elliott, Joe. She's invited you and Harry and Tom to go over and join her boys. They're going fishing on the lake, and I've got this pest-control man coming in this afternoon, so it would be much better for you all to go off with your own friends.'

The trouble with Hanna was that she didn't understand about men. 'The Rat Man? I'd like to talk to him. Do you know how he does the killing? Does he use traps?'

'I don't know. He didn't mention traps. I think he puts some sort of bait down. It's all very hygienic. There's nothing nasty about it.'

'Pity,' said Joe.

'What's bait?' asked Tess.

'Oh, well, I suppose it must be some sort of poison,' said Hanna, 'but I'm sure it's all quite humane these days.'

'Poison?' repeated Tess, then sat silent again for a moment. She put Finnegan down and left the room. Joe heard her go upstairs. Good riddance, he thought.

'I'll stay here and talk to the Rat Man,' said Joe. 'I bet he knows some wicked stories.' He pushed in the ear-pieces of his Walkman, switched on a cassette and turned up the volume to show that the conversation was over. Hanna had to raise her voice above the hissing beat of Joy Division escaping from his earphones to make herself heard.

'I've told Mrs Elliott that the three of you will be over there in half an hour.' And for once she was quite firm about it. Joe had to console himself with the hope that the eldest Elliott boy would let him have a go with his new gun.

★ ★ ★

'Still cooped up in your room, Tess? Why don't you go outside and play while it's sunny?'

'I want to stay here, Mum.'

'No, Tess. You wouldn't go off with Aurora and the Suttons, so you'll have to find something to do outside in the fresh air. At least when you go to Gryphons you'll make some nice new friends.'

'I don't want any more friends. Friends talk all the time and you can't think properly when people are talking round you. And I like listening to the stories inside my head. Friends just get in the way. But I do want to meet the Rat Man. Can't I stay here? Please, Mum.'

'I can't understand why you all have this sudden interest in Mr Ratsaway.'

'I want to make sure he's not going to be cruel to the mice when he gets rid of them.'

'You'll just have to trust me to do that.'

Why didn't Mum know what Gerard wanted? Couldn't she hear him? It seemed to Tess that his voice was everywhere these days, not only inside her head. She couldn't understand why everybody didn't hear his whispering and smell his damp tweed jacket as he moved about the rooms at Martenswood. Would he forgive her if she didn't stay and talk to the Rat Man? She was doing her best, but everything seemed to be going against her.

'When will Aurora be back? And the boys?'

'What are all the questions for, Tess? What is it you're worried about?'

'Nothing. I was just interested.'

If she couldn't talk to the Rat Man and find out how he killed things, she would have to try something else. Time was dripping away. Gerard wouldn't forgive her if she and Aurora went away to school and left Malcolm in possession of Hanna. She had finished what she had to do upstairs and now she must plan her next move.

'The library's open,' she said. 'I'll go down and change my books.' The branch in the village was only open for three days a week, and this was one of them.

The library was hot and smelled of old people. The librarian watched Tess walk up to the desk and turned a welcoming smile upon her. She had a round face, greying hair and red lipstick on her teeth. Tess wondered how to frame her request: she could hardly ask outright for what she wanted.

'Have you got anything about wild flowers and berries and things?' she asked, adding a faint lisp, like Aurora at her most winsome. 'Mushrooms?' She smiled up at her. 'Toadstools?'

Well done, said Gerard. *The world is full of ways of getting rid of vermin if you look for them.*

It was a relief to have done something right.

Tess closed the book she had been reading and gathered the notes she had made into a neat pile as her mother put her head round the door of her room.

'Yes, all right, Mum, I'll go out for a walk now.' She put the notes in the pocket of her jeans, then went down to the kitchen.

'Is it all right if I take some of these plastic bags?'

'The ones I use for sandwiches? Yes, fine, dear.'

DEATHSPELL

'I thought I'd like to make hedgerow jam – blackberry and crab-apple and stuff like that.'

'Are you sure you know what to pick?'

'Oh yes. I've been looking it up in these books I got from the library. They're all about edible fruits from the hedgerow and how to turn them into jam and stuff. It's like recycling and self-sufficiency.'

'It is?' Hanna sounded unconvinced.

'Green is good, small is beautiful,' Tess added. 'And I know just what I'm looking for.'

She watched her mother wind a strand of hair around her finger and tuck it behind her ear. Never mind, if she sorted things out the way Dad wanted, Mum would be all right. She'd soon be happy again, like she was when Gerard was alive. They'd have the old, warm Hanna back again, once she and Gerard had solved all her problems. They'd done it that other time, hadn't they? So they could do it again.

'Don't worry, Mum,' she said, since Hanna was still frowning, 'you know I always get things right.'

She took the plastic bags and walked down the path towards the farm. The hedgerow was bright with hawthorn berries, rosehips and brambles. Elderberries hung in bunches from the trees, green and red and purple all on the same stem. She pulled them off in handfuls and put them into one of the plastic bags.

She could use rosehips, too. There were no crab-apples in this stretch of hedgerow, so she wandered on down towards the river and then followed the footpath up the hill leading to Bennetts' Farm, eating blackberries as she went – after all, it didn't matter, she could easily pick more on her way home. Towards the top of the hill she found the navy-blue dusty-looking berries of the sloe, and black briony with its bright, shiny scarlet berries, and picked them both. And nightshade. She wasn't sure whether it was deadly nightshade or woody nightshade, but she thought that either of them would do.

Death's herb, whispered Gerard. *That's what we need, and plenty of it.*

She had made a drawing of dog's mercury and put it in her pocket and now she checked with the plants in front of her. She hoped that she'd got it right. Meadow saffron would have been useful since her book said that it had actually killed people, but she had never seen it, or anything that resembled the picture in the book, flowering around here. But the magic in the earth was working with her today. She could smell it in the scent of vanilla that gusted in waves from the hedge.

She wondered what the jam would taste like. They said that deadly nightshade was sweet and pleasant to the taste, but some of the other berries that she had picked looked hard and full of pips. She would put in extra sugar in case it was bitter, and add spices – she had seen cinnamon and cloves and nutmeg in the cupboard – to improve the flavour.

The sun was right overhead now, and she ate another handful of blackberries. She hummed her favourite song as she wandered along. She only had seventeen days, but she was at least doing something now, instead of just sitting and suffering, like Aurora.

Seventeen days. It isn't long. But you have me beside you, helping you; and the magic is flying all around us, waiting for you to catch it up and weave it into the right pattern. We'll have him, Tess. He'll swallow the poison as

DEATHSPELL

easy as the trout in the stream take the mayfly.

In the ditch the lords and ladies held up lollipop spikes of orange and green beads, and thistledown floated over the grass in the meadow. The sun started slipping across the sky towards the west before she took the path back to Martenswood with her bulging, darkly oozing, dripping bags.

Chapter Five

Hanna had just finished her pleasantly child-free lunch when she heard the sound of tyres braking on the gravel drive, followed by the ringing of the front doorbell, and she stepped briskly through the hall to open the door, in the sweet belief that at least one of her problems would be solved before she had to face Malcolm again. She was ready to welcome Mephistopheles himself if he would only promise to rid the house of rodents.

In fact, standing on the honey-coloured tiles of her doorstep, leaning against the brickwork of her porch, with a nimbus of sunlit hair surrounding his shadowed face, stood a quite beautiful young man, and she felt a warm and welcoming smile curving her own lips and a sparkle rise to her eyes as she met his friendly and amused blue gaze.

'Ratsaway,' said the vision, and behind him a dark blue Escort estate echoed the name in cursive white letters.

Hanna stared into eyes that were the most amazing blue, like the forget-me-nots you find growing in a shaded patch of the garden. He had long dark lashes of the sort that are envied by young girls and too often possessed instead by young men. His smile lit his face from within and made it impossible not to smile back. He had dark eyebrows, like circumflexes, poised over his blue eyes, giving him a questioning expression as though he couldn't quite take Hanna and her words at face value, but was turning them over in his mind. The eyebrows themselves were soft and shiny and made her want to reach out and stroke them. Hanna was suddenly very aware that she hadn't changed out of her old blue shirt and faded jeans, and that she should have washed her hair that morning. Her face was growing warm under his gaze and she wondered whether her foolish smile had lasted just a few seconds too long.

'Won't you come in, Mr Ratsaway?'

'Steve. It's easier if you call me Steve, don't you think, Mrs Benson?' A low, attractive voice, with the elongated vowels of Oxfordshire. He flashed the smile at her again.

'Hanna, my name's Hanna.' Oh bother! Her name slipped out before she could think what she was saying and stop it, and she could feel the silly smile still on her face. Perhaps she shouldn't have had that glass of wine with her lunch: it must have gone to her head.

Steve was tall, and when he smiled at her she saw that his teeth were pleasantly crooked, like a faun's, and that his eyes wrinkled up at the corners in a way that showed that he liked to smile a lot. With difficulty she tore herself away from this pleasing eye-contact and moved back from the door, through the hall and round into the kitchen, the lightfooted Mr Ratsaway close behind her. There was a soft, outdoor smell about his hair and skin. And something about him that reminded her of Gerard.

'Would you like a cup of coffee, Mr Ratsaway . . .

Steve . . . while I tell you what the problem is?'

'If you're sure it's no trouble.'

'I was about to put some on for myself.' Would real coffee made in her expensive French machine be all right, or would he prefer instant? Oh, to hell with it, she was going to make real coffee for herself, wasn't she? And maybe it would neutralise the effect of the wine.

'I'll put the kettle on for you while you measure the coffee out, OK?' he said.

She liked the deft and unobtrusive way he worked. If Malcolm had offered to help her he would have made sure that everyone noticed what he was doing and he would have dropped a mug, and asked where to find the kettle and the strainer, and totally confused her by now.

When the coffee was made and poured, and she had found an unopened packet of plain chocolate digestives that she had successfully hidden from the children since her last visit to the supermarket, and laid them out on a blue-flowered plate, they settled down at right angles to one another at the end of the table. Hanna decided that the wonderful blue of his eyes was enhanced by the colour of his denim shirt and jeans, and the tan on his neck stood out nicely against his very clean white T-shirt.

She was glad now that she had brought in leafy branches and seedheads to make a new arrangement for the sitting room. The wicker basket looked rural and homely, standing on the pine dresser, and the big, dramatic arrangement, like an overflowing cornucopia, was particularly effective. She didn't like to analyse why she was glad that she just happened to have an example of the one thing she was really good at sitting full in Steve

Ratsaway's view, but when she picked up her mug and started to sip her coffee at the same time as Steve started to drink his, she noticed how close to hers his head had moved, and his hand, when he stirred his coffee, just brushed the back of her hand for a second so that all the tiny hairs on her arm stood up. She edged her chair a few inches further away from his.

'Mice,' she said firmly. 'We've having problems with mice.'

'I'm very fond of them myself,' he said, 'but I can understand that you don't want them moving into your house. So,' and she was treated to another few hundred watts of Ratsaway smile, 'tell me about your problems.'

She was severely tempted to. She wanted to say something like: 'My husband is no longer the cheerful, boyish extrovert I married, but is always finding fault with the things that I do and the way that I do them, and one of my daughters is secretive and frightened of her step-brothers, and my stepsons despise me, and my other daughter thinks she's . . . I'm not sure what.' But she was sensible enough not to spew all this out over her kitchen table, but to tell him instead about the Martenswood mice.

Unlike her interview with Jean Rainbird, when she had listened to the words spurting incoherently from her mouth and the witless sentences tumbling out without her being able to check them, here in the kitchen, talking to Steve Ratsaway, she found that she could be quite concise and articulate. He didn't make her feel at all inadequate. In fact, he made her feel about ten years younger than she had an hour ago, and a good eighty per cent more attractive. He listened to her with great attention and she noticed that the line that bracketed his mouth on one side had a definite dimple in its angle. She resisted the temptation to stretch out a finger and touch it. A smear of chocolate shone on his lower lip for a moment; his tongue, when it snaked out to lick it away, was very red, very pointed, with a line of smoker's creamy fur down its centre.

'Been winding him up, have they?'

She was in danger of losing the thread of the conversation, but she kept her eyes on his mouth. 'To breaking point.'

'Likes gardening, does he, your husband?'

She didn't want to talk about Malcolm. 'He wants it tidied up and under control.' He wants *me* tidied up and under control, she thought suddenly.

'I like a bit of wilderness, myself. Nothing too neat and tame. But it does encourage the wildlife. Mice and that.'

What would it be like to have a man around who liked wild things, who begged her not to comb her hair, who removed her solemn clothes and enjoyed her imperfect body both in and out of her rumpled bed? She reminded herself that she had chosen Malcolm and safety. 'The mice will have to go,' she said. 'But you won't hurt them, will you?'

'They won't feel a thing,' said Steve.

'But you can get rid of them in a day or two?'

'That depends, like,' said Steve.

'Depends?'

'On whether they're your streetwise city mice who know their bait from their elbows, or whether—' and here he gave her another flash of the slightly crooked, crowded upper teeth. White, she thought. So white, like a healthy animal. 'Or whether,' repeated Steve, 'they are in fact your naïve little pink-nosed country mice.' And he lifted the strand of hair that had slipped in front of Hanna's eyes so that they crossed very slightly, and put it back in its place. 'I can lay the bait,' he said, 'but will the little darlings take it?'

Hanna got up and filled the kettle. Unnecessarily, she realised, but it gave her something to do.

When Steve had finished his coffee, she showed him round the house, starting with Malcolm's study and the bookcase.

'You've got your fieldmice coming in here from the garden, by the sound of it,' he said. 'It's unusual this early in the season, but maybe we're in for a hard winter.'

'Do you think it is fieldmice? My daughter thought it was, but the rest of us weren't sure. In fact, my husband thought they might be rats.'

'You can tell by the droppings, see.'

She tried to look intelligently at the black crumbs. They smelled faintly musty.

'Your mouse droppings are quite small, but rats now, they put out cylindrical droppings with pointed ends, oh, up to ten or fifteen millimetres long.'

This was more than Hanna wanted to learn about rodents and she encouraged Steve to move on round the house (avoiding only the boys' bedrooms with their intractable mess and ripening smell of rotting socks). From time to time he bent down and opened a cupboard door or rapped gently on a skirting board.

'Nice place you've got,' he said appreciatively as they walked through the sitting room. 'I like these old houses, myself. Got a bit of quality to them.' He stroked the silky wood of the banister rail in a way that made Hanna, watching it, remember the feel of his fingers on her hand, and she turned abruptly towards the window. 'And plenty of garden. You haven't got your neighbours peering in at what you're doing all the time. Quiet, too. I like that.'

Hanna agreed that Fox Hill was a very desirable residential area.

'Look at the timber there. And those floorboards. Won't find anything like that down on that new estate they're putting up in Waverley Lane. And upwards of 95K they're asking for them.'

Hanna said that, yes, Martenswood was certainly a fine example of Edwardian craftsmanship.

'But then, everywhere has its drawbacks, doesn't it? And we can soon sort you out and put you right.'

'You can?' Hanna felt an immense confidence in Steve Ratsaway.

After he had left, she heated up more coffee for herself and sat at the table, staring at the basket of leaves and seedheads. It was odd that when it came to arranging things like that, her fingers worked by themselves, knowing exactly what to do. It was only when she tried to deal with the children, or cook a complicated meal, that she was so inept. But Malcolm did enjoy his food, so, feeling cheerful after the Ratsaway visit, she decided to have another go at bread-making.

When she first came to live at Martenswood, she had been overwhelmed by a primitive urge to make her own bread in this large, warm kitchen with its Aga and its quarry tiles, but now she had to search through larder and fridge to find the ingredients. The sight and the feel of them always appealed to her: the wholemeal flour in its brown bag with a hand-written label in italic script, the special granary flour with crunchy bits in, bran like sawdust, speckled wheatgerm, the jar of glossy molasses, sticky black sugar and crystals of sea salt. And, best of all, the yeast – fresh yeast like a slab of putty (though hers was now sadly dry, and as wrinkled as a dowager's elbow).

'What are you making, Mum?'

It was Tess, back from her nature walk, standing too close, hair trailing in the bowl of flour.

'I thought I'd have another try at making bread.'

'Oh good. I'll watch, then.'

Hanna longed to tell her to go away but girls, after all, learned by watching and copying their mothers. So she gritted her teeth as Tess stood there for more than an hour while she weighed and mixed and kneaded and proved. When she had slapped the dough into gritty mounds on the deal table, she was uneasily aware of Tess's eyes on her while she pounded and pummelled and stretched it, and Tess's own hands clenching into fists on the edge of the table. Could the child read her mind? Did she know that the uncooked dough reminded her of human skin? She closed her eyes as her fingers dug into its depths. She stopped herself from running a forefinger lightly down its moist outer skin, believing for a moment that the living dough would shiver in response. *Get out of my head*, she shouted silently, blushing at the pictures her imagination provided.

Finally, when her hair was hanging in damp strands over her forehead, and she could feel the sweat glistening

on her cheeks and trickling down between her breasts –
as though she had in fact been indulging in illicit acts of
love instead of just in fantasy – she let Tess help her
mould the sections of dough into baking tins and cover
them with damp, nearly clean tea towels. And then, at
last, Tess left her alone.

By the time the boys and Aurora came home, the
sweet smell of baking was filling the kitchen. She lifted
the loaves from the oven, tapped them knowingly to
hear them ring hollow and put them to cool on wire
racks. But when she cut herself a trial slice, she had to
admit that, once again, her bread was a disaster. In the
past, her loaves had been pale and hard all the way
through, so that she and the children sat round the
table with the sound of crunching and chewing taking
over from the usual noisy conversation. But this batch
was dark and moist and soggy, with a crust like wet
suède leather, and a musty flavour that reminded her
of the mouse droppings. She took a shop-bought loaf
out of the freezer and put it into the oven: the boys
wouldn't bother to ask whether she had baked it
herself, and perhaps Tess wouldn't notice how much
larger and whiter it was than the loaves she had helped
to make.

She hated wasting food, though, so tomorrow morning she would get rid of the evidence of her latest
failure by taking it down to Sudden Cottage for Kay
Parker's chickens. It occurred to her, as she crammed
the loaves into a couple of plastic carrier bags and
stuffed them into the back of the larder, that the next
time she felt like making bread she should stifle the
impulse and spend her afternoon instead getting her

hair fixed by Richard at Mahogany. Malcolm would appreciate the improvement in her looks and the children would prefer the thick white sliced bread which she could buy from the supermarket on her way home, like everybody's else's mother.

Chapter Six

Tess came back into the kitchen before Hanna had a chance to clear up, tracking footprints across a floor already spattered with raw dough like the droppings of some large and incontinent bird.

'If you've finished making your bread, Mum,' she said, 'can I make my jam? They'll go well together, won't they?' And before Hanna could answer, she had taken out the preserving pan and started to boil up the squashed, unidentifiable fruits with pounds of sugar and all Hanna's cinnamon sticks. The child was so insistent that she was making her jam as a present for Malcolm that Hanna didn't like to interfere. It smelled awful, though, even with all the spices in, and she couldn't see herself persuading Malcolm to spread it on his breakfast toast, even to please Tess.

'Perhaps it needs keeping for a week or two,' she said, 'to mature.' She didn't want to kill the child's enthusiasm, but you had to be realistic about these things.

'No.' Tess was at her fiercest. 'It's a special present for Malcolm and the boys. I want them to have it straight away. Well, tomorrow morning, anyway. They can spread it on slices of your bread. And I don't want anyone else to eat it.'

Tess's aim had not been perfect when she filled the jars – smears of jam clung like glue to the table-top, and rough dark gobbets of jam, that had the colour, size and texture of squashed baby hedgehogs, dropped slowly towards the layer of guano on the floor.

Hanna didn't confess to her bread fiasco as she inspected Tess's jam. Once it had settled and cooled in its jars it was, unfortunately, dark, thick and opaque, and when Joe came into the kitchen later, he rushed round the kitchen, holding his nose.

'It looks like dogs' turds!' he shouted. 'It smells like dog shit!'

'Make them eat it, Mum!' hissed Tess. 'It's good for them; full of vitamins and stuff like that. They've got to eat it. It's natural. It's *organic*!'

'Orgasmic jam!' shouted Joe.

Hanna glared at him. She didn't want the girls asking what that meant. 'I'll put it away for now,' she said as she gave the two jars gingham covers and put them at the back of the shelf reserved for jams in the larder. 'I expect it will be delicious on toast.' She closed the door on them and went back to the washing up. Tess looked unhappy about it, but she couldn't always have her own way.

And then there was the very peculiar thing that happened to Harry when, five minutes later, she came out to deal with the boys. Joe had punched Tom and Tom had roared with anger and turned on Harry, hitting him in the chest and kicking his shins and pushing him backwards against the kitchen door.

'Stop bullying Tom,' she shouted at Harry, realising

her mistake too late. Harry roared at the injustice of it and a moment later all three boys were on the floor, kicking, punching, biting and shouting.

'Upstairs with the lot of you!' she shrieked at them, grabbing a handful of T-shirt and trying to pull a squirming body free from the mêlée. 'You can all bathe and change into clean clothes for supper,' she shouted. 'And pick the dirty clothes up and put them in the linen basket.'

Finally, they extricated themselves from the fight. Tom was still purple in the face with fury, and Harry was crying and had a scratch on his cheek. But Joe stood up and circled the table a couple of times, gathering his brothers behind him, then spread his arms like aeroplane wings and led the way out of the kitchen and upstairs.

It was a few seconds later that she heard the wordless wail of anguish from Harry and went hurrying up to see what the matter was.

At first she could not see what was wrong. Harry's teddy-bears were lying in neat rows on his bed. The oldest and best loved had bald patches on their fur, and ragged ears, and missing eyes, and were dressed in an assortment of hand-sewn and knitted garments. She recognised Orly in the grey jumper, and Gatwick in the hat with holes for his ears, and she knew that Round-house was the one with the missing arm, but she had forgotten the names of the ten or more others.

'What's up, Harry?'

He was standing by the bed, his face purple with grief, his fists buried in his eyes, still unable to tell her anything. Perhaps one of the toys was missing. Joe might have kidnapped one, or taken it hostage and teased

Harry with the threat of some awful torture. She knelt down so that she was on Harry's level and put an arm round the jerking shoulders. 'Tell me what's wrong, love, can't you?'

Harry raised an arm and pointed at the toys on the bed. Hanna could see nothing amiss. Then, with mounting dismay she realised what had been done: each beloved teddy-bear was skewered to the bed with one of her own fine-gauge steel knitting-pins. In the centre of the bed was Orly, the bear that everyone knew was Harry's favourite. Not only was he spiked through his round tummy, but his arms were fixed together with an elastic band so that they lay folded on his grey woollen chest like a slain crusader's, and he clasped a crumpled white flower in his balding plush paws. A convolvulus, she saw, when she looked closer. The bruised petals gave off a slight, bitter smell.

When she had sorted out the bears and comforted Harry, and promised to push back the pieces of foam and replace the sawdust and sew up the holes in all the furry tummies, she went out on to the landing.

'I want to see you all downstairs in the sitting room,' she said clearly so that none of them could pretend not to hear.

When they were assembled she stared at each of them in turn. Which of them had done such an unkind thing – and to Harry, of all people? There hadn't been time after the fight, it must have happened earlier in the day.

Tess stood impassively, her face unreadable, holding Aurora's hand. Aurora looked apprehensive and guilty, but that probably meant nothing. Joe had his lower lip stuck out and looked stubborn and aggressive – but then again, that was the way Joe usually looked. Tom stood next to Joe, a small reflection of his brother, with the scratch and a new pink bruise on his cheek. Harry stood slightly apart, his face still damp and blotched with tears.

'So which of you did it?'

There was silence for a moment, then Aurora's mouth turned downwards and she started to cry. 'We haven't done anything, have we, Tess?'

'We don't even know what's happened,' said Tess.

'Harry's teddy-bears,' said Hanna impatiently. 'You must have heard the fuss.'

'Oh, that.' And Tess added nothing more.

Hanna turned to Joe. He could be a nasty little sadist, she thought to her own surprise, but was this the sort of thing he went in for?

'Joe? Tom? What do you know about it?'

'Nothing,' said Joe. 'But we're going to get the people who did it, don't worry.'

'Oh no, you're not!' snapped Hanna, feeling like a character in a pantomime. 'When *I* find out who did it, *I'll* make sure they're punished. Understand, Joe?'

But Joe turned to his two brothers. 'We look after our own, OK?'

Even Harry nodded agreement.

Hanna had to let them go. They had retreated into their tightly exclusive camps, and she knew herself to be the outsider. From behind the wainscoting came scrabblings and scratchings as the mice, too, got on with their own lives. She went back into the kitchen: it seemed to be the only area in the whole house where she still retained some control, though when she looked in the larder, someone had placed another of those horrible convolvulus flowers on top of the jars of Tess's hedgerow jam.

Upstairs, Tom went along to Joe's room. As he opened the door, his big brother threw his anorak quickly over something that was on the bed before he could see what it was.

'Look, Joe,' he said. 'Someone's done something funny to Ted.' Joe took the greyish toy from his brother and examined it. 'So you've made it a funny sort of collar. What's wrong with that?'

'But I didn't make it. And it's not really a collar, it's more like a—' But he didn't want to say the word out loud.

They both looked at Ted. The collar was made of string, or twine, rather, which had been knotted round Ted's neck and which had a long end to it. Tucked into it, like a bow tie, was a faded, crumpled white flower.

'It's just a joke, Tom,' said Joe. And he undid the knot in the twine and threw the flower into his waste-paper basket. 'Ted's all right now.'

'He didn't like wearing that collar.'

'Don't worry, he won't have to wear it again.'

When Tom had gone back to his own room, Joe picked up the anorak from his bed and looked at what he had hidden underneath it. Then he pulled the large wooden knitting pin out of Bruno's neck and threw the ragged white flower away with the other two. For a long time he pounded his fists into his pillow, then stuffed it into his mouth to stop everyone hearing him. Then he put a rap cassette into his Walkman, pushed in the earpieces and turned up the volume.

DEATHSPELL

★ ★ ★

Malcolm bounded into the house in buoyant mood that evening, and after he had downed his statutory whisky Hanna told him about the efficient Mr Ratsaway.

'Great,' he said. 'Show me the estimate when it comes and I'll OK it. And have you told the girls about going to Gryphons, Han? I bet they're pleased, aren't they? It's a step or two up from that potty little convent of theirs.'

'It will take Aurora a little while to get used to the idea.' And then, because Malcolm had enfolded her in a large hug and was chewing at her earlobe, she ventured, 'Don't you think she's a bit young to go away to school? She is only seven, after all.'

'Nonsense. It'll do her good. She needs taking out of herself. You mustn't be over-protective, Hanna.'

He had finished nibbling and was trying out some gentle blowing. Hanna was concerned about their supper, which was possibly cooking to a brown pulp in the oven by now, and after the excitements of the day she was, in any case, longing for a chance to sit down and relax in front of an undemanding television screen. She couldn't tell Malcolm, but her feet were hurting and her head was starting to ache.

'We need some time on our own,' Malcolm was murmuring into her ear.

'We do?' His thumb was tracing out slow circles somewhere low down on her spine, but it was still failing to arouse her in any way at all.

'Yes. We need to get started on that entertaining we were talking about: it'll be much easier with the kids out of the way. You'll really be able to concentrate on *me*, then, won't you, Hanna?' He released her and went to pour himself another drink, and she thought that this was not the time to offer him a slice of home-made toast and hedgerow jam, either; or to tell him about Harry's teddy-bears. Malcolm had to be given a strictly edited account of their lives.

'Have you got a babysitter for this Saturday?'

'Should I have done?'

'It's the Dovers' dinner party. Haven't forgotten about it, have you?'

'It just slipped my mind with all that's been going on.'

'Kay Parker will come in and sit for us, won't she? I'll pop down to the cottage to ask her after supper.'

Malcolm ate his meal with greater speed than usual, it seemed to Hanna, and with little interest in what he was eating. She was disappointed that he wouldn't have a second helping of her crème brûlée: she thought it had turned out particularly well, with a thick layer of very crisp toffee on top and the custard only slightly curdled. The smell of burning sugar would take a little time to clear from the kitchen, but it had been worth it, she felt. She must ask Malcolm whether he thought she should serve it at their first grand dinner party. But Malcolm just spooned it in wordlessly, crunched and chewed hard for a few minutes, wiped his face thoroughly with his table napkin and then went off down the lane towards Sudden Cottage. He was gone for quite a while, and he was in such a good mood when he returned that she assumed that Kay had agreed to babysit for them. But Malcolm looked at her quite blankly when she asked him about it.

Did you enjoy that? Did you like the way it felt when you

pushed the needles into their chests?

'I thought about how I hated them all. I remembered what they had done to us.'

Do you remember Jeff?

'Sometimes.'

You can get anything, Tess. Anything you want, if you put your mind and your magic to it.

She didn't remember Gerard speaking like this while he was alive. Perhaps that was what death did to you.

'How was your day, Jean?'

'Fraught. How about yours, Tracker?'

'Quite interesting. I met your friend—'

'Ann rang first thing this morning to say that she'd have to go over to her sister's place to look after the children while she was in hospital. God knows how long that will be for.'

'But you'll cope with one short, surely?'

'I'll have to get out there on the blunt end of a scrubbing brush until I've replaced her.'

'Not really your style.'

'Someone's got to clean the punters' houses if I'm going to pay the mortgage. I'll go over to Hanna Benson's place tomorrow and work the morning there.' She turned out her bedside light. 'What was that you were saying about your day, Tracker? Something about meeting a friend of mine?'

'Did I say that? I've forgotten now, so I don't suppose it was important.' He turned off the lamp on his side. 'Can't we stop talking about work and get on to something else?'

'You have my full attention, Tracker.'

Chapter Seven

If you ask Tess what she remembers best about her life before Gerard's death, she will tell you about that dreamy summer's afternoon when she went walking across the fields with her father and she made the bullocks disappear. It is as though the whole of her childhood is concentrated in that single day, like the rays of the sun through a burning-glass. And yet, even as she is recalling them, the details shift in their kaleidoscopic pattern and the picture changes. Sometimes she sees a hot afternoon, its blue sky stippled with white cloud, and the gnats swarming in thick clouds along the path by the water, prickling her bare arms as she passes through them. But when she looks again, she and Gerard are wearing their Wellington boots and macs and have scarves around their necks and hats pulled down over their foreheads – and Gerard is wearing his green woollen gloves. Sometimes the muddy earth clings to her boots and pulls at her feet as she walks, and yet at others she is running through long grass in her old sandals, her legs powdered with gold from the buttercups. Did a skylark rise from the ground at her feet, to sing out his desperate and beautiful song? Did she and Gerard perhaps go to the meadows together more than once? Or is it that her memory deceives her?

But however the details merge and change as they pass through the distorting pane that separates today from then, here from her beloved there, always, in the background, drifting into view across the long green grass, come the bullocks. And, always, too, she can hear Gerard's voice above her head, telling her not to be afraid of them. Telling her – she is quite certain of this part now – that everything is possible if she can capture the magic that floats in the air and crouches under the ground. She has only to grasp its power and use it to get what she wants. She watches the bullocks retreat across the field and knows that they are afraid of her. Above her head the skylark sings his heart out to pull her attention away from his nest, and Gerard's light voice floats over the field:

As I was coming over the Kilmagenny mountain,
I met with Captain Farrell and his money he was
    countin'.

And she secretly thinks of him as her own brave Captain Farrell, and joins in with the chorus:

. . . Wack fol the daddyo, there's whiskey in the jar!

And now they both laugh, because they know that Mother Philomena does not consider this a suitable song for a girl to be singing. But, with her father beside her, she, Tess Farrell, doesn't have to worry about the fearsome Mother Philomena any more than she does about the bullocks. If someone threatens one of his family, Gerard will remove him. For a moment a figure appears on the towpath. She tries to shout out a warning, but the sky rains blood from purple clouds. She closes her eyes, and when she opens them again the sky has cleared, and she is back in her sunlit meadow.

She kneels by the bottom drawer of her bedside chest and pulls out the worn glove. Today it smells of summer and of Gerard.

'What was the name of the place where we used to live, Tess?'

They had lived in a lot of different places during the three years that Hanna earned her living as a resident housekeeper and cook, but Tess knew that there was just one place that mattered to Aurora: the tall yellow house in the London suburb.

'Fifteen, Wootton Road.'

Aurora sighed. 'Yes, that's it. Just for a moment I thought I'd forgotten. And Dad? I won't ever forget about him, will I? Only sometimes I can't quite think what he looked like. I can see his eyes, but I can't see the rest of him. And do you remember Mum, too?'

Mum was downstairs. They could go down any time and look at her, touch her face, push fingers through her hair. But Tess knew what she meant. It wasn't the old Hanna down there, but a new and different one; the one that had appeared after she married Malcolm.

'Yes. I remember how she used to be.'

'I've still got—' And from behind her back, where she had been hiding it, Aurora brought out an old cotton dress that Tess recognised as once belonging to Hanna.

The material was soft from frequent washing, but she could still see the pattern of pink and white flowers on the pale blue background, and she remembered quite clearly her mother wearing the dress, standing over the gas stove in the house in Wootton Road, stirring something in a big saucepan.

'She put it out for the jumble sale with all her other stuff, after she married *him*. But I didn't think anyone would mind if I took it back again. No one would have wanted to buy it, would they, Tess? Not someone from Fox Hill.'

'No one.'

Tess buried her head in the soft cloth and inhaled. There was the faint scent of flowers, and it brought back Wootton Road and the old Hanna in a way that no photograph could. She remembered the front garden, which smelled of wet privet hedge, and the back garden where there always seemed to be a cat scrabbling in Gerard's vegetable patch. There were dusty-leaved rhododendrons straggling along by the sides of the path, and wild places where she and Tess could hide and play and dream. A couple of times during the summer, Gerard would get out the lawn-mower and try to bring the grass under control, but he wasn't serious about it, and the grass won every time. There were wild flowers in their garden and the local cats came in daily to chase after mice and small floppy hopping frogs. This, she knew, was what Gerard wanted her to take them back to. She had to keep the picture whole in their heads, and one day – soon, now – she could lead them to the place itself.

Hanna was softer, somehow, in those days, and her clothes felt different to the touch. Malcolm bought her different clothes altogether, as their mother had grown thinner and more angular in the past months. And when she and Malcolm went out together and she put on these new, stiff, padded and pleated jackets and skirts, you had to be careful not to get sticky fingers on them, or wave your felt-tipped pens around near her pale shiny blouses.

Tess handed the dress back to Aurora. It had helped her to know what had to be done.

'Do you think they'll let me take it to Gryphons? I know that Harry takes Orly and Gatwick, but he has to leave the others at home, and I wasn't sure that they'd count a dress like a teddy-bear.' Aurora was sitting on Tess's bed, and had twisted the dress round her fingers. She picked up one of the short, loose sleeves and started chewing it.

'We're not going to Gryphons.'

Aurora took the soggy piece of cloth out of her mouth. 'Not ever?'

'No.'

'I knew you'd think of something; you look after us just like Dad did, don't you?' And then, as an after-thought, 'Why did he die, Tess?'

'I don't know, yet.' Dad would tell her about it one day, when he was ready.

On Saturday morning, immediately after breakfast, Malcolm started on the garden. Tess could hear him, shouting instructions to the boys, chugging around on the ride-on mower and trundling backwards and for-wards to the compost heap with the wheelbarrow.

She watched them from her bedroom window. Their foreshortened figures were amazingly similar, like decreasing images of the same original picture: the same square-faced good looks, with blue-grey eyes, red Cupid's-bow mouths, and short, flattened noses. They all had angled jawlines and firm chins. Their ears were large and aggressive and stuck out a bit, and their feet were so wide that Hanna had to traipse from shop to shop to find shoes for the boys that were broad and deep enough for their square feet, and Malcolm had to get his soft black kid slip-ons from a place off Bond Street. Their skin had turned a glowing brown in the summer sun. When Malcolm disappeared round the corner of the house with yet another loaded wheelbarrow of grass cuttings and leaves and twigs, she watched Joe take his place and order his younger brothers around. And still the lawn-mower throbbed away, devouring long grass and nettles. It chewed its way through clover and rag-wort and mallow, spitting them out mashed and unrecognisable. Mr Slug the Destroyer, she thought. And Master Slug the Destroyer's son. They were tearing through living tendrils and leaves, pulling out brambles and dog roses with their gloved hands. She went downstairs to the larder and stared at the jars of hedgerow jam. Why hadn't Gerard made them eat it?

From the garden came a vicious thrashing sound of mower blades, a sharp *clunk* and then silence, followed by Malcolm's angry voice. The garden was fighting back, after all. The back door crashed against the wall and Malcolm came in, tracking mud across the kitchen floor from his green boots, and with the boys trailing after him.

'I'll have to go and pick up a new blade for the mower,' he said. 'Do you girls want to come to the garden centre with us to choose some seeds and things?'

Four locks of dark hair flopped over four low fore-heads, and four full lower lips jutted pugnaciously over four strong chins. Harry had a smear of mud across his nose and cheek and there was a funny smell rising from his boots.

'No, thank you,' from Tess.

'We'd rather stay here,' from Aurora.

'Suit yourselves. But wouldn't you like to grow some pretty flowers? It's the right time to put in bulbs for the springtime.'

Tess wished Malcolm would stop trying so hard to be friendly: she didn't want to be his friend. 'We hate tame flowers.' And anyway, she could have added, tulip bulbs when eaten are rarely fatal.

'Right, well then . . . Come on, lads. We'll be off, shall we? Leave the girls to their own funny little games.' Four figures turned and four hard, round, denim-coated pos-teriors strutted back out through the kitchen door. Tess and Aurora pulled faces at the retreating backs and then, when they heard the Volvo surge away up the drive, they went out into the garden.

It had rained hard during the night, bringing the slugs out from the long, rank grass and weeds. They were everywhere, wet and slimy. On the path leading away from the kitchen door, one large black slug approached a smaller, dun-coloured one.

'What are they doing, Tess? Why's that slug climbing on top of the little one? Is he hurting it?'

'Probably. I think they must be fornicating.' That was the word Sister Patrick used, rolling the 'r' around on her Irish tongue like a small boiled potato, but Tess wasn't sure it was the right one to use when it came to slugs.

'That's sinful, isn't it?'

'I don't think it's quite the same for slugs. Just people. Can you remember anything in the Bible about slugs?'

'No. But we haven't done much this year except parables.'

They wandered across the grass towards an area that was now mostly reduced to bare brown earth. Malcolm had drawn plans of what he was going to do to the garden so they knew that this was the site of the new vegetable patch.

'Well, there's one good thing.'

'What's that?'

'It's the wrong time of year for planting seeds.'

'I expect he'll think of something.'

While they were all occupied, Hanna retrieved the plastic carrier bags of bread from the back of the larder, and slipped down the drive and along Sudden Lane. She turned in to Kay Parker's gate and rang the doorbell.

Kay kept chickens and geese, ducks and rabbits, and Hanna had heard other, unidentifiable birds and animals calling and squawking and howling in the Fox Hill dawns. Kay was always glad to accept free food for her livestock. Sudden Cottage was considered a terrible eyesore by the other Fox Hill residents – 'Due for redevelopment soon,' they said to each other as they clucked with disapproval at her corrugated-iron hen houses and the patches of nettles and heaps of unidentifiable implements that rotted in the mud around her slatternly cottage. 'Soon,' they said, though they'd been saying it for ten years or more.

DEATHSPELL

Although it was now past ten o'clock, Hanna found Kay dressed in an emerald-green satin dressing-gown, with her bleached hair stiffly sprayed and backcombed, her flea-bitten feet crammed into fluffy scarlet mules, and a cigarette between her full fleshy lips. The figure that was revealed by the gaps in the green dressing-gown was also full and fleshy, and uniformly suntanned. She was polite to Hanna. She accepted her offerings, but she didn't invite Hanna inside to sit on the black plastic settee and drink an early gin with her, though she did remove the cigarette from between her lips before thanking her. But Hanna didn't entirely trust the expression in those grey-green eyes: there was a condescension there, as though Kay was party to some secret from which Hanna had been excluded.

As Hanna walked away from the cottage door she averted her eyes from Kay's washing line and the black satin and lace undergarments that jiggled so suggestively in the breeze.

Chapter Eight

Kay Parker ate her breakfast a couple of hours later than the Bensons, and she wasn't pleased to be interrupted by Hanna. Kay's bread came in plastic packets, was white and thickly sliced and produced – with no effort on Kay's part beyond its insertion in the toaster – very good toast indeed. She and Malcolm had eaten a couple of slices, thickly coated with cholesterol-rich butter and Tesco's coarse-cut marmalade, during the stolen hour the previous evening after their vigorous exertions between Kay's purple nylon sheets.

Very enjoyable, her sessions with Malcolm Benson. Brief, of course, but he had a briskly unimaginative style in bed which suited her well. She didn't go in for too much fore- and after-play, herself. Since they both knew what they were there for, they might as well get on with it. So, forty-five seconds after he rapped at the cottage door and strode impatiently into her lounge, she slipped out of her satin dressing-gown and helped Malcolm's fumbling fingers to unbutton his shirt and take off his shoes. After ten strenuous minutes of slithering about on the slippery sheets they were sitting up in bed for a fag, before coming downstairs for their snack in the kitchen, made with proper bread from a packet, none of that wholemeal muck like the boot-faced Hanna baked for him.

'Even the sodding chickens won't eat the stuff,' she told Malcolm. She sometimes wondered if he didn't feel more guilt about the sliced white bread, the butter and the supermarket marmalade than he did about their illicit heavings in the double bed upstairs. So it amused her to be polite to Hanna when she came calling, like Lady Bountiful, with food for the livestock. Hanna should have seen the twenty-pound notes that her husband had tucked under the pillow the previous evening.

'Go on, Kay, treat yourself,' he had insisted when she had shown reluctance. And then they had a cup of tea, laced with gin, and he had told her a very funny story that he had heard that lunchtime at the pub.

She woke feeling warm and cheerful, her skin gleaming with satisfactory sex. But now, though the sun streamed as brightly as ever into the kitchen through the gaps in the curtain where the hooks had come off the rails, Kay's mood had been ruined by the morning's post.

When she had got rid of Hanna, she read through the letter again, then she made herself a third mug of strong instant coffee (Tesco's Gold: she'd got into the habit of buying only the best since she'd known Malcolm), and lit her fifth cigarette of the morning. While she swallowed the coffee, puffed at her cigarette and took absent-minded bites at another slice of toast, she flattened out the stiff sheet of paper with the solicitor's name on the top and tried to make sense of its unfamiliar language. She could get the gist of it all right. Those sods, her landlords, wanted to develop the site which included

Sudden Cottage, and they wanted her out. They'd been talking about it for years and now they'd decided to go ahead. But she had the feeling that there'd been something in her lease about it. She'd have to find the bugger and check it out, and maybe Malcolm would see her home after her babysitting and take a look at this letter for her.

Meanwhile she had another visitor to prepare for. She would tidy the house and feed the birds and animals so that they didn't howl and screech in their sheds and cages. She didn't want to put him off on his first visit. She'd change the sheets on her bed, too. Not that she'd invite a man up to her bedroom the first time he dropped in for a cup of tea, of course, but still you never knew how these things might develop. He had lovely eyes, that bloke. Really deep blue they were. And when he'd stopped to ask her the way to Martenswood, she knew it was because he wanted to get to know her better and she'd allowed the green satin dressing-gown to reveal a glimpse of cushioned thigh as she gave her high-pitched giggle.

'Know them up at Martenswood, do you?' he asked.

'You could say so, I suppose.'

'Don't suppose you have much trouble with mice at your place?'

'Me? Not likely!'

'But if ever you need a man – for the mice, that is – you'll know who to phone for now, won't you?'

It seemed natural after that to ask him to call in for a cup of tea next time he was passing, and she noted where he put his blue gaze while she was talking to him. Yes, she'd have the house looking nice and she'd put on her red dress for him: give his eyes a treat. Mustn't try too hard, though, she thought, as she sprayed Impulse behind her knees. Not the first time. It might give him the wrong idea. Then, as though placing an each way bet, she sprayed up behind her thighs and into the rich dark forest of her pubic hair.

'I told you he'd think of something.'

Aurora and Tess watched as Malcolm unpacked the car and gave the boys their orders. He had found a garden centre to sell him trays of vegetable plants to put into his new plot, even this late in the season.

'Cabbages,' he said proudly.

And, 'Leeks,' as the next trayful disappeared into the back garden, carried by Harry.

'Lettuces. For salad,' he added helpfully.

'Oh, really?' said Tess sourly. 'I thought they must be for pudding.'

'Special variety,' said Malcolm, ignoring her, 'goes on cropping right up to November.'

'I hate lettuce,' said Aurora.

'When we've planted out this lot, we'll be going back for shrubs and things,' Malcolm said happily, passing by with yet another tray.

'What's wrong with the shrubs we've got?' Tess asked Aurora. She supposed that Malcolm would be in there with his pruning saw and his grubbing tool (or whatever the thing was called) and he'd destroy completely the lovely dark green tunnels and rooms where she and Aurora had played during the summer, safe from the boys.

They had cleared secret paths through brambles and

arranged overgrown bushes and overhanging branches so that they had their own world which, until the boys came home on holiday, had been private and entirely theirs. They had watched the grey squirrels springing through old dried leaves, with a scrunching noise like eating Rice Krispies. And there they had played the games they used to play in the garden at Wootton Road, in that summer world when Gerard was still alive and Hanna was forever waiting in the kitchen for them wearing one of her old dresses and cooking something on the temperamental gas stove.

They might have come to regard Martenswood as their home if they could have kept away from Joe and carried on playing in their shrubbery. It didn't smell of privet – that, Tess decided, was a special, London smell – but still, there were red and orange beech leaves under-foot, and the rich Christmas-pudding smell of warm wet earth after rain. And although they chirruped to differ-ent tunes, there were some familiar small brown birds, too.

'What's that one called, Tess?'

'It's a sparrow.'

'Well, what about that one, over there?'

'That's a sparrow, too.' Everyone knew that small brown birds were called sparrows. But then she had gone to the library and got some books out, and had per-suaded Malcolm to buy some more advanced books for her, so that she now knew the names of quite a lot of the small brown birds that hopped and peeped and chook-chooked around them. And if he weren't so busy destroying her entire world, invading it with his bullying, masculine voice and the snarl of his machinery, she would have asked Malcolm if she could have a pair of binoculars for Christmas.

'He had shrubs on his plan,' said Aurora. 'He showed it to me. He's putting in a straight line of them, over there, and another straight line of them along by the drive, up to the gate.'

'I hate straight lines,' said Tess.

'Malcolm likes them,' said Aurora.

Joe had grown bored with planting things. One set of green leaves looked much like another, and with Malcolm around he couldn't boss the other two as much as usual. He had seen Steve's blue van parked in the lane and now was out looking for him. He found him at the side of the house away from Malcolm and the others, examining an airbrick.

'Have you killed any yet?' asked Joe, getting to the point.

'Needs replacing,' said Steve, ignoring the question. 'It's probably where they're getting in.'

'Are there any corpses I can look at?' persevered Joe. 'Have you got some in those plastic bags?'

'Nothing yet,' said Steve.

'Have you thought of shooting them?' asked Joe. 'I'm going to get a gun soon and then I'll be able to go out hunting rats.' He had thought of hunting the girls, too: he and Harry and Tom, creeping through the woods with their new guns, and the girls running terrified through the bracken and the brambles. That would be really wicked.

'We use poison to get rid of vermin,' said Steve, scowling at him.

'I want to see the effect of that stuff when they eat the bait,' said Joe. 'Do they swell up and explode or—'

'No,' said Steve. 'And get your hands off those bags,' he added sharply, grabbing back a plastic packet containing a measured quantity of bait. 'It takes some time before they'll eat it. They're cautious creatures, rodents, and you have to gain their confidence before you can con them into eating your poison.'

Joe grinned at him. 'I'll come back tomorrow, then. Maybe there'll be something to see by then.'

'Don't bother to hurry back,' Steve muttered under his breath.

But Joe was whistling as he sauntered back round the corner and in through the back door: Steve, for all his cleverness, had failed to notice the packet of poison that he had slipped into his jeans pocket.

Finnegan was out hunting again. There was too much activity going on for his liking near the house, so he slithered under the bottom of the gate into the lane and made off down to the ditch and the hedge. At first he could smell only shrews. They had a musky scent and left an unpleasant taste in his mouth, even if he was careful about not piercing their skin with his teeth. He moved further along, through the hedge and into the wheat. Fieldmice were still his favourites, and this was a good place to find them. And when he had caught one he brought it, clamped firmly but bloodlessly in careful jaws, into the house, flowing through his catflap while Hanna wasn't looking. And there he released it, sitting back on his haunches to watch it disappear into the cobwebbed darkness beneath the bookcase.

★ ★ ★

That afternoon a light rain started to fall and Malcolm, in spite of his new Barbour, his tweed hat and his shining Hunters, gave up his gardening efforts for the day and retired to his study with a freshly purchased copy of *The Economical Gardener's Guide to the Gardening Year* and a bottle of whisky.

'I expect,' said Tess, 'he didn't want to get his new clothes wet.'

She and Aurora wandered outside in their anoraks and cut-offs, kicking over a stack of empty plant containers and examining the devastation that had been wrought on their garden.

At the end of each straight row of plants was a hand-written label saying what it contained. And sprinkled at exactly the recommended density were the blue pellets that were necessary if the slugs were not to demolish the lot. Already a couple of slugs, drawn no doubt by the succulent green leaves, had unwisely set their slimy stomachs to Malcolm's plot and had met their inevitable ends.

Tess hunkered down to examine the survivors. Aurora bent down to watch them, too.

'Look, Tess, that one's just like Malcolm.'

She saw what her sister meant. There were slugs of all different sizes and colours: small and large, gingery and grey. But this one was a particularly large slug, glistening with healthy moisture. It was black, like Malcolm's hair, and when Aurora prodded it with a small twig, they saw that its underbelly was a soft, pinkish colour, like Malcolm's face. Its back was ribbed and scaly, its head flattened and smooth.

DEATHSPELL

Malcolm had burned some of his garden rubbish on a bonfire, only a few feet away from where they were. The wet grey ash scented the air like incense.

Aurora's face lit up with a sweet smile. 'Let's kill it, Tess,' she said.

Somewhere overhead a blackbird made his August popping noise. Tess felt a tingling in her arms as though the thin skin had peeled away, leaving her nerves exposed to the moist air.

'For practice, you mean? Or as a sort of . . .' She didn't know a word for it, but it seemed to her that if they could kill the slug, then Malcolm might drop dead as well. 'Wait,' she said. She knew they had to get this right. 'First of all he has to be properly prepared. Fed. Looked after.'

The slug inched towards the row of tender lettuces. In his path lay two blue pellets. Tess removed them.

'We'll have to get rid of all the slug pellets, or he'll never last, not even till tomorrow morning.'

They worked carefully and methodically to remove every one.

'Next,' said Tess, 'we have to get rid of all the other slugs, or there won't be enough food to go round.'

Aurora had to borrow a pair of her mother's rubber gloves from under the sink in the kitchen, but Tess picked up the slugs in her bare fingers. There weren't that many of them, for few had managed to penetrate Malcolm's pellet barrier. They carried each one across to the long grass and dropped it in. The grass by the hedge swayed and rustled and Finnegan appeared, his tail arched high over his back. When they had finished they saw him sitting watching them from the path.

Leaving their slug – the one that they had by tacit agreement named Malcolm – in solitary enjoyment of the young vegetables, the girls built a barrier round the vegetable patch with the blue pellets to prevent any others from encroaching on his path.

'We've forgotten something,' said Tess. 'Wait here,' she said, 'and don't let Malcolm go away.'

She ran up to her room and took what she needed from her treasure drawer. Back in the garden, the rain stopped and Finnegan moved closer to the action. Tess knelt on the path and leant over the raked earth. She put down a candle stub, pushing it in so that it stood firmly. Then she took a tattered book with a dark blue cover and tore out some of the pages, shredding and crumpling them and building a pyramid over her candle stub.

'That's Malcolm's book, isn't it?'

'It's the one the mice ate. He threw it away and I rescued it, so now it belongs to me.'

Finnegan pushed his head through the angle of her arm so that he could sniff at the blue cover. When she had built the structure to her satisfaction, she struck a match and set light to the candle wick. Then, as the paper caught and flared, she produced a flask with a gold stopper and squirted something at the flames. There was a spitting and crackling and a flare of yellow sparks, and then the air was full of the heavy smell of Hanna's new perfume. She pushed the top down again and again.

'What was that for?'

'It's a sort of sacrifice.'

As she breathed in the fumes, Tess felt dizzy for a moment.

DEATHSPELL

That's my girl, Tess. We'll soon have her back with us. Where she belongs.

The candle sputtered to its end, and she started singing:

'I first produced me pistol, and then I drew me sabre,
Crying, "Stand and deliver, for I am a bold deceiver!" '

Tess gathered up her belongings and they took a last look at their handiwork before going back into the house. There was, of course, a risk that Malcolm – the slug Malcolm, that is – might try to escape from his lonely kingdom, but, as far as they could tell, he was as happy as a slug ever is as he started on the first of the lettuces, and the possibility seemed a remote one.

Hanna spent the afternoon going through her wardrobe, trying things on and then rejecting them, deciding on a suitable outfit to wear to the Dovers' dinner party. She would have been comfortable in a cotton dress in this sultry weather, but Malcolm expected her to look like all the other wives. She washed her hair and dried it vigorously with a towel, then looked at her reflection in despair. She rubbed moisturiser into her already shiny face and applied three shades of pink to her eyelids. It was lucky that the children were being so good and quiet, leaving her in peace. They were engrossed in the new gardening project: at last, she thought happily, they were all settling down to live together as a proper family.

Chapter Nine

At half-past seven, Kay Parker settled down in the
sitting room at Martenswood with a cut-glass tumbler, a
freshly opened bottle of whisky, a packet of cigarettes
and the television set turned up high so that she couldn't
hear the children. The Bensons had left for their dinner
party, with Hanna all tarted up and Malcolm smirking
at Kay behind his wife's back. Kay was wearing her new
turquoise and lemon Lycra tracksuit with white plastic
ankle-height aerobic shoes. She had no intention of
taking any serious exercise while she was wearing this
outfit, but she felt it was just the thing for an evening's
babysitting. The children had disappeared upstairs, and
as long as they were in bed and asleep by the time
Malcolm and Hanna returned, Kay would, in her own
opinion, have done the job she was being paid for. What
the children did in the meantime was their own business.

'Right,' said Joe, sitting on the end of Aurora's bed, and
watched from the doorway by a grinning Tom and an
apprehensive Harry. 'Now I'm going to demonstrate the
new, improved, Humane Mouse Exterminator.'

'What does exterminator mean?' asked Aurora, who

never learned not to ask Joe that sort of question.

'Exterminator,' said Tess, appearing behind Harry and Tom, 'means a killer, a destroyer. Like Malcolm, and like Joe.'

'That's right,' said Joe. 'It means a killer. A mouse killer, Aurora. Like the Rat Man's going to use on all those furry little fieldmice.'

'You don't have to believe him, Rory,' said Tess. But Aurora was watching as Joe brought something out from the cardboard box he was holding.

'Here, ladies and gentlemen,' said Joe, 'you have Part A.' He held up a block of wood about eight inches long, three inches wide and two inches thick, with a white letter A painted on one end. 'And here,' he said, 'you have Part B.' He produced from the cardboard box another block, marked this time with a white letter B. Then he smiled at Aurora. 'Now, here's the crucial bit, so watch very closely, Aurora.' Aurora blinked, twice. 'You take your mouse and place it on Part A, like so,' and he placed a lump of grey Plasticine about the size and shape of a fieldmouse on the block in his left hand. 'Then, taking Part B firmly in your right hand, you bring it down—'

'Don't look, Rory!' cried Tess, but she was too late.

The *thwump* as wood squashed Plasticine sounded clearly just half-a-second before Aurora's scream. In the following silence they could hear the television set downstairs blaring out the closing music of a popular quiz show.

Even then, Tess didn't react quickly enough to stop Joe. 'And just to show you what it can really do,' he continued, speaking in a normal tone so that Aurora closed her mouth and listened to him again, 'here is one that I dealt with earlier.' And before Tess realised what he was doing, he pulled from the cardboard box a small, dangling object that he held by its tail. It might once have been a mouse, but now it was crushed and its entrails spilled like coils of vermicelli from its ripped abdomen. Its fur was blotched and clotted with bright blood. Translucent pink ears stood incongruously intact above its distorted and broken mask. Joe swept his arm in an arc and stopped so that its dead eyes were just in front of Aurora's face.

'Piss off out of here!' Tess shouted. She picked up the wooden blocks and landed a furious blow on Joe's shoulder and a less vicious one on Harry's disappearing back, before throwing them both at Tom as he hurried from the room. As she sat on Aurora's bed with her arm around her sister's shoulders, she could hear the shrieks and whoops of triumph coming from Joe's bedroom.

'Don't worry, Rory, he was making it all up. That's not the way the Rat Man gets rid of the mice at all. Mum was telling me he's a real animal lover, so there's no way he'd do anything cruel to them.'

She sat there for some time, with the light off, until Aurora went to sleep. From Joe's room came the crash and shriek of a heavy metal group, while from the sitting room arose the sound of shouting and gunfire as Kay switched over to an American crime series. Tess closed the door behind her and walked along to her own room.

'Did you see them?' she asked Gerard.

I saw.

'Did you see what they did?'

They deserve no mercy, the little devils.

She saw that Gerard had his knife in his hand, the blade lying across his thin white fingers. The three rivets shone silver against the black handle.

'Will you help me?'

You feel it in your hands when you have the power. A drop of blood appeared at the point of the knife, as it had that other time. She had forgotten about it till now.

'I must do something. I must try. Come with me?'

You know when I'm with you.

Tess put on her anorak and went downstairs in her socks, though Kay probably wouldn't have heard her even if she had been wearing walking boots. From the cloakroom she took her wellies, pulled them on and opened the back door. No one saw her as she walked across the garden and out through the gate.

Hanna was relieved when Malcolm approved her appearance.

'You're looking very smart, Han,' he said, but then added, 'Why aren't you wearing the perfume I bought for you? Don't you like it?'

She had muttered that she couldn't find it, and of course she liked it, Malcolm. But she couldn't really blame him for being annoyed – the stuff had cost a bomb, and she couldn't understand why the bottle was empty. She remarked, quickly, how distinguished Malcolm himself was looking in his new charcoal-grey suit with the faint stripe, the hyacinth-blue Sea Island cotton shirt and red and blue Liberty silk tie. The journey would take only a couple of minutes, since the Dovers lived just a few hundred yards down the lane, but Malcolm said that they should drive there in the Volvo, although the massive estate car brushed against the hedges in the narrow lane and Malcolm, she knew, worried about the paintwork.

The Dovers' hall was large and panelled, with Persian rugs on the polished floor. Moving carefully in her high heels, Hanna approached Jenny Dover with her hand outstretched, realising only at the last moment that her hostess expected a kiss on either cheek. Off balance, she caught her heel in the fringe of the rug and fell into Pearce Dover's arms. He was not very tall, but luckily stocky enough to hold her upright, and the two of them danced a sort of embarrassed *paso doble* before Hanna regained her balance.

'Lovely to see you both,' murmured Jenny, diplomatically ignoring this mishap and smoothing cream wool crêpe down over slim hips.

'Expect you'd like a whisky, Malcolm,' said Pearce. When Pearce brought her own dry sherry, Hanna took the drink out of his hand (a gin and tonic, she discovered – was it perhaps Pearce's own?) and passed on into the pink-papered drawing room.

There were at least sixteen of them to dinner. Some – the older ones – had always lived on Fox Hill and looked condescendingly on the newcomers (though they envied their money); the younger ones were of the same thrusting, successful kind as Malcolm. Hanna exchanged bored stares with painted cows in a painted meadow.

'Good investment, those, Han,' said Malcolm from behind her. 'House value's risen forty-seven per cent in the past eighteen months, too. Smart man, Pearce Dover.'

She had to admit that the room and indeed all that she had seen so far of the house was, like the Dovers, very smart, and perhaps it was true that you couldn't invite people from Fox Hill into your house until it had been

Technicleened into a similar state of smartness. The thought of ever getting Martenswood to this state depressed Hanna. The idea of keeping it like that for ever seemed impossible.

'Malcolm, darling, come over here and talk to us!' shrieked a female voice from across the room, while Jenny took Hanna firmly by the arm and led her over to a group of ancient tortoises.

'This is Hanna Benson,' she said, and left.

Little shortsighted faces swayed precariously towards Hanna on scrawny, wrinkly necks, then retracted into brown carapacious clothing as they continued their conversation.

It was a relief when dinner was finally served in the dark dining room by the Dovers' au pair, a plain girl who followed each plateful of food with hungry eyes.

They started with a portion of raw vegetables, arranged in a daisy pattern on a puddle of clear red sauce on a white octagonal plate. Hanna tuned in to the conversation.

'Funny how attractive a powerful woman can be,' a male voice was saying. 'You'd think it would turn you off, wouldn't you?'

'I don't know about that,' said a dark-haired, over made-up woman in a wide-shouldered sequined and draped bodice at the far end of the table from Hanna. 'What woman in her right mind wants the slog of going out to work every day and worrying about the mortgage? No, leave power to the man, let him dominate as much as he wants – and I'll have his gin and tonic waiting for him when he gets home in the evening. And I won't be wearing a shapeless old pair of jeans when he gets there, either. I know how to manage a man, I can tell you.'

'Bet you know how to manage his bank account, too, Diana,' said a voice on Hanna's left, but pianissimo.

'Does power necessarily mean dominating other people? And do money and power always go together?' Hanna ventured, addressing her remarks towards the quiet voice on her left.

'I can't think of any other kind for the moment,' replied the voice, and she realised that she was speaking to her host, Pearce. 'Though women like Diana use the power of sex. But what's the point of it unless it brings you a wealthy partner?'

'What about talent?' asked Hanna, wistfully. 'Using your talent can bring satisfaction, at least. Talent has power, doesn't it?'

'Not unless it has money behind it. Talent alone won't get you anywhere: a good business brain is what you need.'

'People don't want power, what they really want is to be told what to do.' This was a new voice joining in the discussion. 'Your man in the street doesn't want to have to make his own decisions – hasn't got the mental equipment, anyway.' The speaker was on Hanna's right, a red-faced man who slurped his words like tomato soup: Russell, the naval commander, she remembered.

'But I still think,' said Hanna, 'that people want the freedom to decide their own destiny.'

'Power? Freedom? Destiny? What big words you use, my dear Mrs Benson . . . Hanna . . .' Russell's hand moved damply over her knee and she could feel its plump pressure through her skirt. 'But a fascinating subject,' he said, slurping his words more than ever. 'And so tell me what sort of power it is that you want, my dear?'

'I'd like to feel in control,' said Hanna, swallowing her wine and trying to remove a hand like a beached jellyfish from her leg without appearing to be aware of it. 'I'd like to wake up in the morning and know that I could do what I wanted – that my time wasn't dictated by other people's needs. I'd like to transform my house so that I could walk through it without tripping over a skateboard, and then I'd like to look in the mirror and know who I was.'

'You're nothing but a little pleasure-seeker, aren't you?' said Russell, getting bolder.

Hanna drank the rest of her glass of wine and wished that she'd packed a hatpin in her evening bag. Then an elderly woman with a small but very ripe gooseberry for a mouth glared at Russell so that he removed his hand from its position halfway up Hanna's thigh, and asked loudly whether anyone had read the shortlisted Booker novels yet. This flummoxed most of them and the conversation subsided to a general buzz again.

Hanna took a mouthful of green mousse swimming in a pool of transparent yellow sauce and garnished with a feathery leaf. A second mouthful, and it was gone. Perhaps in the kitchen there had been dishes piled with mashed potatoes and baskets overflowing with hot herb breads, but all had been eaten by the starving au pair as she waited to bring in succeeding courses. She drank another glass of the very good white wine and returned to her own thoughts. She wished that she could understand this mystery about power. Why was it that Gooseberry Mouth could quell Russell with one glare, whereas she would have gone on ineffectually pushing his hand off her thigh for the rest of dinner if it had been left to her? If only she could grasp some of this power they were all talking about for herself – just a very small fistful of the stuff would do – then she could gain control over her own life as well as over lecherous male hands. She would tell the children to do something, and they would all go away and do it. She would put a meal in the oven, tell it to cook itself, and it would – without sticking like tar to the dish. The house would not look like the municipal tip (Malcolm had a point there, she conceded, as she started on another glass of Pearce's really excellent wine), but would conform to the high standards of Fox Hill. These people all around her, stupid as most of them sounded, obviously knew something that she didn't: she should be paying attention to what they were saying.

'. . . about time they privatised the education system, if you ask me,' Russell said. She returned effortlessly to her own world as yet another plain white plate was placed in front of her by the au pair: slivers of chicken, two mangetout peas, and this sauce was beige with green dots. Gooseberry Mouth prodded at hers, red lips pursed. Hanna was looking forward to the thick peanut butter sandwich she intended eating when she got home. Meanwhile she was relieved to see that Pearce had refilled her wine-glass.

Tess had stuffed a torch into the pocket of her anorak before leaving the house, and now she pulled it out and switched it on. It wasn't easy to make her way along the footpath in the pitch dark. There should be a moon tonight, she knew, but it was hidden behind the thick banks of cloud that streamed across the darker backcloth of the sky and pressed with their rain-laden weight on her head and back. At least the torchlight saved her from falling into the worst potholes and showed her the stile at the corner of Bennett's field. Once over it, the long wet grass clung uncomfortably to her bare legs above her Wellington boots. Bleached white buttercups starred the field and she inhaled the sour smell of waterlogged earth.

'Are you there?'

He often joined her on the other side of the stile. She had grown so much taller in the past three and a half years that he didn't need to help her over it any more. But tonight there was silence and she felt very much alone. Her plans wouldn't go right. She had got that book out of the library and had turned straight to the last chapter, Plants to Avoid. She had skimmed the story about the couple who made soup out of water hemlock and then nearly died – she wasn't sure she could identify it from the picture, it looked just like cow parsley to her. But a lot of the other plants she did recognise and had found on her walk. Someone else's magic – evil magic – must be working against her, since in spite of all her efforts, no one was lying in a coma at Martenswood, or having plastic tubes stuck into them at the John Radcliffe.

She tasted the coppery flavour of the coming thunderstorm on her tongue as Gerard joined her and swung silently along beside her as she made her way towards the river. There was a light wind and the trees added their cascading rustle to the chatter and gurgle of the stream beyond the pollarded willows.

Where the path joined the river bank, there was a small gravelled bay and Tess climbed down and stood there, listening to the river and turning her face to the sky to catch the first huge drops of rain.

'You've got to help me. I know that you could destroy them for me if you wanted to.' She tipped her head back to speak to the weeping clouds and the dark figure that lowered above her. 'Are you listening?'

Don't I always hear what you say?

'Then do it!'

Don't you feel the power rising?

'No, I feel nothing but the rain on my face.'

Just hold on to my hand and I'll make the stars whirl and dance for you.

The rain was coming down in earnest now and Tess's hair hung down in dark fronds, sticking to her face and dripping down her neck. She turned round so that she was facing the hill where Martenswood stood, its lights just visible through the surrounding beech trees. A little further along, to the left, she could see the lighted windows of the Dovers' house where Hanna and Malcolm were sitting at dinner. Then from beyond the hill she saw the first snake of lightning and a few seconds later the thunder rolled down the slope towards her.

'We did it before, didn't we? You showed me the magic and I made them disappear.'

That's not all I did, is it? So trust me.

For a moment nothing happened. Then the thick black sky shivered and further over the hill, past the Dovers' house, a second snake of lightning leapt to the ground, followed by a fiery starburst and a crash of thunder that seemed to echo and roll all around her. When she looked up, she saw that the lights in Martenswood and in the Dovers' house had gone out, as though the two houses and all the people in them had ceased to exist.

'Thanks,' she said. 'I knew you were listening really.'

We can go home now.

She walked back up the field. If anyone had been listening, they would have heard her singing:

'She sighed and she swore that she never would
  deceive me,
But the devil take the women for they never can be
  easy.'

The beam of the torch was swamped by the torrential rain, but, in her triumphant state, Tess was sure-footed. Gerard joined in the chorus of her song as he strode along beside her, before he left her at the stile. She heard his voice behind her, singing the next verse as she walked up the path towards Martenswood. There was something in the back of her mind that nearly pushed forwards into consciousness and she knew that she didn't want to know what it was. Then she forgot it again as she thought about the joy of winning the battle against Malcolm and the boys, of making them disappear for ever. She knew that the knife would be in its place in the drawer when she got back to her bedroom.

'What's happened?'

'Where the hell are the candles, Jenny?'

'Maybe it's a fuse. Have you got the fuse wire?'

'Do you think it's the sub-station gone? Must have been struck by lightning.'

'Rather fun, this, don't you think, Hanna?'

'Ouch!'

'Everybody stay where they are! Jenny and I will sort it out in a minute—'

'Fancy seeing you again, Malcolm—'

'Haven't you found the torch yet, dear?'

'That you, Dishpot? Never expected to meet you here—'

Jenny Dover had drawn together the thick velvet curtains before dinner, so the room was now completely black. But Hanna could hear the rustlings and whisperings of people moving quietly about.

'Do you think the children are quite safe?' she asked the room in general.

'You just hold on to me, old girl. The Navy'll see you right.' But she didn't think the Commander was speaking to her. It was difficult to tell who was speaking to whom, or indeed who anybody was in the dark.

'You're looking pretty good yourself—'

She caught a whiff of stale cigarette smoke as figures shifted place.

'I've found the candles. Has anyone got any matches?'

'Here, Jenny, have these.'

'Diana? Trust a smoker to have a light handy!'

A match flared briefly, illuminating a bright lipstick mouth and dangling earrings. But was the hair fair or dark? Hanna couldn't be sure in that short glimpse before the match died again. The voice was slightly common, she thought.

'I've got the matches, darling. I'll bring them out to the kitchen.'

'You're looking very prosperous, Malcolm.'

Was it the same voice? Not local, she thought. Essex, probably.

'I'm so sorry, was that your foot?'

'Jenny! Where have you got to with those matches?'

'We must get together again some time—'

'Come on, Jenny! Why are you taking so long?'

'—so much to talk about—'

'I blame the weather forecasters, myself. Never get the thing right.'

'—I could meet you there on Wednesday.'

'Thursday. In the afternoon. Up at—'

'Thursday.'

'Here we are, everybody. Lights again at last.'

'You're a marvel, Jenny, darling.'

There were candles in silver candlesticks and candles stuck on to old saucers, giving a soft light that was kind to faces that were flushed and shining from a combination of much wine and little food.

'Oh, well done, Pearce. This is wonderful.'

'I thought it was rather fun, myself.' That was the Commander, who had doubtless been pinching thighs and searching for soft bosoms since the moment the lights went out.

'Now, dear, how about bringing on the pud?'

Hanna brightened. Pud sounded substantial, but it would probably turn out to be two teaspoonfuls of sorbet and a blackcurrant leaf.

'Good idea. Why don't you pour everyone out another glass of wine, Pearce?'

Heads moved closer together, conversation hummed confidentially. She thought that several people had changed their places at the table.

The sorbet was wrapped in a minute parcel of almond pastry, and there was no blackcurrant leaf, just a white sugar flower. It reminded her of a convolvulus, and she shivered. Two modest mouthfuls and she was free to listen to the increasing volume of conversation around her and try to single out one particular voice. Gooseberry Mouth was complaining about Godless bishops and women priests; the Commander was trying to get a bit closer to the blonde who had come with one of the spare men; there was a woman whose name she hadn't managed to catch talking to Malcolm at the other end of the table. It was no good, she couldn't distinguish names, faces, voices; and in the fitful candlelight, expressions were distorted and eyebrows danced and lips curved in unfamiliar shapes. Which of them could possibly answer to the name Dishpot?

Kay Parker didn't care about the thunderstorm, but she did notice when the lights went off and the television screen went blank.

'Shit!' They had good films on the telly Saturday evenings, and she wanted to know what happened at the end of this one. She wondered for a moment about going upstairs to see whether the kids were all right in the dark. Better not, she didn't know her way around up there and would probably fall over and break an ankle. Aurora was always whining about something, anyway, so it wouldn't make much difference.

Luckily she remembered quite accurately where she had put the bottle of whisky on the small table, and she managed to pour herself out another one without spilling too much. Then she lit a cigarette and waited for someone to switch the power back on.

All night the rain fell upon Malcolm's vegetable garden like grapeshot, beating delicate green leaves into a pulp and ruining his fine tilth.

Next morning he saw that his row of lettuces had practically disappeared – and so had the slug pellets, in spite of the manufacturer's assurances on the label that they were resistant to rain. The air was thick with white butterflies, swooping and dropping on to the remaining cabbages and Brussels sprouts. He would have to take Monday off from work to repair the damage and replace the plants. When Hanna came out to hang up the washing, he off-loaded some of his irritation on to her by shouting, 'You'll have to think about returning the Dovers' hospitality.'

'Don't you want to wait until—'

'Get that Technicleen woman moving. I want to see this place under control. And, Hanna—'

'Yes, dear?'

'Start thinking up some new decorating ideas, will you? Take a look around, see if you can find—'

'Don't tell me, something like the Dovers' stuff. All right, dear.'

Malcolm didn't like having his sentences finished for him, so he said, 'Good. Well, what have we got for lunch?'

That was enough to send Hanna hurrying back to the kitchen and out of his sight. Shortly afterwards the smell of scorching potatoes floated through the open window.

Chapter Ten

Hanna sprang from bed half an hour early on Monday morning, knowing there were things she had to do that she would never get finished. This was the morning of the Technicleen invasion and she started picking up toys, books and newspapers from their resting places on the floor and cramming them into cupboards and on to shelves before returning to the bedroom to get dressed. She dealt with washing up that had mysteriously appeared overnight and then panicked because there would be breakfast for seven to clear before she could allow the Technicleeners into her kitchen. She tried not to feel annoyed that Malcolm had taken the morning off, she shouted at the children to get up, nagged them to put their discarded clothes away, seeing the house all too clearly through the eyes of critical strangers.

Jean Rainbird arrived promptly at half-past eight, driving one of her bright green vans and dressed in matching overalls. Her companion was a big girl with forearms like a weightlifter's, who unloaded metallic equipment from the back of the van and carried it into the house.

Within five minutes her aggressive use of a vacuum

cleaner had driven Malcolm from the folders of papers in his study and out into the garden. Hanna crept about the house while around her machinery whined and hummed. She flattened herself against the wall as green figures passed her on the stairs, and hid in the kitchen while implements with long handles and odd-shaped brushes whispered around her ceilings and picture rails, ingesting dust and cobwebs. Finally, admitting to herself that her presence was of no practical use, she sent the boys off to the Elliotts' lake for some fishing again and begged a lift from Malcolm for herself and the girls to go into town shopping for their new school uniforms.

She hunched in the front seat of the car, clutching the Gryphons clothing list, while Aurora grizzled in the back seat next to a silent Tess. She felt useless and worse, she felt like a traitor. She was deserting Martenswood, betraying it to strangers. She felt a thick, strong, but invisible elastic band joining her to the house so that the further the car carried her away from Fox Hill, down the bypass towards the city, the stronger the backwards pull of Martenswood until, as she stood at Carfax and watched the Volvo disappear down the High Street, cold gusts of panic swept through her. She had been wrong to want the house transformed. It was lovely the way it was – familiar, safe, friendly. She didn't want to impose smart new decorating schemes on its scruffy interior.

'Come on, Mum,' said Tess, at last, taking one of her hands. 'We can't stand here for ever.'

So Hanna took the other small, damp hand that was Aurora's, and they pushed their way through a noisy thicket of French schoolchildren, through diesel fumes and discarded hamburger trays, past the beggars and the buskers, towards the shop where the girls, too, would be transformed. But even as they dodged between two minibuses and an express coach, above the noise of their engines Hanna fancied she could still hear the throb and whine and slap of the machines that were eagerly ravishing Martenswood.

Steve parked his car round the back of Kay's chicken shed, as befitted his status as an invited guest. Tea on Saturday had been very enjoyable, even if it had halted at a minor skirmish on the simulated-leather slopes of Kay's sofa, and now he was back for Monday lunch, before moving on to deal with the Martenswood mice in the afternoon.

Kay put two plastic bags to boil in a saucepan of water, and they had twenty minutes to wait before the meal would be ready.

'Had any ideas about my problem?'

Kay had explained on Saturday about Sudden Cottage. She would have welcomed Malcolm's advice, but unfortunately she hadn't had a chance to mention it to him after the babysitting on Saturday night, what with all the fuss about the power cut and that kid Aurora screaming her head off about dead mice or something.

'It looks to me as though they'll be able to get you out of here in the end, but not right away,' Steve answered, when he'd taken another look at the letter and at the lease. 'They'll have to go through all the legal crap with eviction orders and that before you need to pack up and leave.'

'Thanks. You're a great help. Friend of the landlord, are you?'

'I didn't say you just had to sit there quietly and wait for the JCBs to arrive, did I? Look, it's going to cost them, taking you to court, not to mention the time they'll have to wait around before they can start demolishing or building and that.'

'So?'

'So, you offer to leave, nice and easy and no fuss – but at a price.'

'What sort of price, do you reckon?' When it came to money, Kay was quick enough, he noticed.

'Must be worth 5K to them, mustn't it? Maybe more.'

'Here, I'll go and look at the lunch, see if it's ready.'

'Don't be daft! What's to see with boiling plastic bags? You could find us a couple of tubes for while we're waiting, though.'

'Cheeky bugger!'

But the look she gave him from under her mascara'd lashes was still encouraging. Later, Steve, later, he reminded himself. Stick with the main point for now.

'What about your friend up at Martenswood: can't you touch him for a bit?'

'Why would he pay anything?'

'Dish up the boiled plastic, Petal, and we'll work on it.'

Later that same afternoon, Hanna sat with her sewing basket, the pile of new clothes and the name-tapes, in her clean and tidy, and now unfamiliar, small sitting room. She was trying not to notice what Steve was doing with boxes and tins while he trod his light-footed way around the house and garden, whistling softly through his teeth.

DEATHSPELL

At four o'clock she asked him whether he would like a cup of tea and was treated to the full wattage of his smile. She was ready this time, with three different sorts of biscuits, just in case he didn't like plain chocolate digestives. She had successfully hidden them from the children for two whole days.

They sat at the kitchen table, like last time. She was wearing her new soft green shirt with the pattern of dark green leaves and pink berries. She had put on some lipstick, and a clear gloss over the top, and washed her hair that morning. But was the blue eye-shadow perhaps too much for the daytime? She wasn't sure, but she thought that Steve sat just an inch or so closer to her than he had before. She tried to control her breathing, but it still sounded fast and shallow and far too loud.

Steve's eyes finished their assessment of the room and returned to her face. 'Been here long?'

'I've been here since we were married, last spring.'

'Divorced, were you, before that?' The blue eyes looked so sympathetically into hers that she didn't feel that the question was at all impertinent.

'Widowed.'

'Oh, sorry.'

'That's all right. It happened over three years ago.' Then she added, 'His name was Gerard and I do still miss him.'

'Tell me about him.'

What a very peculiar conversation this was. Why did she feel that she could talk about Gerard to the Rat Man? And how did he know that she had been longing to talk to someone about her dead husband? For no one, after all, wanted to hear about their housekeeper's personal problems, and it hardly seemed appropriate to talk to a live husband about his dead predecessor.

The silky circumflex accent rose a few millimetres. 'Well?'

'Oh, what can I tell you? He was unpredictable and difficult; he was bossy and he was jealous, but he was free and we were more alive when he was around. I feel so buffeted these days by everyone else's demands that I've forgotten how freedom feels.' She picked at a strand of hair. 'Maybe it's the price I pay for security. When Gerard had a pile of bills and no money, he just told people to bugger off and took us all for a day out. But money used to worry me.'

'That doesn't sound like freedom to me.'

'Have another biscuit. The ones with jam in the middle are rather good.'

'Cheers.'

'He covered his fecklessness over with a layer of charm, if I'm honest about him, but at least he wasn't always trying to change me into something different, and I still miss him.'

A sun-browned finger skimmed down the back of her hand for a second, in a comforting way.

'And Malcolm? What about him?'

'I'm very lucky to have Malcolm. Really. He looks after all our needs. But oh, Steve—'

'Any chance of another cuppa? And you're right. The biscuits with the jam in the middle are the best.'

So that was it. The money all belonged to Malcolm. Pity, that. He could have quite fancied her otherwise, even though she was a year or so older than him. Gerard had probably kicked it leaving her nothing but two small kids, a load of debts and a few good memories. What did Malcolm see in her, if she was so poor? Maybe it was those cool blonde looks: you'd try like hell to see whether you could get her to drop the ladylike act and behave like a real flesh and blood human being, if you had the chance, preferably while lying beside her between lavender-scented linen sheets. He realised he was starting to find her a challenge, and reminded himself that without money she wasn't for him; he couldn't afford a Hanna Benson.

She wasn't as dim as she looked, though, landing something as substantial as Martenswood. How much were houses on Fox Hill worth now? Nothing up here went for much under a hundred and fifty thousand, and Martenswood was no run-down cottage. If Malcolm were to have the heart attack he looked as if he was due before he nudged his forty-fifth birthday, she'd be worth a bob or two. Now then, Steve, she's nowhere near being a widow yet, so stop dreaming and keep your thoughts and your hands to yourself and your eye on your real goal.

His gran had lived up here on Fox Hill, in one of the terraced cottages along Ridley Way, before they'd been tarted up with name-plates and Austrian blinds. He felt he owed it to the old girl to get himself back here, out of the flat he shared in the crowded street off the Fridesley Road. He owed it to himself, too, of course: Steve Tracker was going to make it one of these days.

'What's that stuff you're putting down?'

It was the thin, witchy-looking one, interrupting his train of thought in the irritating way that kids had. 'It's called warfarin. What're you called, then?'

'I'm Tess. That stuff looks like little blue beads. Is it really poisonous?'

'If you had four paws and a pair of hairy ears, it's what you'd call lethal. Deadly. Seriously dangerous.'

'But not to people?'

'That depends how much you took, how often and for how long,' said Steve, wondering how he could change the subject. He didn't think it was a suitable one to be discussing with a small female. But this child was crouching down beside him, dipping a finger into a bag.

'Here,' he said. 'Don't do that! It can go in through your skin, you know. Look at me, wearing gloves: you wouldn't catch me sticking my fingers in the stuff like that.'

'Sorry,' said Tess. 'But that means it does hurt people, even if they haven't got hairy ears, doesn't it?'

'A man would have to eat a lot of it all at once—'

'How much is a lot?'

'About sixty pounds.'

She looked blank, so he explained. 'Think of bags of sugar, right? Now think of thirty of them.'

'All that much, at one meal?'

'Couldn't do it, could you? But if you ate much less than that – oh, half a bagful, maybe – every day for a week, then you could do yourself some real harm. Especially,' he said severely, 'a little kid like you. Probably would need less to finish you off, you being a lightweight. So keep your fingers out of it, all right? And make sure those brothers and sisters of yours keep away from it, too.'

'Thanks for telling me about it, Steve, I'll remember

what you said,' and she smiled at him. She's really quite a sweet little kid, he thought. And she'll be a looker one of these days, too.

'Steve, I wonder if you could give me a hand for a moment?' It was Hanna, looking as fragile and helpless as a tall, healthy woman ever could. 'Sorry to interrupt you,' she said, pushing back a strand of hair. 'But this box is rather heavy for me to lift on my own. Do you mind?'

He never minded showing off his shoulder muscles to a woman and he followed her into the house. When he got back to his bait-laying, the little girl – Tess, was it? – had disappeared again. She must have taken his warning to heart.

'Don't you like your tea?'

'What? Oh, it's great.' It was just that he'd had three cups of tea and half a dozen biscuits in the past hour and wasn't feeling like any more. But he could hardly tell Kay that. And he had another meal to face when he got home. Christ, he'd be putting on weight if he went on like this.

Half an hour and some anaerobic exertion later, lying in bed smoking a fag, he was a lot more relaxed. Kay was smiling with satisfaction and he thought he could risk some more direct questions.

'Tell me about Malcolm,' he began.

'What's there to tell? He's a good bloke, I suppose. Generous.'

'Still, it's been peanuts you've had from him up till now, and what you're going to need is some real money.'

'But what's it to you, Steve? That's what I can't make out.'

'I'm fond of you, aren't I, Petal? I'm looking out for you.'

She lit his last fag. He'd have to go out again soon and get them some more: Kay Parker smoked too much. But he said, 'And don't undersell yourself. You make the best cup of tea—'

'Is that what you call it!'

'—on Fox Hill, and I'd like to help you.'

'Don't get me wrong, I'm not turning you down. But what do you reckon we should do?'

'I wondered when you were going to ask me that,' he said gently. 'Now, Petal, here's my plan . . .'

Malcolm saw that there was nothing he could usefully do to his vegetable patch until the soil had dried off considerably. He shouted at the girls to keep away from it, too. He couldn't understand why they were fascinated by it now that there were hardly any plants left, but he kept seeing their heads, one molten gold and the other liquid honey, bent over the ground, prodding something with a twig. Funny things, girls. He turned to the area where he was going to put in a row of shrubs, in carefully decreasing sizes. He set off with gloves and fork and trowel and wheelbarrow for the place he had marked out on his squared-paper plan.

An hour later and he was sweating underneath his Barbour and words that he thought he had forgotten years ago rose to his lips.

Bindweed. It was everywhere. It had crept in from the surrounding fields, over and under and through his fences and hedges. It sidled across lawn and flowerbed. Just when he thought he had followed the long stringy stems to their source and rooted them out, another head pushed up out of the earth with its furled leaflets, ready to take over a section of his garden.

He pulled at tangled skeins of weeds, and saw the cuts and scratches that they left on his hands. This stuff! He'd never imagined anything like it. It had a mind and a will of its own, like some fast-breeding animal, rather than a simple weed.

And it didn't help his temper when he looked up to find that the girls were standing there watching him. Tess was smiling at his efforts to disentangle his fork from the bindweed stems.

'Why don't you,' he said grimly, 'go and help your mother with the lunch?'

'Because it's three o'clock in the afternoon,' said Tess.

'Then why didn't someone call me in for a meal?'

'We didn't like to disturb you.' They turned back towards the house and he heard Tess say to Aurora, 'Have you noticed what hairy ears Malcolm's got?'

As Malcolm stamped back to the house he caught up with Joe.

'What's that you've got?' he asked sharply.

Joe stuffed the small plastic bag of blue granules into his pocket. 'Nothing.'

'Have you been messing about with that Ratsaway's gear?'

Joe faced up to his father, both hands stuck into his pockets, belligerent chin stuck forward. 'Well, if I had a gun I wouldn't need this poison stuff, would I? I could shoot the mice' – he pointed his arm at imaginary rodents – 'bang, bang!' he said. 'And I could get that scraggy cat, too,' he said, pointing a digit at Finnegan.

'And you could break a few hundred pounds' worth of windows,' said Malcolm, looking up at the shining glass of Martenswood and the greenhouse next to the garden shed. 'And I could have bills from the neighbours, too, I expect, every time they broke a window and blamed you for it.'

'Vermin,' said Joe, doggedly. 'I could get rid of vermin for you, Dad.'

'I've told you,' said Malcolm, his voice rising, his face taking on the colour of a newly baked brick, 'that we'll talk expensive toys when you've come back from Gryphons with a decent report at the end of the term. No more of that rubbish about not paying attention and being a disruptive influence on your classmates.'

'Form, Dad, not class. Like we call it prep instead of homework.'

Brick was deepening to pimento. Joe decided to call it a day and get back to his other amusements, so it was Hanna who bore the brunt of Malcolm's fury.

'Snot-nosed bugger isn't going to make me use those poncy words,' he said as he sat down to a plate of cold mashed potato and warm ham. 'I'll show him who's master in this house.'

'How's Malcolm?'

'He's doing all right. Look.'

They weren't talking about their stepfather. They were standing close together by the vegetable plot, watching their slug.

'Has he got enough to eat, do you think?'

'I think so, as long as he likes leeks. He's nearly finished the lettuces.'

126

DEATHSPELL

The slug had grown as thick as Malcolm's thumb, like a tentacle of squid that had become detached and now lived an independent life. He was looped over a leaf and draped down into the tender heart of the last lettuce.

'Yes. And most of the cabbages have gone,' said Aurora.

'I think that was the rain. I don't think he can have eaten the cabbages as well. He isn't big enough.'

'He's very greedy, though. And he is pretty big, isn't he?'

'Bigger than yesterday.'

'Can we kill him soon?'

'Yes.'

'When?'

'Not long, now.'

Chapter Eleven

'I'm taking the car for an hour, Malcolm.'

She knew he didn't like that sort of bold statement; he preferred to be asked, very politely, but just for once she didn't care. She had heard the children chatting away together and the conviction surged over her that everything was going to be fine now. All they needed was the chance to get to know each other. Once they learned to get along, to stop that constant teasing and squabbling, then they would be fine and could start to grow into happy, independent young people. If they got to know Malcolm better they would come to love him. White wine, she thought, had a less depressive effect on her spirits than red. She hardly noticed that Malcolm was frowning at her.

'I'm not sure about that, Han.'

'What?'

'The car. I might be needing it later.'

'That's all right. I'll be back before you want it.' She was behind the wheel before he could object further, smiling at him, switching on the engine, shifting into gear. She accelerated away, turned right at the top of the lane and then left at the junction, joining the traffic on the bypass. He kept telling her how generous he was, so now she would take him at his word. And he would love what she was going to do to the house, once he got used to it.

It was a large garden centre, stretching over an acre or more. She walked quickly through rooms full of plastic flowers and imitation grasses like pink and green candy-floss. She passed pottery rabbits in mobcaps, hedgehogs with parasols, cats with pink fur and painted blue eyes. She strode through a rain forest smelling of damp compost until she reached the section she wanted. And there she gathered up enormous glazed pots, and even larger unglazed ones, and took them to the check-out. She bought wicker baskets and armfuls of cut flowers, then she moved on to buy containers of shrubs and small trees and things with green leaves that trailed or crept.

The man at the till recognised the name on her cheque card and accepted it without question, sending out a couple of youths to help her to fold down the seats and pack everything into the back of the estate car. The tallest of the trees pushed out through the sun roof like a personal standard. For the first time since she had married Malcolm she felt the heady power that comes from being rich. She could, in that instant, see why Malcolm had worked so hard and so long to earn his money and why he was now so fond of it.

When she reached Martenswood with her loot, she found that Malcolm had retired to one of the further corners of the garden to sulk about her kidnapping of the car. She left him to it and set about transforming the clean and impersonal rooms, with their chemical smell, into bowers and jungles and forests. She hadn't realised until now that she could impress her own personality on her surroundings. In fact, until this moment she had been unsure whether or not she possessed such a thing as a personality of her own: she had spent so many years reflecting back what other people expected of her. All it had taken was one enormous cheque – and, perhaps, her own talent.

'This is one thing that none of you can do as well as I can!' she shouted at the empty room.

'Are you there?'

Tess had closed the door and pulled the curtains, shutting out the daylight, and now she lit the candle in front of the photograph. The flame reflected off dead black pupils so that they flickered into life.

'You can hear me, can't you? You know what's happening, because you can see it all from over there. Are you angry now you've seen what Joe and Harry and Tom have done? And Malcolm? Make them stop, Dad! Even Mum is behaving as though she belonged here, as though she wanted to stay.

'Do you remember that time by the river? It was that afternoon we went for a walk together and the bullocks were in the corner by the gate. You were wearing your green gloves. I've still got them, you know – well, one of them, anyway. It was cold that afternoon, and raining. And one of the bullocks was bellowing at us so that I was frightened. He had stretched out his neck and opened his mouth wide, and he was pawing the ground. You held my hand and you shouted back. And you said that I was safe as long as I kept holding on to your hand.

You said that you would always keep me safe, because I belonged to you. We still belong to you, don't we, Dad? Me and Aurora, and Mum. Most of all Mum. You said that she'd never belong to anyone except you. It was dodgy for a while when Jeff came along, but not for long. Did it happen that same afternoon? I've forgotten so much about it, but I remember we can destroy them – wipe them out. You showed me how to do it, but don't make me do it on my own.

'I've got a new idea. I'm sorry the jam didn't work. But I'm not giving up. I think the new idea is better, anyway. I think I know what to do now, but it's easier when you help me. And like you said, I've been practising.'

I'm here. I'm always here when you need me.

'And you'll come with me? Look at this stuff, Dad. I took it when he wasn't looking and no one knows I've got it. But it could be what we need.'

I'm the power in your arm and the anger in your heart.

'Soon, Dad. Make it soon.'

'Tess.'

It's a quiet voice: Harry. What does he want?

'Yes?'

'Can I come in and talk?'

There's nothing threatening about Harry when he's away from the other two.

'OK.' Tess puts down the book she is reading and Harry comes into the room and sits on the upright chair by her desk. 'What is it?'

'It's just that I wanted you to know about Gryphons—'

DEATHSPELL

'So?'

Harry has one of his smallest teddy-bears with him. He rarely goes anywhere without one of them these days. Tess sees that Hanna has sewn up the hole in its furry chest, but there is still a round bald scar where the knitting needle went in.

'It isn't always as awful as Joe makes out, you know. Not if you can keep clear of the big ones. Sometimes we have quite good fun. And—'

'Yes?' She still isn't being very friendly, but she thinks that Harry is the best of the three and she isn't throwing him out of her room, yet. She knows that she is going to stop them being sent away if she can, but, even so, things don't always turn out the way you want, however hard you work at them.

'I could help to look after Aurora, you know,' Harry is saying. 'She'd be all right with the two of us, I expect.'

'Thanks, Harry.' That's hard to say, but it's not a bad thing to be three against two, even if one of the two is Joe. 'I can look after Aurora all right by myself, but you can be our . . . friend . . . sometimes if you like.'

Saying that word takes a very big effort, but Harry seems to appreciate it, for he smiles his twitchy little smile at Tess before leaving her room.

But Gerard is frowning at her.

Don't go forgetting what you have to do.

She sighs. She would have liked to stay in her room and read a book, but she goes downstairs instead.

'Mum, do you think I could try making some bread? You've got all the stuff I need, haven't you?'

'Well, it's not very convenient just at the moment, Tess.'

133

'Healthy food, Mum. You're always on about how we should eat properly instead of that junk stuff they have at the supermarket.'

'I am?'

'Yes,' lied Tess.

'I don't think I've got the time to show you how to do it today.'

'That's all right. I know where the recipe books are, and I've watched you doing it often enough. Don't worry, Mum. You go and get on with what you wanted to do and I'll make the bread.' She added the clincher. 'I'll clear up after myself, OK?'

'Oh, all right then. If you're sure.'

'I'm quite sure.' She smiled at her mother. 'I'm going to make a mixed-grain loaf, Mum. You use several sorts of flour, instead of just the wholemeal.'

'Oh well, I suppose it can only be an improvement on my efforts.'

'It'll be great when I've made it, Mum. Magic, I promise you.'

'I'll have to be going in a minute. Have you got all that clear?' Steve Tracker stole a quick look at his watch – Christ! This was taking for ever!

'Can't you stay a bit longer then?'

'I've got another job to get to. Got to earn my living, love.'

They were lying in bed again, the tired purple sheets crumpled beneath them and twined, snake-like, round their legs. He hoped that she would have changed them for fresh ones before he came to call again: he was fussy about that sort of thing. He was getting rather bored, too, with explaining his plan over and over to Kay. She was greedy, but not very bright.

'Make us another cup of tea, Petal, why don't you, while I have a shower and get dressed? Then we'll go over it again, downstairs. OK?' He'd have to make sure he was clean and Kay-free before he went home. He just hoped that she didn't go in for some unfamiliar soap. Jean would be sure to notice if he came home smelling of something foreign, and then there'd be trouble, and he wasn't ready to leave her flat just yet.

Fifteen minutes later they were both at the kitchen table with a sheet of lined notepaper and a biro, going over the points that Steve had made.

'I still don't see why he'd pay. After all, what's it to him if Hanna walks out? She'd take those two whining girls of hers too, and good riddance to the lot of them.'

'Look, Petal, we're in the nineteen-eighties here. If she walks out, she takes half his house, a third of his income and most of his pension with her. Now, you and I may think that he can afford it, but look at it from his point of view: he loses his precious Martenswood; he loses God knows how many thousand a year in maintenance payments; he gives away more thousands to the lawyers—'

'How come you know so much about it? Been divorced often, have you?'

Steve stopped himself from losing his temper. Instead, he opened his blue eyes very wide and looked straight into Kay's slightly bloodshot ones. 'I'm trying to help you get yourself a decent place to live, so stop getting at me, OK?' He wished he'd got a fag left, he could really do with one at this minute. 'Now, this is the tricky bit.

You've got to write a good letter. Got to let him know that we mean business. Don't be too specific right at the start, OK?'

'I'm to set up a meeting.'

'Make it Thursday, in the afternoon. Three forty-five. Up in Ruskin Wood. He's to park his car by the sawmill then walk up the path for half a mile. They've been cutting wood along there, you can't miss it. He's to wait until I get there. He's not to come looking for me. I'll find him. Clear? And no names. There's no need at all for him to know who I am.' Malcolm Benson would be unlikely to recognise him. He wasn't the matey kind who try to be friendly to the workers.

'Got it. I'll deliver the note this evening.'

'Right then, I'll see you.'

'Tomorrow?'

She shouldn't have said that. He didn't like his women trying to call the tune, getting some sort of commitment out of him. 'Can't make it tomorrow. See you Wednesday.'

'See you, lover.'

At least she'd seen sense on that one: some of them tried to argue.

Malcolm seemed very subdued all through dinner. He didn't comment on her flower arrangement, the size of a small tree, that sat in one of the new wicker baskets and filled up the unused hearth. His mind seemed to be miles away. Maybe it was the continuing row with Joe over the shotgun. The two of them seemed at permanent loggerheads this week, and Hanna was finding it very wearing. They were so similar in their pigheaded way, that it was no wonder they couldn't come to any agreement over it. She hoped that it wasn't a warning of adolescent storms to come. She thought of five children, all going through awkward teenage phases, and quickly shut the thought out again.

Or perhaps there was something at work that was worrying him – a note had been hand-delivered to the house that evening and he had said that it was business – though in that case he was unlikely to have taken a couple of days off.

He spooned in a large helping of lemon meringue pie, the topping a dark caramel colour that wept syrupy tears, absent-mindedly refused a second, and then said, 'I think I'll go out for a bit of a walk now. Clear my head.'

'Really? I'd have thought you'd had plenty of fresh air today, dear. Why don't you sit down and read the paper instead?'

'Oh, for goodness' sake, Han, do stop questioning me and arguing about everything.'

'But I wasn't—'

'And don't contradict me!'

But even as she subsided back into her chair, she felt his heart wasn't really in his grumbling. Well, let him go off and leave her in peace for an hour: she could get on with some chores while he was out. Or put her feet up. Or fall asleep.

'Right. Well. I'm going out now. I'll see you later.'

'Have a nice walk, dear.'

She cleared up the dinner things and settled down with more of the name-tape sewing and a glass of wine to cheer herself up. Malcolm was out for a very long time, it seemed to her. He didn't get home until it was nearly bedtime. And then he appeared to be in an even worse temper. She tried to cheer him up by telling him how Tess had made a loaf of healthy, cholesterol-reducing bread just for him, but though she spread it thickly with butter, he didn't seem too keen on eating it. Tess should have kneaded it longer, she thought. Or maybe Malcolm had a headache or was sickening for something.

'Jean?'

'Not tonight, Tracker. I'm wiped out.'

'So what naughty things have you been up to today, my love?'

He slides an arm under her unwilling shoulder and fits her head into the hollow under his chin.

'Give my back a rub, will you?' she asks.

'Everything fine up on Fox Hill? Getting on well with Mrs Thing, are we?'

'Just an inch or so lower, Tracker. Yes, that's the spot. Great. What? Oh, I hardly spoke to her. I think she was terrified of my vacuum cleaners. She took the girls and ran off into town, anyway. Spending more money, I should think. What about you, Tracker? What have you been up to?'

'Oh, this and that, Jeannie, this and that. Shift down a bit and I'll do your neck, too. A bit of wheeling here, a little dealing there. All part of life's rich tapestry.'

'Secretive bastard.'

'I'll do your shoulders now, if you like.'

'Fifteen days.'

'You what?'

'Fifteen days.'

'What is?'

'I've just remembered. There was this piece of paper pinned on the wall, just above the black candle and the photograph. Fifteen days, it said.'

'Are you sure you're not working for the Fox Hill coven?'

'Not at all sure, now you mention it.'

'Oh, well. As long as they invite us to a few of their parties. Midnight. In the woods. Leave your clothes at home. That sort of thing.'

'Very funny, Tracker.'

'So why aren't you laughing?'

Next morning, Hanna tried again to persuade Malcolm to eat a slice of Tess's bread. He heaped it with margarine and marmalade and bit into it.

'It's a funny colour, isn't it?' he said. 'How soon can we send that child for some proper cookery lessons? Don't they run kids' summer schools where they teach them a bit of cordon bleu?' He examined the slice of bread on his plate and sniffed at it. 'A big of basic egg boiling and vegetable peeling wouldn't come amiss, either.'

'But you won't say anything to Tess, will you, Malcolm? You'll tell her how good it is?'

'If I must. But toast me a couple of slices of real bread now, will you, Han? And dump this stuff in the dustbin.'

She wondered whether she could persuade the boys to eat it, but thought that they would be less tactful than Malcolm if they didn't like it. No, it was another trip down the lane to Sudden Cottage for her, once all the children were out of the way, and a lie to Tess about how many slices of the delicious stuff Malcolm had wolfed down. Kay would have the fattest chickens on Fox Hill at this rate.

Chapter Twelve

Tuesday afternoon was heavy and warm, the heat settling into the canopy of the trees and enfolding Martenswood in its steamy embrace. Steve had finished his work an hour or so earlier, and was watching the house and its occupants, noting their comings and goings, the pattern of their lives, as another man might study the habits of birds or wild animals. He had left his car out of sight, a hundred yards along the road to the bypass, and now he approached the house on foot. Even on the gravel his feet made no sound. Lovely old house you are, he thought as it displayed itself in its dark veil of September leaves. Why did I think I'd settle for anything less? You're what I've dreamed of, old girl. Always, down the years, a house like Martenswood. You're a local, like me, and one day you'll be mine, I promise you. I'm like the mice that live under their floorboards and behind their wainscoting: I'm watching them, and when I find their weak spot, I'll use it. Somehow, one day, you'll belong to me.

It was cool and dark inside the house. Steve knew that there was a good chance of finding Hanna alone. He had seen the girls playing one of their odd games in the garden before moving off in the direction of the river. Joe and the youngest boy had gone to Ruskin Woods; he had heard them talking in their loud prep-school voices about how they were going to trap and kill some small animal. That left one unaccounted for, but he was unlikely to hang around indoors on his own. And sure enough, as Steve entered the house (thoughtfully leaving the boxes with the tools of his trade in the cloakroom by the front door) he met Harry on his way with a fishing rod and a canvas bag.

'I'm going fishing,' said Harry, unnecessarily.

'Wish I could go with you,' said Steve, easily.

'I've been invited by the Elliotts,' said Harry. 'I'm not sure that they'd like it if you came too.'

'Not to worry. Maybe I can go another day.'

'I'll ask them for you, shall I?' said Harry, always eager to please.

'Cheers. You do that.' Steve watched the dark-haired figure disappear off up the drive. Malcolm and the Volvo had left early that morning – doubtless speeding office-wards to make up for yesterday's day off – and, unless Hanna had acquired yet more children since yesterday, she should be alone in the house. And this, Kay darling, is the part of the plan you'll be happier knowing nothing about.

And then: There's something different about the place, he thought, as he looked around him. In the wide entrance hall someone had placed a heavy wooden Doric column topped with a bowl of cascading greenery: some sort of fern with small pale green leaves that caught the light like glittering coins; in the empty hearth was an arrangement of grasses and leaves in a brass cauldron; a terracotta pot sprouted a four-foot-tall tree; wherever he looked, greenery trailed and flowers bloomed in muted shades of cream and gold. He brushed past a starry white jasmine, switched on his smile and put his head round the kitchen door. Hanna was still sewing on name-tapes.

'Any chance of a cup of coffee?'

'Oh! Steve! Goodness, I hadn't realised how late it was. You do work hard for us, don't you! I must put this away and think about getting the supper on.' She stood up, scattering white cotton threads, picked up an empty wine bottle and dropped it into the rubbish bin, then hurried her wine-glass out of sight into the sink. 'Of course I'll make some coffee. Or would you prefer tea? Come in and sit down.'

She was filling the kettle, getting out cups and saucers. He sat down and watched her. He would have liked a fag, but knew she wouldn't like it. 'Coffee. Instant will do me fine,' he said. He didn't want her fussing around for too long. He wasn't sure how much time they had together on their own before another child appeared, demanding her attention.

'Really? It's not trouble to grind the beans.' She had the various pieces of the coffee-maker in her hands and she looked as though she would never successfully reassemble them. Her cheeks glowed and her eyes were unfocused.

'Really.' And he stood up to help in his neat, deft way. When they carried the cups across to the table, hers slopped over on to the floor and made a milky ring on the clean surface of the table when she put it down. She was one of the messiest ladies he'd met.

He had found in the past that the way to win with tall, strong-looking women was to treat them as though they were very tiny and fragile. You carried their bags and pulled out their chairs and generally made them feel like little delicate pieces of china. But with Hanna, now, there was no pretence about it. Hiding inside that five-foot-eight-inch frame there really was a small and frightened child who needed comforting and looking after. She wasn't fit to be let loose on the world, he thought fondly, as he sipped the dreadful coffee and wished that she had offered him a glass of her wine, instead. And although she wasn't Harry's natural mother, they shared the same anxious, eager-to-please expression of life's victims. She seemed to be inviting him to take advantage of her, treat her badly, let her down; and then, he was sure, those lovely wide-set greenish-blue eyes would turn on him reproachfully, fill slowly with tears, and forgive him. Irresistible. And he did believe, too, that there was a slight smell of lavender flowers in her hair, so what happened next just wasn't his fault.

He put down his mug next to hers on the table and pulled her very gently round to face him. Her hair was newly washed and fell across her left eye. She went to push it back with her usual nervous gesture, but he took her hand in his right one and pushed the hair back into place himself, allowing his fingers to idle over her eyebrow and on her temple. It was her mouth that made her look so vulnerable, he decided. It lacked definition, as though at any moment it would smile or pout or droop as he directed it. And the upper lip was slightly swollen, as though someone had just kissed it. This close to her, he could smell her pleasantly wine-laden breath, see that there were freckles on her nose, and that her eyelashes were a sandy-gold colour. He kissed the nearest freckle, gently and briefly, and then wrapped his arms around her in that safe, protective, *unthreatening* way that women always fell for. He was afraid that she would leap away like a startled animal, but, although he could feel the tension in her like a charge of static electricity vibrating from the top of her head (which fitted in comfortably just below his nose) down to her feet in their scuffed white sandals, she resisted him for less than five seconds. She relaxed against him and her arms wound hesitantly around his neck. She trusts me, he thought happily, and set about some serious seduction.

'Why don't we go upstairs?' he asked, eventually.

To his disappointment, she led him past the open door of her bedroom, with its king-size bed and exciting scatter of discarded clothing, and into a smaller back bedroom that, from its ill-assortment of bedcovers and rugs and curtains, was intended for visitors. But the mattress was a good one, and the sheets, if not exactly linen, still had the crisp feel of new polycotton.

Some time later, he lay on his back looking up at the ceiling and admiring the plasterwork round the cornices and the central rose.

'We'll have to think about moving, Steve.'

'Hmm?'

He didn't feel at all like moving. He could lie here in her cool, crunchy sheets all afternoon and dream about being the owner of Martenswood. And if he could only have a cigarette to smoke, life would be quite perfect. A dig in the ribs brought him awake again. She had remarkably sharp elbows for such a soft and sinuous person.

'There's a shower over there.'

Oh good, he didn't have to tiptoe naked down the passage in search of a bathroom. Lovely house, you are.

'We could use it together, if you like.'

Now that was a suggestion to get a man out of bed with a bit more enthusiasm.

Once they were dressed and downstairs in the kitchen, Hanna noted the dreary pile of clothes that still lacked name-tapes, the oddments of washing up waiting to be done, and changed her mind about getting on with the preparations for supper. Let them cut sandwiches for a change. Let them come in and find the house lacking a mother to whine at, grumble at, bully and demand from. The sunshine was still bright, there would be a breeze out on the hills, and she felt charged with enormous energy. I am reborn, she thought fancifully. I haven't discovered yet what I am reborn as, but I don't think it's a wife-and-mother.

So she and Steve climbed the hill together, Hanna springing up the path. Now they stood, arms casually around one another's shoulders, looking back across the fields.

'Look over there at Martenswood,' said Hanna. 'Isn't it a marvellous house?'

But it's *just* a house, thought Hanna, seeing as though for the first time its red-tiled roof above the cream rendering of its walls. You don't own me, I am not your slave, after all. From up here its shrubberies were mounds of varied golds and greens. Sunlight danced on clean windows. A splash of vermilion geraniums spilled out of a terracotta pot on the terrace.

'Yeah, that's it then, isn't it?' said Steve. 'Your little bit of England.' His hand tightened on her shoulder. 'One of my all-time favourite houses, Martenswood.'

Another romantic, thought Hanna. Men were far more sentimental than women. 'It's more than that,' she said impatiently. 'It's mine.'

'I thought it belonged to Malcolm.'

'All right: mine and Malcolm's, if you insist. Half mine.'

The house seemed so close that she could almost smell the beeswax polish and the peppery fragrance of the flowers, and she stood there, leaning against the gate, not caring that the lichen was staining her skirt, and inhaled as though she could draw in Martenswood's very essence. 'A million? Half a million?' she said. 'It must be worth that, don't you think?'

'Four hundred thousand, I should think,' said Steve, practically, but Hanna wasn't listening to him. Why had she never thought about it in these terms before? Up till now it had been one enormous chore that she could never complete, and while it protected her from the outside world, still it held her in its own demanding grip. Today she felt as though chains had been cut from her feet, and all because she knew for the first time that Martenswood belonged to her, not she to it. She turned her head to look at Steve.

'You don't really know what that means to me, do you? It's freedom from the everyday worries about how to pay the next round of bills, how to educate the girls, how to see that they have a better chance in life than I did. Nothing to say to people but "yes, sir" or "yes, dear", in case they reject me or fire me.'

Steve's face was blank. He didn't understand. Men never did.

'I spent more of my time thinking about money than anything else.'

'Don't we all?'

'I'm starting to see now that Gerard was the free spirit, not me. I was stuck at the sink with the washing up.'

'Isn't that what most women want out of life?'

'Not for ever. And I'm talking about money. Money equals power. I'm learning about that.'

'Money,' said Steve, 'equals property, too. You just see it the other way round from me. You want to convert your property into power, whereas I . . .'

Hanna wasn't listening to him, so busy was she trying to boil down into words all the muddled thoughts and feelings of the past few years. 'Can you imagine the awfulness of it? Me, the world's most hopeless cook and housekeeper, trying to earn my living doing just that, always terrified that we'd be out on the pavement, me and the girls, homeless. Roofless.' She wanted to weep at the sadness of it all, and wondered if some of the emotion that was overwhelming her was down to the wine she had drunk at lunch (and, if she was honest, for the next two or three hours as well). 'When you're poor you can't take risks.'

'I suppose not,' said Steve. 'So you moved in with Mr Benson.'

'You think I married him for his money?'

'No, no, of course not. You wouldn't do a thing like that, I know.'

'Wouldn't I? Romantic love wasn't a luxury I could afford. Though I did love Malcolm, in a way – until I found out more about him . . . well, never mind about that, it isn't relevant to the story. No, he solved so many of my problems, and he seemed to be so sure of himself, that I just didn't see any of the drawbacks.' Solid, dependable, *boring* Malcolm, with jowls and paunch threatening to spoil his looks. Hadn't she stopped and wondered about him and his needs? But that would have been just another luxury when her own needs and those of Tess and Aurora were so pressing. And then there had been Gerard's wicked laugh in her ear and his soft voice whispering, *Take the money, Hanna, me darlin', and run . . .*

'You made the right decision there!' Steve's voice broke into her thoughts.

'You think I'm selfish?'

'I think you're a warm and lovely person, Hanna, you know that.'

'Oh, that's got nothing to do with it,' she said. Why did men always have to fit you into that insipid ideal of theirs? 'I'm tired of being what some man wants me to be. I'm changing, and this time I'm going to decide what I change into. Tess and Aurora want me to be one thing – some sort of mother-in-aspic – but I shan't let them put fences round me like that. When they're away at school . . . when all of them at last are away, out from under my feet, then I shall sit and work it out.'

'Shouldn't we be getting back?'

The air was cooler now, it must be getting late. She hadn't bothered to put her watch on. 'I suppose one always has to go back in the end.' Perhaps you only got freedom in small portions, like the Dovers' food. She'd have to go back and pay for today's heaped plateful by being wonderfully motherly and wifely this evening. 'Coming, dear,' she said to herself. 'So sorry I'm late. I don't know what came over me.'

That evening, as she struggled with the never-ending chores and with Malcolm's touchy mood, the great feeling of confidence in her rebirth seeped out of Hanna, and the familiar exhaustion took its place, made worse by the dull headache that didn't improve when she opened another bottle of wine. Perhaps it was the claret that didn't suit her: she'd give the Sancerre a try, for a change. But after a couple of glasses all she longed for was her bed and the wonderful feeling of being horizontal and able to close her eyes and stop listening to endless requests for her time and attention. Why can't I be free? But freedom, she thought, as she drifted off into sleep (having first removed Malcolm's hand from her hip), isn't something that you can take in one large piece and hang on to and say, 'Now I own this: this is mine.' It was more like a ball of fleece that you plucked out strand by strand through the meshes of a string bag and painfully teased and spun into a long unending yarn. And then, she thought, burrowing her head into her pillow and hugging her knees, you could dye it any colour and knit it into the world you fancied. There seemed to be, she thought, as she floated between layers of sleep like thick clouds, rather a lot of knots and breaks in her own length of thread, and it looked sadly grubby. She didn't have the trick of spinning her freedom yet, but maybe, if she practised, it would get easier. A little practice every day, that was what she needed.

Next morning there was none of the crispness that you might expect in early September but instead the clammy air hung over Fox Hill like a shroud.

'I don't like the smell in here, Tess. It goes up my nose and prickles my eyes.'

'It's just the animals: it won't hurt you.'

'Can't we go home? Why do we have to stay here?'

'We have to watch and learn.'

'Watch the animals? Why?'

'No. Just shut up a minute, will you? It's her. She's the one we're watching.'

Kay came out of her back door, green satin robe draggling in the mud, and hurled a bucket of kitchen scraps in the direction of the hens. There was a clucking and squawking and an intensification of the ammoniac smell as the birds shuffled their wings and stirred up the detritus on the ground with their scaly claws.

'Get off, you stupid buggers!' Kay shouted, as they came pushing and pecking around her feet. She put down the bucket and pushed a grimy hand inside the top of her dressing-gown to scratch an armpit. 'Bloody cat must have fleas again,' she muttered.

'I don't see what we're supposed to be learning from her, Tess.'

'Those chickens don't look well to me. Do you think they're getting overfed?'

'Not as overfed as her.'

Tess had made them put on green and brown clothes

that melted into the green and brown backcloth to
Sudden Cottage, and they crouched behind the fence to
Kay's garden, peering through one of the gaps between
the boards.

Kay went back inside the cottage and they could hear
her loud voice sliding around the notes of an unfamiliar
song. Water gushed from the upstairs overflow pipe,
steam clouded the bathroom window and a round figure
bounced pinkly around behind it.

'What are we supposed to be learning *about*, Tess?'

'Haven't you noticed how she gets people to do what
she wants? Things happen for her.'

'Like you with the magic, you mean?'

'But magic doesn't always work out, does it? I can feel
I've got the power in my hands, but when I let it go, I
can't tell what direction it'll fly off in. But Kay's got
something different, and she sort of ties people to a
string and then pulls them in and makes them dance for
her. I don't know yet what she's got, but I'm going to
find out.'

'I think she's horrible. Fat and horrible.'

'Yes, she is. But if I knew how she did it, I could use it
too.'

Upstairs, Kay's voice rose to a crescendo as she
informed them that she would stand by her man. There
was more gushing water and flushing of the lavatory,
and then a long silence. It was really very boring, but
Tess wouldn't allow Aurora to go home.

And then at last something happened: a Ford Escort
slid in through Kay's rickety gate and parked by the door
to the henhouse.

Aurora's mouth opened. 'It's—'

'Steve,' said Tess. 'Mr Ratsaway. I knew Mum shouldn't trust that man. What's he doing here, do you think?'

'Maybe Kay's got mice.'

'Of course she's got mice. And rabbits and rats and beetles, I expect. But she wouldn't bother about getting rid of them, would she?'

'Perhaps he's a friend of hers.'

'You're such a baby! Just watch what happens, will you?'

At the sound of Steve's car, Kay came to her front door. The girls crawled round behind the fence until they were in a better position to see what was going on. Kay was now wearing a scarlet angora sweater and a black skirt that garotted her knees and creased into contour lines around the plump hillocks of her bottom. Her hair was a newly dyed gold and her lipstick exactly matched her sweater. She had just lit a fresh cigarette, and when she withdrew its long, white length from her mouth, they could see that the filter tip was stained a bright wet scarlet.

Tess and Aurora craned forward as she approached Steve. The flexing of her knees almost made up for the increased height given by her heels, but she needn't have worried, for she was still several inches shorter than he was. Kay's head cocked sideways; she dropped her heavy lids and then looked up at Steve through her eyelashes, and let the last lungful of smoke from her cigarette dribble out through her shiny, parted lips.

'What's he doing that for, Tess?' asked Aurora, as Kay, having undulated against Steve for a moment, moved sharply back again, crying, 'Just keep your hands to yourself, you dirty bugger,' and flounced back into the house with a look over her shoulder that even the girls recognised as an invitation. As she pushed the door open with her right hand, she paused for a moment, and her left hand, apparently innocently, moved up to caress her breast. Then she disappeared inside, Steve following quickly behind her. The door closed and, since nothing more happened during the next ten minutes, Tess gave up trying to keep Aurora quiet and they made their way back up the lane to Martenswood. As they went, Tess practised Kay's small steps: her knees bent, her bottom pushed out, her head pushed forward and tipped sideways.

'You look really stupid like that,' said Aurora. Tess pretended to hit her, and they ran, chasing and shouting, back to the house.

'What's for lunch, Mum?' Tess asked when they got back to Martenswood.

For once Hanna wasn't in the kitchen, ruining another batch of food, but was in front of the mirror up in her bedroom, pushing her hair this way and that. Her bed was piled high with clothes and the floor littered with shoes. She was wearing her familiar old blue jeans, but instead of her usual T-shirt, she had on a pale pink satin blouse with diagonal draping across the bosom. When she turned towards them, letting her hair fall back into place, and said, 'Lunch? Oh, I thought we'd have a bit of salad and some cold ham,' they were shocked to see that her mouth was an unfamiliar, richly glistening red.

Chapter Thirteen

Hanna overslept on Thursday, which was a pity because she had invited the Elliott children to play in the morning and promised to give them lunch. Then Joe took it into his head to get up early to launch his assault on Malcolm.

'Think of the things I could kill, Dad! Pigeons – you can eat them, you know. And rats and mice and squirrels. You could fire the Rat Man: it would pay for itself. I could shoot slugs, maybe.'

'With a gun?' scoffed Malcolm. 'Think of the way you could show off to your mates. If you want me to spend that sort of money on you, you'd better make sure you get yourself a better report next term. I'm shelling out enough money on you as it is.' He caught his son a light blow with the flat of his hand across the back of his head. 'I've told them to stand no nonsense from you this term: discipline, that's what you need, I've said. I want to see you getting into Palgrave when the time comes. You're going to have the chances I missed in life whether you like it or not. And take that bloody Walkman off when I'm talking to you.'

But Joe turned the volume up so that the music

poured tinnily out through the earphones and blotted out Malcolm's words. Hanna could almost see it spilling out and lying around in muddy puddles on the floor, pulsing away with a life of its own, shouting out its violent message, urging Malcolm and Joe on. She felt detached from what was going on between her husband and stepson, and yet unable to leave the room.

Malcolm stared at Joe for a moment, his face the colour of corned beef. Then he leant across and wrenched the earpieces away from Joe's head and hauled on the wires until the lightweight machine jerked away from his belt and skimmed across the floor. Joe scrabbled after it on his hands and knees.

'You old shit!' he roared. 'You'll pay for this! F—' before Malcolm stopped him with a blow across the mouth. Then his father bent down and picked up the Walkman.

'I'm giving this to the first kid I meet in the street,' he said, as he put it into his jacket pocket. 'In future, anything else you want, you go and graft for, same as me.'

Hanna came out of her state of shock at the point where Joe lost control and battered his fists against his father's chest and kicked out at his ankles and shins with his trainer-clad feet, mouthing obscenities. Joe wasn't yet as tall as Malcolm, or even Hanna, but he was young and powerful and in such a rage that he was stronger than either of them. She wasn't sure that the two of them could have restrained Joe in that state, but the postman and milkman both turned up at the back door while they were struggling with him.

'Need a hand?' said one.

'Shall I call the police?' said the other.

'Help me with his arms,' shouted Malcolm.

'Get off me! I'm going to kill you!' howled Joe.

While one pinioned his arms, another grabbed him round the knees to stop him from kicking, and the four of them finally bundled Joe upstairs and confined him in his room.

'Bit of a temper, that lad's got,' said the postman, who was a charitable man.

'Right little bugger, if you ask me,' said the milkman, who wasn't, and whose ear had come into contact with Joe's flailing fist.

Breakfast was punctuated by shouts and roars and stamping from Joe's room, but Malcolm told Hanna to take no notice. Half an hour later, as he was leaving the house, he handed her the key to Joe's bedroom.

'You can let him out in another hour. And I want a decent apology from him when I come home. Which reminds me, Hanna, I'll be back for lunch today.'

Hanna wished that she, too, could stride from the house and drive away in a powerful car, while behind her someone else dealt with the frightening wild animal that was Joe, transformed the house into a civilised place to receive the incoming Elliott children and rustled up a meal for eight – or was it ten? – people.

Upstairs, Tess listened to the shouts and grunts.

'Don't worry,' she said to Aurora. 'It's only Malcolm and Joe having a fight. It's nothing to do with us. And perhaps they'll kill one another. That would be nice, wouldn't it?'

Hanna's hands were still shaking when she started to

prepare breakfast for the children. She couldn't cope with violence. She couldn't face anything to eat, but she wondered whether she could pour herself a brandy to calm her nerves. It was a bit early, but then it was an unusually tense start to the day, even for Martenswood. Later, when she again tried to work out how many people would be there for lunch, she kept losing count.

'Is it time to kill him?'

'Yes. But just wait a minute, will you?'

'Come *on*, then, Tess. Why can't we go and do it *now*?'

The Elliott boys and their sister (who was supposed to be a nice friend for Tess and Aurora, but whom they detested) had arrived a quarter of an hour before, and at any moment Tess knew that they would be forced to join in with some game that the Gryphons children all knew how to play and win at which would reduce Aurora to tears and herself to a fury of frustration. She saw that her sister was dancing from foot to foot, impatient to be away, but she made her wait a little longer: there were things she had to do first. She went to her treasure drawer and chose what she wanted. *You must do things in the proper way.* So, candle and matches, and finally, Gerard's photograph.

'Why do you need Dad's picture?'

'He wants to watch.'

'They'll be up here looking for us in a minute if we don't hurry.'

Tess put everything in a shoe box and then she made Aurora change her sandals for boots, for although it was warm outside, the ground was still very wet. She considered asking Harry to join them, but perhaps he wouldn't understand why they had to kill Malcolm: it was his father they were planning to murder, after all. So they walked past the door of his room without saying a word. As they passed the playroom they could hear a very loud banging and a rhythmical chanting that sounded like 'Ra-ver, *ra-ver*, RA-VER!' followed by wild laughter.

'Joe must have recovered from his tantrum,' said Tess as they escaped into the garden.

Tess put the box down by the vegetable patch, ordered Aurora to start looking for Malcolm and went off to the shed to find the slug pellets. She took down the green tin, poured out a handful of the slug killer, measured the quantity by eye, judged it to be sufficient, put the top back on the container and dropped the pellets into her pocket. As she placed the tin back on the shelf she read the warning printed on its side: 'Dangerous to pets and animals. Keep out of reach of children. These pellets are poisonous.' She stopped and thought for a moment before pouring out another handful and putting them in the other pocket of her green dress. Then she went in search of the rest of the things she needed.

Bindweed. It wasn't hard to find. It seemed to be flourishing after Malcolm's efforts the previous day: perhaps pruning was good for it. The white flowers shone in the morning sun as she chose three perfectly unblemished blooms.

'I've found him. Look,' called Aurora from the vegetable plot.

The slug was larger, fatter and glossier than he had been, and reminded them both even more of their stepfather. Finnegan appeared from nowhere and wound himself round Tess's legs, purring and rubbing his head on her feet.

'Hello, Vinegar. I bet you hate the horrible Elliotts, too. Have you come to watch?'

'Where shall we put him?' Aurora had no time to spare for the Elliotts or for the cat: she was crouching down, intent on the slug.

'Here.' Tess indicated a space in the centre of the vegetable garden and picked Malcolm up in her bare fingers and put him down in the middle of it. She pushed the candle stub into the earth a couple of feet away from him, then balanced the frame holding Gerard's photograph a foot or so to the left of the candle and at right angles to it, so that he could see properly.

'Now, watch carefully.'

Aurora obediently made a concentrating face. The slug waved its stubby antennae at her.

Tess knelt down on the wet soil and drew a five-pointed star in the soft earth, then she joined the five points so that they rested on a circle. She took the pellets from one pocket and dribbled them out on to the ground, following the lines of her pattern, enclosing the slug in a network of blue poison. The slug was sitting on bare earth, but, a few feet away, out of his reach, were the remnants of Malcolm's vegetable purchases from the garden centre. Tess placed one of the bindweed flowers within the circle next to the slug, and another outside the circle, near the ravaged cabbage plants. Very slowly, Malcolm set off, unravelling his silver trail across the wet earth. Finnegan settled on the grass a few feet away and watched.

Tess lit the candle and placed her remaining bindweed

flower in front of Gerard's photograph. Malcolm slithered away from the candle flame and towards the cabbage.

Facing the picture, Tess took Aurora by the hand.

'We have to sing a hymn.'

'I don't know many – not all the way through.'

'How about "All things bright and beautiful"? You must know that one.'

'All right. I know some of it.'

They started to sing:

> 'All things bright and beautiful,
> All creatures great and small,
> All things wise and wonderful,
> The Lord God made them all.'

Tess had a lovely voice, true and clear.

'Not too loud, we don't want the others to come and find us.'

The candle flame danced in Gerard's eyes and lifted his long, thin lips into a smile.

'I can tell he's enjoying it,' said Tess, her eyes on Gerard. She and Aurora still had their backs to the slug. 'Now we can sing another verse.'

Aurora couldn't remember all the words of the second verse, but she did her best. When they had finished, she said, 'I'm not sure that I want to look at Malcolm. Do you think it's all over yet?'

'Not quite, I shouldn't think.'

'What shall we do?'

'Keep holding my hand, and we'll leave him to it for a bit.' And she led Aurora past the candle and away from Malcolm, without turning her head to see what was happening. She didn't think that slugs could scream or anything – not like the bird that Joe injured up in the woods last week – but she didn't want to look at Malcolm again until he was quite dead. In any case, there was no need to stay, since Gerard would be there, looking after things for them.

They went into the kitchen through the back door so that they would miss the Elliott children in the play-room.

'What's for lunch, Mum?' The smell of baking bread still lingered in the room, though Hanna had just finished cleaning out the bread bin and was drying it with a cloth.

'Something cold and simple, I thought. Salad, per-haps. And ice-cream for afters. But you're not hungry already, are you? There's hours to go yet. And Malcolm said he would pop in for lunch, too, so we'll have to wait for him.'

'Oh good. I was wondering if I could do anything to help.'

'I'm glad you're getting on better with Malcolm these days, Tess. And if you really do want to help, you could make a sauce for the ice-cream.'

'Chocolate sauce is his favourite,' said Tess, running the slug pellets in her pocket through her fingers. 'I know how to melt the chocolate over a pan of hot water, Mum. I'll make the chocolate sauce.'

'Lovely, darling,' said Hanna. 'You can be getting the things out on to the table while I go and see what those children are up to. There's an awful lot of noise coming from the playroom. I do hope no one's getting seriously hurt.'

DEATHSPELL

As Hanna left the room, Tess got the small pestle and mortar down off the shelf. She'd better be quick, or her mother would start asking her what it was that she was grinding up into that smooth powder. She thought about feeding chocolate sauce to Joe and Tom and the Elliott children; she was strongly tempted, but she couldn't be sure that there would be enough to go round so many people. The packet hadn't said how much you needed per person. She'd better concentrate on the main target for today: she would make a special dish of it, just for Malcolm. The rest of them could be dealt with later, if it was still necessary.

An hour later, Tess had not only made the chocolate sauce but had cleared and washed up after herself, so she had been allowed to escape from the enforced sociability of the playroom and was out in the garden again. She wandered back to the vegetable patch and stared down at what was left of Malcolm. He must be dead, with all that shining trail ending in a puddle of slime. But just to make sure, Tess picked up a stone the size of an egg but with sharp edges. She brought it down on Malcolm's remains with force. Then she lifted it and brought it down again and again until the puddle of slime and the piece of black India rubber that had once been a slug called Malcolm had disappeared into the earth and were indistinguishable from it. Only then did she put down the stone. She went back to the house to tell Aurora that everything would be all right now.

'Is it over, Tess?'

'Oh yes, he's quite dead now. There's nothing that anyone can do for him.'

163

'Good.'

'Don't you want to see for yourself?'

'No. I don't like slugs. And I hate it when they go all squishy and slimy when they die.'

'There's nothing much left of the candle. I'll have to make another one for next time. But I must take the picture of Dad upstairs and put it away. I think he's seen enough of Malcolm.'

'Do you think it will really work? Will it stop us going to Gryphons? Will everything be all right?' The insistent voice followed Tess.

'I'm sure it will,' she soothed. 'You just have to believe, now. And wait.'

'OK.'

At one o'clock Hanna came out of the kitchen, where she had been preparing lunch for herself, Malcolm and eight children. There was a series of staccato bumps coming from one child's bedroom, roars and shouts from another, and heavy running footsteps along the upstairs hall.

'After him, Hugo!' someone yelled, and the noise level went up another few decibels.

Two rock bands competed for air space, someone had left green handprints up the banister rail and muddy footprints tracked up the stair carpet. Another tenner on the Technicleen bill this week, thought Hanna, calmly, and drew in a lungful of breath to shout that lunch was ready and would they all wash their hands before coming down to the dining room. There were several more yells and a lot of noisy splashing before they eventually appeared. No one had turned off the music, which still thumped and pounded contrapuntally upstairs. Never mind, thought Hanna, as she picked the tomato from the salad for the Elliott girl who ate no greenery, heated up a tin of baked beans for Harry, who didn't like tuna fish, told Joe to stop punching Hugo, and opened endless giant bottles of Coke for them all: in two weeks they'll be back at school, and I'll be free. Free. I'll have a clean, quiet house all to myself and time to think and to plan and to do something with my life.

'Can we have some more crisps?' interrupted one child.

'Mum, Harry's spilt his Coke over my salad,' whined another.

'Never mind,' said Hanna, a sweet smile on her face as she dreamed of peace and silence, crumb-free floors, child-free meals and a life where she didn't feel permanently exhausted.

'Where's Malcolm?' asked Tess. 'I thought you said he was coming home for lunch.'

'He is, but he won't be here till about half past, so I thought we wouldn't wait for him. I'll serve the ice-cream now. Who'd like chocolate sauce on it?'

'I'll bring it in, Mum. I've poured some over Malcolm's already and put it in the freezer, so we can finish all of this.' No one would notice now, she thought, that Malcolm's chocolate sauce was a different colour from everyone else's.

Hanna was still smiling when Malcolm turned up at one thirty, changed out of his suit into pressed blue jeans and an old sweater and joined the children at the table.

'Yes, dear,' she said. And, 'Just coming, dear.'

'I want an apology from that child,' said Malcolm, as he sat down.

'Which child?' Hanna could only cope with the problem of the moment.

'Joe.' And Hanna felt that responsibility for Malcolm's children had subtly switched from their father to herself. She called Joe in.

'Well?' asked Malcolm. 'I'm waiting for an apology. Don't they teach you any manners at that school of yours?'

Joe's face was turning red, and Hanna felt that in a minute he might burst into angry tears. It was hard on Joe to humiliate him when his friends were here, she thought.

'Yeah, well, all right. I'm sorry. I suppose.'

Malcolm should have left well alone at that, in Hanna's view. He shouldn't have pressed his son to offer a more gracious apology. He shouldn't have hit Joe once and threatened to thrash him thoroughly that evening. And he really shouldn't have provided the Elliott children with such a colourful scene to describe to their mother when she arrived later to pick them up. The shouting couldn't have been good for Malcolm's digestion, either. Thank goodness that in the middle of all this there was one child who had done something kind and thoughtful.

'You can bring in Malcolm's pud in a minute, Tess,' she called, when the others had all thundered upstairs out of Malcolm's reach.

'Can't you get those children to make a bit less noise, Han?'

'No, Malcolm. I have tried, but they don't take any notice. Their mother is picking them up in an hour or so, though, so you won't have to bear it for long.' And when they've gone, she thought, and Malcolm is busy doing whatever Malcolm does, I shall pour myself a glass of the Sancerre that is chilling in the fridge and forget all about the waves of aggression that are washing around in this kitchen.

Tess looked at Malcolm carefully when she brought in his dish of ice-cream. 'Are you feeling well?' she asked him.

'Yes, of course I am,' he said, surprised. 'Why?'

'Oh, I thought you looked a bit off-colour,' she said. 'Are you sure you haven't got any unexplained bruises?'

'Of course not! Why should I?'

'Well, they sometimes go with bleeding gums.'

'And I haven't got those, either,' said Malcolm, laughing and showing a mouthful of strong white teeth and perfectly healthy pink gums. He spooned a heap of vanilla ice-cream topped with glistening chocolate sauce into his mouth. 'I can't think what's wrong with you kids today.'

At two-fifteen Steve came to the house. He realised from the whoops and howls and blaring rock music that there were a load of kids there but, hoping for a quiet word with Hanna to arrange a time to call back, he put his head round the kitchen door. He withdrew it quickly when he saw Malcolm.

Hanna strode out after him, slightly pink, rather breathless. 'What are you doing here?' she whispered fiercely. 'Couldn't you see Malcolm's car?'

He had approached the house from the footpath and across the garden, so he hadn't noticed the car. 'Sorry,' he found himself saying, to his disgust: he never apologised to women.

'I'll have to go back now, but please make sure you don't walk in again when my husband's there.'

Steve didn't enjoy being put in his place, and he went back down the footpath and then turned left into the lane towards Sudden Cottage. He'd get a better reception from Kay, and it would just serve Hanna right – all he'd wanted to do was fill her in on Malcolm's bits on the side. She should be grateful to him: he was giving her great ammunition if she wanted to be free of the man. If she played her cards right she could find herself the owner of this lovely house, and if she was really lucky he'd agree to come and share it with her.

When Hanna got back to the lunch table, she found that Malcolm and Joe had started fighting again, with an interested Elliott audience.

'I'm not having them say those things about a son of mine,' Malcolm was shouting. 'Not at the fees they charge. You'll pull yourself together this term, my lad, and forget this nonsense about mountain bikes and shotguns. Have you any idea how much they cost?'

'You can afford it,' said Joe.

'Don't you speak to me like that. I didn't have things like that when I was your age, I can tell you.'

'Yeah, yeah. That old story,' said Joe, and spilled some more Coke on the table.

Hanna hastily told Joe to leave the room before he and Malcolm started getting physical again.

'I'm not playing with those kids any more,' he said sulkily. 'I'm off out.'

'Where, Joe?'

'Just out,' said Joe.

Hanna let him go: the Elliott children had quite

enough gossip to spread around the other Gryphons parents for one afternoon. She made coffee for herself and Malcolm and joined him at the table, littered now with oddments of discarded food and spilled drink.

'This ice-cream tastes disgusting,' he said, when she sat down.

'Don't tell Tess that, she made the chocolate sauce specially because she knows you like it.'

'Well, put it down for the cat or something, Han. I can't eat any more of it. It's making my mouth feel sore. And I'm off out now.'

'Here,' said Hanna. 'Give it to me, Malcolm. I'll eat some of it. I'd hate to hurt the child's feelings.'

Malcolm was right. It did taste disgusting, as though horseradish sauce had got mixed in with the chocolate.

'You're in a hurry, Tess! Where are you going?'

'Out for a walk.'

'I don't like you wandering around the countryside on your own. Why don't you stay and play with the Elliott children?'

'I don't want to. Aurora's here, she can play with them.'

'I'm not sure—'

'Mum! I've got to go – there's something I have to do.'

'Well, wear an anorak, will you? That's a thin dress and it looks as though it's going to rain later. It's oppressive enough for another thunderstorm.'

'Don't worry. The lights won't go out this time.'

'What a funny thing to say! How can you be so sure?'

'I just know it. But I've got to go now, or I'll be late.'

'Tell me where you're going, first. Down to the river?'

'Yes, I expect so.' Tess wasn't absolutely sure where she

was going, but her quarry had gone off in the direction of the woods, and it seemed safer to say she was going somewhere else. If it stopped her mother's questions it was good enough. 'There are all different sorts of butterflies down there and I'm trying to learn their names,' she invented: it was the sort of thing that grown-ups liked to hear.

'I expect they'll wait while you put your anorak on.'

'They only come out after lunch,' said Tess, pulling a darkish anorak from its hook in the cloakroom – Joe's, but it didn't matter – 'and they disappear again by teatime.' She had the back door open now, looking out for the broad figure in its white pullover. 'Bye, Mum!' And she was off across the garden and through the gate into the footpath.

There must be a good reason why Malcolm had come home to lunch and had sat wrapped in his own thoughts, with the skin of his forehead furrowed like that of the Elliotts' basset hound. She could see his bright blue jeans against the pale gold of the stubble, and his white pullover against the dark backcloth of the woods. She was better camouflaged than he was, in her green dress and brown anorak, but she'd have to be careful that he didn't see her following him across the open ground. When he reached the woods she'd have to run to catch up with him or she might lose him completely. She had to know why he had dressed so carefully in these clean, neat, casual clothes, and looked so guilty when he had left after lunch. Why hadn't he gone back to his precious office? What was he up to? And when would he drop down on to the woodland floor and melt into a pool of slime as a result of eating all those chocolate-flavoured slug pellets?

Chapter Fourteen

Malcolm was easy enough to follow, even in the woods. She paused, slightly out of breath, and searched until she saw his white pullover moving among the trees. He had taken the main ride and was stepping carefully round puddles and over ruts, his head lowered. She relaxed a little: he was deep in his own thoughts and wouldn't notice her, and she slipped along behind him, keeping to the silent muddy parts of the path, avoiding the twigs and loose stones that might give her away. Her old gym shoes with their worn soles served her well.

They went on for another mile or so, and although they were still in the woods, the trees had thinned out on their left, and she could see the adjoining meadow of grazing sheep. Where the woodland ride joined the narrow lane up from the village there was an open circular space by a stile, its floor beaten flat by the wheels of cars into a small parking space, for no vehicles, other than those belonging to the Keeper and the timber merchants' lorries, were allowed in the woods. And here Malcolm stopped. After a minute or so he looked at his wrist, paced up and down, glared at the sheep. Tess moved off the ride and into the woods, stepping on soft leaf-mould, until she had circled round and squatted at the base of a tree, hidden from Malcolm by the thick foliage that was only just starting to rust at the edges, but still able to see when she needed to, and close enough to hear anything he might say.

After ten minutes, in which nothing happened, Malcolm's pacing was growing more nervously rapid, and Tess was glad that she had found herself a comfortable place to hide. It was all very boring so far, but she wasn't going to leave. She still had the stubborn feeling that something interesting was going to happen and that it was important for her to be there to see it.

Malcolm kicked the bottom of the stile and said, 'Bloody woman! Why does she always have to be late?' He stamped over to the sheep in the field and said, 'And baa to you too, you stupid buggers.'

Then from the bottom of the hill Tess heard a car engine and the grunt as it shifted down a gear, and a red Metro nosed slowly out of the tunnel of leaves and into the parking space to come to a stop close by the hawthorn hedge. A woman Tess had never seen before, with dark hair piled high on her head and spilling down into curls around her forehead and neck, climbed out of the driving seat. She was wearing a blue jersey dress that looked as though she had weighed ten pounds less when she bought it, and a lot of bright make-up. Tess thought of Hanna, pale and fair-haired, with the grey smudges of tiredness under her eyes, and she felt a jealous anger mounting until she wanted to go running out into the clearing and punch and kick at the two of them. She buried her head in her arms for a moment until she felt better. When she looked up again, the woman was scowling down at the muddy ground and the deposits on her spike-heeled shoes. She's ruined them, thought Tess, pleased.

With a smile that showed a lot of large, yellowish teeth, the woman spoke. 'Hello, Malcolm,' she said.

'Hello, Dishpot,' said Malcolm, and stood for a second or two looking pink and sweaty before leaning forward and kissing her on the cheek. 'Shouldn't call you that thought, should I, Diana? How are you, then?'

The woman laughed, a dry, heh-heh-heh noise, and said, 'I'm just great, Malcolm.' So, this must be the Dishpot Malcolm was once married to, thought Tess: Joe and Harry and Tom's Mum. And, briefly, she felt sorry for them.

Malcolm pushed his hands through his hair so that it stood up on the crown of his head, took a step away from Dishpot and relaxed slightly.

'Funny the way we bumped into each other after all this time.'

'You don't think I left it to chance, do you? I wangled that invitation on purpose. Just so that we could get together for a little talk.' She took a packet of cigarettes out of her white handbag. 'Cigarette?'

'No thanks. I've given up.'

'Pity the way people always put on weight when they give up smoking.' Then, with another flash of the yellow teeth, 'Not that it doesn't suit you.'

Malcolm's expression had changed again, Tess noted. Now he had the look of concentration he wore when he was reading the financial pages of the newspaper.

'Come on, out with it then,' he said. 'What is it you're hoping to get from me, Diana?'

'What's your hurry all of a sudden? Can't we talk a while for old times' sake?' Malcolm turned half away from her as she lit her cigarette and blew a thin stream of blue smoke up into the air. The three of us, thought Tess, are locked up in this woodland room, cut off from the rest of the world by the trees with their autumn foliage of dark, dusty green. She watched Diana draw in another lungful of smoke and place her left hand on her hip, tilting it towards Malcolm. Like Kay.

'Don't try to tell me that you went to all this trouble for a bit of social chat. What is it you're after?'

'Isn't it normal for me to wonder about the boys? How are they, Malcolm? How's little Tom?'

'After nearly three years? You walked out on them fast enough, didn't you, when Terry asked you to go off to Dubai with him?'

Now it was Diana's turn to look uncomfortable.

'And how is lover-boy Terry? How are you two getting on?'

'We're not.' She scuffed her white shoe on the ground, as though trying to remove some of the mud from the white leather. 'In fact, if you must know, we only stayed together for just over two years – and that was more than enough of that place, I can tell you. He's gone off to Canada now and I haven't even got an address for him.'

'He's left the country? Smart bloke!' barked Malcolm.

'Yes, well, I'm back in UK now, and I'm staying in Kidlington.'

'That close?'

'And I thought I'd like to see a bit more of the boys. Come and visit them every week, maybe.'

Somehow, Diana had regained the upper hand, Tess

saw. Cogs turned in Malcolm's brain as he processed this new idea.

'Come on, Malcolm, they are my kids too, you know. And it's not unreasonable of me to want to see them, is it?'

'You think a court would be on your side if you tried to play the grieving mother, do you?'

'We're not talking solicitors and courts.' But the unspoken word 'yet' hovered over her head like the thought bubble in a strip cartoon. 'But I'd like to get to know them again. Have them to stay for a little while, that sort of thing. You know, weekends, holidays.'

'Come off it, Diana. When did you ever have any time for them?'

'Now look,' said Diana, and Tess saw two vertical lines furrow the skin between her eyes, 'you've just got to listen to what I'm saying to you. I know I haven't been a particularly good mother, but I want to start again. I'll try a bit harder this time. And any court,' she looked Malcolm straight in the eye as she said this, 'any court, Malcolm, would give me the benefit of the doubt. You know that, don't you?' She put a hand on his arm, and for a moment he left it there, before pushing it away. 'Don't let's quarrel about it, Malcolm. There's nothing to make a big fuss about, is there? You and Hanna would enjoy a break from the boys, I'm sure.'

'And I imagine,' Malcolm said quietly, so that Tess had to lean forward to hear what he was saying, 'that you'd like a contribution from me towards their upkeep when they're staying with you.'

'Just a small one.'

'I'll think about it, let you know.'

'Well, don't think too long, or I might have to get my solicitor on to you, after all.'

'Look, you stupid cow, I owe you nothing. Nothing, do you understand? And what sort of place have you got for my kids to stay in, Diana? Living on your own now, are you? Or have you got—'

'Bastard! I'm on my own, OK? And, yes, if it makes you happy to know it, I'm living in a grotty little two-room flat with a shared bathroom and a gas ring in the corner of the lounge.'

They both had red faces now, with mouths pulled into ugly shapes.

'I warn you, Diana, I'll be on to my solicitor as soon as I get back to the house. I'm not having you walking back in to take my money off me. I suppose you've checked, have you? Found out how much I'm making these days and thought you'd like to get your snout in the trough?'

Diana showed a lot of thigh as she climbed back into her car. She took one last drag at her cigarette before flicking the butt out of the open window of the car. It lay, starkly white and incongruous on the damp ground, with glistening scarlet lips to match her own. When she had driven off, Malcolm stood watching the space where her car had stood. He was breathing heavily and sweating, Tess noticed, and he was really quite a nasty colour. 'Bitch,' he said. 'Fucking bitch isn't going to get her hands on my money and my kids.' Then he shouted down the lane into the blue exhaust fumes of her car, 'You're not going to get the better of me! Bitch! Fucking bitch!'

Then Tess watched as he crossed his arms over his

stomach and bent double as though he was in pain. His knees sagged slightly and his forehead was bright with a sheen of sweat.

At Martenswood, Hanna had just been sick for the second time. When she first started feeling ill, she had swallowed a glass of wine to help her digest her lunch, but it hadn't helped. Verna Elliott arrived just as she staggered out of the bathroom. She told Hanna how ghastly she looked, then clamped a muscular arm around her shoulders and took control of everything. She insisted that Hanna should lie down on her bed while she made her a pot of tea. She said that Hanna was not to get up until she was feeling better and meanwhile she, Verna, would look after Hugo, Emily, Daniel, Harry, Tom and Aurora. Hanna remembered that Tess was out after butterflies, but she wondered vaguely where Joe had got to.

'We'll play a round of Raver,' said Verna Elliott. 'The children will love that and it will keep them out of your way until you're feeling better.'

Emily and Hugo appeared at the door.

'Mum,' said Emily, unable to wait to give her mother the news. 'Joe was fighting with his father, Mum. And we heard them shouting at each other.'

'Twice,' put in Hugo in the cause of accuracy.

'Not now, children,' said Verna Elliott. 'You can tell me all about it when we get home.' And Hanna knew that this time the Elliott children would do what they were told. She wanted to say something to stop the children from talking about that awful row. Everyone on Fox Hill would know about it if Verna heard the story.

Then she felt another wave of nausea flooding over her, and she stopped caring about Verna or anything else.

Steve was gently day-dreaming as he drove his van up to Ruskin Woods and parked it on the flat piece of ground behind the Lodge. He didn't want Malcolm to see the name on the side and associate Kay's blackmailing friend with the nice Mr Ratsaway who was removing his rodents. Until this lunchtime they had never been closer to one another than the width of the garden, and even now he didn't think that Malcolm had noticed him at all as a person. And he would broaden his accent, like he did when he was speaking to Kay.

He didn't walk up the carriage drive, where the Warden's Land Rover had left deep ruts in the soft ground, but vaulted lightly over the stile and started up through the middle of the pasture where the sheep were grazing and the blackberries were ripening in the hedges. He knew he was going in the right direction because he could hear the distant buzz of chain-saws and smell the newly sawn wood, its unmistakable scent drifting down on the warm damp air.

Last week Joe had found a book on country lore in Malcolm's bookcase. Malcolm must have picked it up in a job lot of books he bought at an auction. In this book it explained in detail how to construct a snare, and where to place it, and how to kill and skin and gut your rabbit when you had caught it. He and Tom had often seen rabbits, their white scuts disappearing into the dusk up on the open heath above Ruskin Woods, and he knew that was a good place for snaring them. It would be even better when he had his gun, of course. He liked the idea of shooting and killing things until the anger he felt at his father had all soaked away.

Yesterday he had taken some of Hanna's fuse wire to practise with, and his father's wirecutters, and had reproduced one of the illustrations in the book with no trouble at all. Now he was off to see what he had caught. He wanted to try laying out some of the mouse bait, too, to see what he could catch with that. Later he'd tell Aurora about it. She'd be really upset by the idea of killing nice fluffy little bunny rabbits.

Malcolm found that it was a long way, and all uphill, to the place – Haggett's Copse – where he was supposed to be meeting this friend of Kay's. He had meant to be here earlier than this, but the set-to with Diana had taken longer than he had expected and now he was getting these cramping pains in his guts. There must have been something in his lunch that disagreed with him. Sour-tasting bile filled his mouth, but he fought it down. He had no intention of being at a disadvantage when he met this blackmailing shit.

He checked the note Kay had sent him one more time. He would have to hurry. He took three or four deep breaths: that was better. He started running up the path, which rose in a series of undulations towards the top of the hill. The part he was on now was particularly steep, and he could feel his heart thudding and the sweat running down his face as he gulped down more air. For a moment the trees swung giddily round in an arc and back again before coming to a standstill. But he couldn't slow down: he still wanted to get to the meeting-place in time to look around him and gain the advantage. No one, but no one, was going to get away with putting one over on him. First Diana, now this other one. They were all the same: all out for his money. But he would get the better of them. He always had done before. He lowered his head and put on a small burst of speed. He wouldn't give in to the sickness. His feet in their Wellingtons were heavy and made of some unfamiliar nerveless material so that he could hardly lift them free of the sticky, sucking earth. The sweat trickled down his back under his pullover and he heard a faint rhythmical squeaking in his ears as he drove himself up another incline. He wished he hadn't worn his pullover, but he had no time to take it off. The only important thing was to get to the top of this unending hill, to reach Haggett's Copse. The air felt oppressively close and warm, as though it was going to start raining again soon.

Now he caught the unmistakable smell of the cut wood and saw the high piles of logs stacked up on either side of the path. A bonfire of waste logs smouldered beside the path. He could hardly hear the rustling of the leaves and the preep-preeping of the birds in the branches overhead, the blood was pounding so loudly in his ears, throbbing against his temples, bursting to get out through the bones of his skull, while a steel clamp closed around his gut. And the leaves and the logs were blurring as though the air was already thick with rain or mist. His ears filled with the sound of rushing water.

Ahead of him he sees a break in the wooden corridor, a view across a long green field dotted with the grey shapes of grazing sheep, and he lurches off the path towards them. The air there will be easier to breathe. He is having trouble with his breathing.

Pale green bark merges into green leaves of beech trees and soft green grass. The greens are fading in and out of focus in time to the pounding in his head. There are such deep puddles here where the Land Rovers have been turning and the ruts have filled up with rainwater that it makes it difficult to keep his balance.

He lies on the grass and stares up into a green sky. The bark on the log beside his head is a mosaic of pink and red and orange and the scent of the sawn wood fills his nostrils and his throat and his lungs like aromatic treacle so that he gags and retches to try to free himself from it.

Someone is standing next to him. He cannot see who it is. He tries to call for help. The figure raises something in both hands, blotting out his view of the trees, and then swings it down towards him. He wrenches his head to the side to avoid the blow, and the wood billet catches him on the side of the neck, just below the ear. He makes one last effort to shout for help and, as the heavy object connects with the first cervical vertebra, he hears from a great distance the sound fly up to the green canopy of the trees above him and lodge there, and die.

Chapter Fifteen

He was lying with an arm outstretched, and his head thrown back and turned to one side, so that a lock of dark hair fell over his forehead. His feet, in the still new and shiny green boots, were sunk into the orange soup of a puddle.

Steve might not have found him, but in the soft ground his footprints had been simple to follow, each one exposing the bright yellow clay through the dark crust of the moist earth. Malcolm must have staggered off the main path, it seemed, and into this grassy ride, and fallen just behind one of the stacks of logs. Already there was the whine and buzz of a fly as it explored the filmy surface of an eye. Steve waited for the eye to blink. His own eyes crawled and itched in sympathy as he watched the spindly legs of the fly moving in their busy, tickling motion across and round and over that staring eye.

He's quite dead. There's nothing you can do for him, Steve. Run away now while you can. No one need know that you were here. That you were going to blackmail him. No one need ever know.

'Is he dead?'

'*What?*' He hadn't heard anyone else approaching. He turned round without his usual light-footed grace.

'Is he quite dead, do you think? He looks it.' It was that witch-child, Hanna's daughter. Her face was very pale and her yellow eyes looked enormous in her expressionless face. Her hair was darker than usual, misted by the recent rain and clinging in elf-locks to her face and neck.

'His chest isn't moving up and down, is it? Doesn't that mean that he's stopped breathing?' she asked him.

'Does it?' Steve couldn't cope with this one.

'I think you're supposed to give him the kiss of life. And heart massage.'

'*No!* It's too late. He's gone. No, I couldn't do that.' Not to a dead man.

'Well, what do you think we ought to do then?'

Run. He made an effort to unfreeze his brain, to plan.

'I think,' he said, putting as much authority as he could muster into his voice, 'that you ought to walk back to the Lodge' – then he remembered where he had left his car – 'no, not the Lodge! Umm, there may not be anyone there. No, you cut across the field and over the stile and go to Martenswood. They can phone from there. There's bound to be someone in who can phone for the police and an ambulance. Yes, that's it, you go down to Martenswood, there's a good girl.'

'What are you going to do?' She was looking up at him through her long, dark lashes, her head tilted to one side. She smiled a slow smile, as though she had been practising it. For a moment, there, she reminded him of Kay.

'Oh, I'll stay here with the body and wait for the police and the ambulance to get here.'

'All right.' The eyelashes were raised and lowered again, slowly. What was this kid? Only about ten, wasn't she? Where the hell had she learned these tricks?

'If that's what you really want me to do, I'll go for help. But I don't think there's anything they'll be able to do, not if you won't try the kiss of life.' She was standing with legs apart, one hand on her non-existent hip. 'Won't you try it, Mr Ratsaway? Just for a minute or two. We'll be learning how to do it at school next term, but that will be no use to Malcolm.'

'*No*. You'd need proper equipment to bring him back now. Oxygen and all that stuff.'

'So it's too late, you think? It's really all over for him?'

'Yes. Yes, I do. Really. I'm sorry.' Was she upset? She was showing no signs of it.

'I think you should close his eyes. Cover him up with something. It's more respectful.'

She had something in her hand, and she threw it down on to the body, then she turned back down the path, away from the Lodge. He looked to see what she had thrown: it was a crumpled white flower. Just a weed, but perhaps she felt something for the man, and for his death, after all, in spite of her odd manner.

'Don't forget to stay until the police get here, will you?' she called back to him.

He waited until she was out of sight before he started running: on up the hill, away from Martenswood, in the opposite direction from Tess. He burst out of the trees and into the flat grey sunless light. But it was enough, all the same, to remind him that he was still alive and that it was some other poor sod who lay back there with his boots in the mud, dead.

★ ★ ★

Tess and Gerard meandered down through the woods and across the fields, listening to the heartbreaking song of the skylarks. There seemed to be a thick pane of green glass standing between Tess and the real world, protecting her from the tears and pain that she guessed would be waiting for her back at Martenswood.

Nobody saw her as she slipped in through the back door and went up to her room, nor again when she went into the kitchen and picked up the things she needed. They were all busy, it seemed. Or perhaps she was invisible behind her screen.

She was halfway back up Sudden Lane when she heard a police car and ambulance wailing their way up from the bypass, along the lane and into the woods. She wondered who had let them know about Malcolm. Perhaps Steve had rung after all. But she could have told them that there was no point in all that haste: no amount of oxygen and urgency was going to help Malcolm now.

Another police car was parked in the drive of Martenswood. Hanna, her face pale, her hair dropping over her eyes, stopped her as she came in to the house.

'There's been an accident. Malcolm . . .'

'Is he hurt?'

'I'm afraid so. Joe found him up in the woods.' Hanna's speech was more disjointed than usual.

'Joe? Was he there? What was he doing?'

'Goodness knows. But, Tess, I'm counting on you to look after Aurora now. Mrs Sutton will be here in a few minutes to sit with you all while I'm out.'

'What's happening? Where are you going?' She mustn't

leave them. She belonged here with them now, more than ever.

'I have to go out, darling. The police need me to . . . Well, they need me, anyway, and I have to go now. Be good, darling, and don't let Aurora get upset.'

'Don't worry, Mum. I always look after Aurora.'

When Hanna had left in the police car, Tess went up to her room. She met Joe on the landing.

'I found him,' said Joe. 'He was just lying there.' He stared at Tess, but she didn't think he saw her. His eyes were still focused on that scene in the woods. 'I didn't know what to do. Do you think if I'd done something I could have saved him?' His face had lost its usual definite lines and was blurred around the mouth and eyes as though he would start crying at any moment.

'I shouldn't think so,' said Tess. 'I really don't think so, Joe.' She felt the screen begin to crack and an unwilling pity for him make its way through the barrier, and there was a hot, dry feeling around her own eyes, as though the skin had been scoured with sand. 'No, Joe,' she said, as if by repeating it often enough she could force him to believe it, 'I'm sure there was nothing you could do for him. You did your best: you called the ambulance and the police, didn't you?'

'From the Lodge,' said Joe. 'I ran up to the Lodge and told them what had happened. They phoned while I went back to the path to show the ambulance where to stop.'

He squeezed his lids shut, but the tears ran down his face. He wiped them away with hands that were still smeared with the dried blood of the rabbit that he had snared and gutted that afternoon. The sickly, metallic smell of death followed Tess into her room, even though she closed the door behind her. She had lifted another candle from the store in the kitchen. She hadn't got time to melt it down and mix it with the black ink and then remould it around the wick, but Gerard wouldn't mind, she thought. Not after today. She placed the bindweed in front of his picture and lit the candle. As usual it made his face come alive and smile at her. It was such a relief when he was pleased.

'Did you see him? Did you see what happened? I know he's dead – really dead – now. And she's ours again. She'll be like she always was, just yours and mine. And Aurora and I can stay here. We won't have to go away to Gryphons. We're coming back to you, Dad, like you wanted.'

The room was thick with her father's presence. She could feel him all around her, she could hear his breathing and his laugh and his voice, whispering:

You're my own dear girl and you're safe now. No one will ever be able to take away the things that belong to me.

But there was an oddly hollow feeling inside her. Was Gerard really pleased with her? Would he ever be satisfied? Or would he always have some new task for her to perform? She remembered Malcolm's smile as he thanked her for the chocolate sauce for his ice-cream, and she picked up the large book with the colour illustrations of British birds that he had given her when she had asked for it and leafed through the pages. It was some time before she put it back on the bookshelf and went out on to the landing.

'Are you there, Aurora?' she called. 'Everything's going to be all right now, like I promised you.'

DEATHSPELL

★ ★ ★

'Where were you working today, Jean?'

'Down in Waverley Lane, then a couple of houses in Franmore. Why?'

'Oh, no reason, but I wondered whether you were passing through Fox Hill.'

'No, but I'll be back at Martenswood tomorrow. Why the interest all of a sudden?'

'Just something I caught at the end of the local radio news. I thought the names sounded familiar, but I missed what it was about.'

'They mentioned Mrs Thing?'

'I don't suppose it's important.'

'Well, stop wandering about and staring out of the window like that. You're making me feel nervous.'

'Right. I'm just a bit on edge, that's all. I'll smoke a cigarette in the next room and then I'll be fine. Don't wait for me.'

'Goodnight, Tracker.'

Chapter Sixteen

Joe dawdled along the animal paths that wound their way through sheep pastures and woods. Sometimes the narrow track doubled back so that he turned away from Haggett's Copse as though he had changed his mind about where he was going. And all the time his mind was filled with pictures of Malcolm's grey face.

'Sing!' he shouted into the trees. 'Why won't you fucking sing?' If only the birds would drive the pictures out of his head with their noise. But they were silent except for one that squeaked like chalk on a blackboard and another that made brief popping noises. He pushed his way through four-foot-high nettles which brushed his arms with their dusty leaves and ragged threads of green flowers, raising painful weals. He watched the rash appear and concentrated on the pain, but then Malcolm's face pushed into his thoughts again: now, although still grey and dead, it wore an accusing scowl.

Joe's feet found a path that ran downhill. Good. He needn't go to the copse. He needn't see again Malcolm's body in its white pullover, lying on the grass, Malcolm's green boots trailing in the ochre mud, and Malcolm's dead eyes staring up into the treetops. And yet something urged him to go back, whispered that this time he might get there and find Malcolm still alive. He could do something for him – give him the kiss of life. He might be given a second chance. He picked up a stick and beat at the bed of nettles until their acid smell filled the air and they lay in tattered rags around him, then he turned away.

In the end, wrapped as he was in his thoughts, he came upon the place unexpectedly. It was curiously ordinary, unmarked by yesterday's tragedy. He looked at the path, at the pile of logs, at the mud. There was nothing here to speak of Malcolm's death: too many feet had trampled the ground to see clearly where he had staggered and fallen. He closed his eyes. Perhaps Malcolm – or whatever it was that remained of Malcolm and drifted on the damp woodland air – might speak some last, comforting, uncharacteristic word.

'Dad!' he shouted, then waited for a reply. Malcolm's dead voice would be soft, a mere whisper. But he heard only the squeaking of the birds and the distant whine of chain-saws. And then, in spite of his efforts to stop the unreeling pictures, his mind showed him a close-up of another blade. This one had a serrated edge and as he watched, it ripped into Malcolm's unprotesting body as it lay on the mortuary slab. He had read about an autopsy once. In fact, he remembered following Harry round the house and reading aloud the descriptions to him. Harry had pressed his hands over his ears and perhaps had not heard all the details, but they were printed in his own memory. He wished now that they weren't. The pictures were as sharp as one of his own drawings, with shadow and half-shadow produced by cross-hatching in black ink, highlights put in with strokes of soft white pastel, like the one of the dog on the beach that he gave to Aurora. But he couldn't tear this picture up and throw it on the floor, as Little Precious had done. The surgeon's saw opened Malcolm from sternum to groin. Another blade sliced neatly around his scalp, while hands in thin rubber gloves pulled the flap of his face away from the skull as though skinning a chicken. Joe bellowed out 'No!' and pressed his fists into his eyes to block it out. Then he wrapped his arms around his body, hugging himself and swaying backwards and forwards like a fretful child left alone in its cot.

'Is this where you found him?'

Once he realised who it was, he was grateful to Tess for interrupting the flow of pictures on the screen of his mind.

'I keep seeing him,' said Joe. 'He won't go away.' He stood up and walked a little way off the path, deliberately turning away from the place where Malcolm had lain. Tess followed him. Her face was as pale and as stiff as a mask, and polished as though she had spent hours scrubbing herself in the bath. Her freckles stood out like the marks of some contagious disease and she smelled of soap. She stared at him.

'Here?' she asked. She looked all round, as though searching for Malcolm among the unresponsive trees. The smell of woodsmoke hung on the air and in the distance the chain-saw stuttered and died. 'Is he here? Can you see him now?'

'I wanted to see him,' said Joe. 'In a way. I might have done something for him. There were things I wanted to tell him.' He wanted to say, I thought I might be able to save him this time, but he couldn't get the words out. Yet Tess might know what he was talking about, after all. Her own father had died: didn't that make some sort of bond between them? She must remember how it felt. 'Do you see him?' he blurted out.

'Malcolm?' She looked more terrified than ever.

'Your father. After he died, I mean. Did you go on seeing him? And did he ever go away again?'

She was shredding the leaves from a twig.

'Sometimes,' she said at last. 'When he's got something to tell me.'

'I wish . . .' started Joe, 'I wish Dad would tell me it was all right. It feels as though it was my fault.'

'It can never be all right,' said Tess. 'It'll never feel like it did before. Not once you know. It's like learning a tune: once you can sing it, it's there in your head, even when you're tired of it.'

'I keep hoping he'll walk in and tell me that it wasn't my fault. If I could have yesterday all over again, I could get it right this time.'

'On the other hand,' said Tess, 'he might tell you that it was all wrong and it was your fault. Then you'd have to spend the rest of your life making up for it. He might tell you there was something you had to do to put it right, but you couldn't, however hard you tried. Then you'd just have to spend all your time trying to forget about it.'

Joe stopped listening. 'I shouldn't have shouted at him,' he said. 'I knew I could upset him when we argued, but somehow I couldn't stop. And then I kicked him.'

'You can't kill people just by kicking them,' said Tess.

'Not if you're wearing trainers.'

It should have been a comforting thought, but it wasn't. 'No,' said Joe. 'It wasn't just the fight. It was the stress. He told me so. I did it.' And for the first time, Joe felt strong again. It was frightening, but it was better than the awful way he had been feeling up till then.

'I don't think so,' said Tess.

'What do you know about it?' Joe was starting to shout. 'We had that row and he went rushing out of the house and the next thing we knew he'd died of a heart attack.'

'Oh no,' said Tess. 'I think he died from being hit on the head.'

'What are you talking about? I didn't hit him on the head.'

'With a block of wood,' said Tess.

'What block of wood? You're talking rubbish.'

'You can get rid of wood by burning it,' said Tess, 'on a fire like that one back there.'

And they both sniffed the woodsmoke that had become so familiar that they had not registered it until now. Behind them the chain-saw screamed into life again, whining through the logs, reducing them to neat, compact, heavy, lethal instruments.

'You made it up,' said Joe. 'You're always making up stories.'

'I thought you must have done it,' said Tess. 'After all, who else was there around? And you keep saying how it was your fault.'

Joe thrust his hands into the pockets of his anorak as though to stop them from doing something violent. His fingers found hard granules of some unknown substance and he rubbed and fretted at them until they were reduced to a coarse grit. Tess had stopped the picture play inside his head all right, but now she had replaced it with a new nightmare. He wanted to stop thinking about what she was saying. For a moment he had thought she knew what he was going through, but she was the same witch-bitch as ever.

'Don't they say that?' the light voice was going on. 'The person who finds the body is usually the one who done it. Did it. I expect you got into one of your tempers and picked up a big piece of wood, like that one over there, and brought it down on Malcolm's head. If you did it hard enough, I expect that would kill him.'

'Shut up. You're talking crap.' He wanted to take hold of that thin neck and shake her. He wanted to pick up one of those lumps of wood and beat her over the head with it.

'And then you got rid of it by burning it. I expect it's turned to ash by now.'

Joe turned round and went running off down the hill, leaving her standing there with her pale face and odd hair.

'Stop blaming me!' he shouted at the trees as he ran. 'It wasn't my fault! I couldn't help it!'

When Joe got back to Martenswood Hanna was on the phone, fielding another enquiry about Malcolm's death and the date of the funeral. She found it impossible to utter the words 'not until after the autopsy', and so was burbling in an incoherent way to this latest caller. The doctor had explained it to her: until a cause of death was established, the body could not be released to the relatives. Meanwhile Hanna had to carry on looking after the house and five children, although the centre of the revolving plate that was her life had disappeared with Malcolm's death and the unimaginable 'after Malcolm' phase of her life could not properly begin. It had come to her during breakfast that Malcolm was not there and never would be again. She had, she realised, in spite of formally identifying Malcolm's dead body, been listening out for the humming of living-Malcolm's razor, waiting for him to come down the stairs to his burned toast and his newspaper. And before she had been interrupted by the ringing telephone, she had been upstairs in the bathroom, looking at Malcolm's electric razor, at his two toothbrushes, one for the morning, one for his evening assault on his teeth. There was the dental floss that they had shared, and the toothpaste that they had not. And on the floor by the window, clearly outlined in fungicidal powder, was the print of Malcolm's foot, as though he had only just thrown his damp towel down and walked out of the room. She looked at the shape with its broad big toe and almost non-existent arch and for the first time she felt his loss. Then she swept all his toilet things off the shelf.

'They've got to go, haven't they?' she said out loud, to no one in particular. 'Just as soon as the police tell me I can go back to normal life, I'll get rid of them all.'

As she turned away from the phone, she faced an angry Joe, thudding down the stairs, shouting.

'What were you doing up there? You can't touch those things! They belong to Dad. You're not to throw them away.'

He really was getting more like Malcolm every day. She could see him in a few years' time, his voice booming from his bedroom demanding a clean shirt, his heavy step on the loose floorboard.

'It was just his toilet things from the bathroom,' she said. 'His razor, his toothbrushes. I don't like his brand of toothpaste,' she added apologetically.

'You threw them on the floor,' said Joe accusingly. 'All his stuff.'

Less than two weeks, thought Hanna. They'll be back at school then and I can do exactly what I want in the house. In *my* house, the infant assertive voice inside her head told her. She had a whole supply of black rubbish bags. Somewhere there was a tip where the public could take their rubbish to dispose of it. Somehow she would locate both bags and tip and deal with all the living pieces of Malcolm that still ruled over Martenswood. In two weeks' time. She followed Joe upstairs and meekly replaced what were, for just a little while longer, Malcolm's belongings on Malcolm's bathroom shelf.

'What will happen to us now?' asked Harry. They were in Joe's room. 'Will Hanna go on looking after us? We'll be living here, won't we, when we come home for the holidays?'

'We don't wait for her to tell us,' answered Joe. 'We make our own plans and tell her what we've decided.'

'But what *are* we going to do?' wailed Tom, who had taken to sucking his thumb and walking round clutching a teddy-bear, like Harry.

'We go back to Gryphons,' said Joe. 'Then we go on to Palgrave, like Dad wanted us to. Then, when we're grown up, we come back to Martenswood. Because it's ours. It belongs to us. Or at least,' he amended, 'it's mine. I'm the eldest, so it belongs to me. And when I'm eighteen I can take it over. But I'll let you live here, too. And we'll have someone to look after us.'

'Who'll look after us?' asked Tom.

'Not Hanna.'

'She's all right, though,' said Harry, doubtfully.

'She's got to learn that she doesn't belong here any more,' said Joe. 'The fifth of March, 1994, I'll be eighteen and all this will belong to me.'

For the moment Harry and Tom were comforted, for they believed him.

Gerard smiled down at Tess from his photograph. He had been with her when she went up to Ruskin Wood. He had urged her to follow Malcolm out of the house and had shown her where to hide when he was talking to Diana. And afterwards he had been beside her as she took the short cut up to the top of the hill and watched Malcolm come into view, panting like an inefficient steam engine, the sweat standing out on his grey face in large pearly beads.

And after she had done what needed to be done, Gerard had told her to pick up the crumpled piece of paper from beside Malcolm's body and he had walked beside her – 'No need to hurry, now,' he had said, as she went over to the break in the stack where the ride crossed the carriage drive and sloped down towards the sheep pasture. She didn't think Malcolm had seen her as she stood over him with the block of wood, though he had twisted away from her as she had brought it down on his head. She didn't think he had heard her reply, either, after he had shouted out to the sky that last time for help. She didn't believe he could have heard her when she did, eventually, reply because Gerard told her he was dead, and Gerard of all people should recognise death.

It was surely Gerard who had told her that she must check that the lump of wood – a slice from a tree trunk as flat and as hard as the cushion Hanna had once embroidered, but many times heavier – was burning properly in the foresters' bonfire before she left.

After that he had led her away from the still figure and had shown her the marbled white butterflies and the small blues out on the open, sandy heath at the top of the hill, to take away the sour taste from her mouth and the ugly pictures in her head. Then he drew her into the dappled light under the trees and pointed out the butter-flies with the dark brown velvety wings that she couldn't find in her field guide. But finally she had gone back to Malcolm in his old white pullover and with his green boots trailing in a puddle, in spite of Gerard's voice calling her away and his weightless hand pulling at her sleeve.

It was odd about Steve Ratsaway. She must find out what he had been doing there, and why he had been so worried when he found that she was there too. And why had he run away afterwards? He had been afraid of the dead body, she knew, but she didn't think that that was all there was to it. Perhaps it had something to do with the letter.

When she crept unseen into Martenswood she had taken the last few crumbs of slug bait from the pocket of her dress and transferred them to the pocket of Joe's anorak before hanging it back in the cloakroom. Then upstairs she removed her old green dress and gym shoes, bundling them into a plastic carrier bag that she found at the bottom of her cupboard. She knew from watching television that the police could tell all sorts of things from your clothes and skin, so she stood under the shower in the spare bathroom for ages, scrubbing at herself and letting the water flow through her hair. When she had finished she dressed in clean underpants and cut-offs and put on yesterday's T-shirt. She buried her discarded underpants and socks at the bottom of the dirty linen basket.

There was no one in the kitchen, so she took the end of her home-baked loaf, together with a couple of rock-hard rolls and a desiccated scone, and put them in another bag. She let herself out of the back door with her plastic carrier bags.

At Sudden Cottage, Kay had already put her dustbin out for the next morning's collection, so Tess lifted the lid and pushed one of her packages deep down among the empty freezer food containers and plastic bags until it was indistinguishable from the rest of the garbage. She knew that it would be ages, if ever, before Hanna noticed that one of her old dresses was missing. And who could ever count the odd black plimsolls that lay around at Martenswood, let alone know which ones belonged to which child, and whether there were two more – or two fewer – than yesterday? Then she had knocked at the door of the cottage.

'I've brought you some scraps for the chickens,' she said to Kay. 'There isn't an awful lot of it, but it's a pity to waste food, isn't it?'

Kay peered at the fossilised offerings and grunted at Tess without removing the cigarette from her scarlet lips. 'Buggers'll think it's their birthdays,' she said. She was walking towards the door of one of the sheds as Tess left through the gate.

Just one meal won't hurt them, Tess assured herself, as she walked back to Martenswood. And chickens haven't got fur, anyway. Yes, Gerard must have been with her all that time.

Steve stayed away from Martenswood. He had plenty of other work on, and he could pick up the threads of his relationship with Hanna when the mystery of Malcolm's death had been cleared up. She'd be glad to see him then, he supposed. He'd call in on Kay, make sure she was sensible enough to keep her mouth shut about their plan. He'd keep her happy for a week or two before moving on.

Kay put the bucket of scraps down by the shed door. The chickens were oddly silent, so she opened the door for a closer inspection. All the birds were looking poorly and some of them looked dead.

'Must have overfed the buggers,' she said to herself as she went inside to make a phone call to the local butcher. 'What can you offer me for half a dozen free-range chickens?' she asked him. She'd have to start looking around for some extra income now that Malcolm had died. His death had come at a really inconvenient time, but then in her experience men always were selfish bastards.

DEATHSPELL

The Chief Inspector was a busy man and it wasn't until late the next morning that he looked through the preliminary report that the pathologist had sent him on what had looked like a typical middle-aged heart attack case. Then he passed it across to his sergeant.

'Usual procedures,' he said, not being a talkative man.

'Any ideas, sir?' asked the sergeant, when he had read it.

'I'd put my money on a kid. A frantic, angry kid. First he tries poison – things he can get his hands on easily – then he hits him and catches him at just the right angle to kill. What was the name of the one who found the body?'

'Joseph Alexander Benson, sir. Born 5 March, 1976.'

'Eleven and a half. But a big lad for his age, with a nasty temper. Had a fight with his father just that morning, apparently.'

'Nasty little bugger, I thought. And did you notice how his hands were covered with blood?'

'But not his father's. It came from a dead rabbit.'

'Let's go and talk to him.'

Hanna found that there were more questions to be answered than she could have imagined.

The policemen who turned up in unmarked cars and sat in her armchairs and refused her offers of tea had short haircuts and white shirts, dark suits and expressionless faces, and they watched her with hard, assessing eyes. They had brought a woman police constable with them, who sat silently and deferentially on an upright chair and didn't remove her hat.

Hanna made a statement that was written down by the

policewoman, and when she read it back before signing it it seemed to be written in words that sounded nothing like her own, but which she supposed must mean the same thing. She couldn't, anyway, tell them much, she said, since she had been very sick after lunch yesterday.

'Yes,' said one of the detectives. 'We have corroboration of that by a Mrs Verna Hazel Elliott.' Hanna wondered what else she had told them.

They spent a long time searching her house, and when she looked out of the window, she could see that there were more of them in the garden and in the woods, scratching and sifting.

Chapter Seventeen

The police left the house some time in the early evening. They took with them a lot of things that seemed quite bizarre to Hanna in their irrelevance, and also specimens that they scraped from surfaces, or picked up on sticky-backed tape.

When she had fed the children and persuaded them to bed, Hanna sat down and poured herself a glass of Malcolm's whisky. She considered diluting it with water, but rejected the idea since it involved too much effort. She was only halfway down the tumbler when the door-bell rang.

'I'll come straight to the point,' said Diana Kinch, pushing into the room ahead of her and planting herself on the sofa. 'We have met, at the Dovers', but we weren't properly introduced: I'm Malcolm's first wife. The boys' mother. And if you want rid of them, you and me will have to come to an agreement.'

'Shall I make us some coffee?' asked Hanna.

'Haven't you got any whisky?' Hanna poured her what Malcolm would have called 'a proper drink', and then topped up her own.

'I don't suppose you'll want the boys here much

longer,' Diana said, accepting the drink. She sat back into the sofa and crossed well-shaped legs down which a single varicose vein snaked its way beneath the sheer smoke-coloured tights. She wore a dark blue skirt and jacket which gaped open to display a well-supported bosom in a shiny cream blouse.

'It's not a question of not wanting them,' Hanna replied, wishing she could hide her own bare legs and disreputable sandals. 'But I imagine that both you and they will be much happier when you're all living together under one roof.' She was about to say, 'You are their mother, after all,' but thought better of it since in all practical senses, Diana Kinch had been nothing of the kind for over three years.

'And there we come to the little problem,' said Diana, lighting a cigarette and then removing a small crumb of the filter from between her two front teeth.

'How do you mean?' Whisky, Hanna decided, had a relaxing effect on the nerves: she scarcely winced as Diana's exhaled smoke blew in her direction.

'No roof. Or, just so that you're quite clear about it, no doors, no windows, no furniture. No house.'

'Ah.'

'So you see, I really can't take the boys off your hands.' She swallowed the rest of her whisky down and stared straight at Hanna with her slightly protuberant light blue eyes. 'Get on well with them, do you? Find them easy to handle?' The smoke was filtering out through the gaps between her teeth, and Hanna wondered whether their back surfaces were thick with tar.

'Not particularly. In fact, I'd say that your eldest, Joe, had the makings of a real problem.' Perhaps she shouldn't have had the whisky, after all: it was too easy to say just what was in her mind.

'Yes, you may be right. I never liked him much, myself. In fact, if this is the time for true confessions, I was glad to leave all three of them behind when I left Malcolm. Of course, they were younger then. They're not quite so much of a pain now that they've got older. I can't stand small kids. But you wouldn't want Joe around those two girls of yours in a year or two, would you?'

'No. But then I don't have to have him around. I'm not their mother, and when I married Malcolm, I didn't take on a job for life as the boys' keeper.' Inhibitions were dropping by the minute, Hanna noticed, and she scratched the itchy bit above her knee that had been irritating her all evening. 'After all, they have a perfectly good mother of their own.'

'Only if I chose to stick around. But I could get on the next plane to anywhere, couldn't I? And then, dear, you'd be lumbered.'

Hanna tried to think how Jean Rainbird would have dealt with this scene. She would have stayed cool and in control. (She probably wouldn't be scratching herself as she sprawled in the armchair.) She said, 'I suppose it is expensive trying to keep a roof over yourself and three boys. And, of course, Malcolm did provide for them.'

'Now we're getting to it. How much?' Diana leant forwards, knees apart.

'He set up a trust fund. And this house will come to them eventually, too.'

Pale blue eyes popped further. 'Martenswood?'

'Yes. But it's mine for life. My life, that is. And so is the income from all the rest of his capital. But there's a respectable sum – you'll have to check with the solicitors, they know all about it – for their education and upkeep and that sort of thing.'

'So just tell them to hand it over to me, OK?'

'Oh no, they won't do that. They can't. There are trustees who decide how it's to be spent – but I'm sure they'll be reasonable. They have the boys' interests at heart, after all.' She went across to the pile of papers and letters that hid her desk. 'I'll write down the name and address for you. It'll be best if you contact them direct.' She scrabbled about a bit until a biro appeared. 'I'll look after the boys for the rest of the holidays and get them off to Gryphons. And then you can arrange all the practical details after that.' She wrote the name and address down on the back of a used envelope.

She had managed to say this without looking Diana in the eye. But now that she came across the room and handed her the solicitor's name and address, she could see that the other woman was pale in the face. With shock, perhaps. Well, it would be a shock to find that you were suddenly landed with three boys like Joe, Harry and Tom after being footloose for three years.

Footloose, she thought, as Diana silently tucked the paper into her handbag. That's what I shall be in my lovely silent house.

'I'll see what the estate can manage,' she said, in a rush of gratitude. 'I expect we can provide you with some sort of lump sum to tide you over, even if it's only a loan. Until you get yourself settled in a job, that is.'

Diana Kinch rose, pushing her foot back into an escaped shoe.

'Don't think I'm going to take this lying down—'

'Why not? Lying seems to be your speciality,' said Hanna, admiring her own quick wit.

'You're not getting away with this. You'll have to come up with a better offer, lady, or I'm away.'

'Think about it,' said Hanna, whose mind was settling back into its usual fuzziness. 'I'm sure you'll see it's for the best.' She opened the door. 'Do drive carefully down the lane, won't you? It's a dangerous right turn at the top there.'

Gravel spurted as Diana Kinch accelerated away. Just like Malcolm, thought Hanna. Oh dear, and she still hasn't said hello to the boys. She returned to her whisky and so didn't hear the screech of brakes at the end of the drive.

'If you turn your headlights off,' said Tess, 'we can talk in the car without anyone seeing us.'

She had thought for a moment that Diana wasn't going to stop in time, but she was wearing a white T-shirt and had been quite visible when she had jumped out from between the rhododendrons and waved her arms.

'You've got to take the boys away,' she said, settling herself into the passenger seat. 'They can't stay here. Not now.'

'That's up to your mother,' said Diana Kinch, recognising an opponent who would speak her own language. 'If she pays, I'll go and I'll take the boys with me. But I'm not doing that unless she makes it worth my while. I want at least half the value of that house and a proper income for me and them.'

'That sounds like an awful lot,' said Tess. 'But you

don't want any trouble, do you?'

There was the flare of a match as Diana lit a cigarette. 'What trouble? There's no trouble.'

'But there would be if I told the police that you met Malcolm up in the woods and argued with him and shouted at him. And threatened him,' she elaborated.

'What's that got to do with it? It's not as though he was murdered. He died of a heart attack or something, didn't he?'

Tess pounced on the hesitation. 'Oh no. Not a heart attack. Someone hit him on the head.' She turned innocent eyes on Diana. 'I suppose it might have been you.'

'You can't go round saying things like that—'

'No, of course not. But I must tell the police what happened, don't you think?'

'Here, you're making it up about someone hitting him on the head, aren't you?'

'Oh no. That bit's true. But the police don't know about how you met Malcolm in Ruskin Woods. Not yet, anyway.'

'Why should they believe you?'

'Because I could show them where you parked your car, and where your footprints are and where you dropped your cigarette stub. I could tell them a lot, really, if I wanted to. Sister Patrick says I'm an unusually articulate child for my age.'

'Says you're a little liar, too, does she?'

'Inventive, she says. And it won't look good when Mum and I both tell them how you turned up at the house this evening and demanded money and stuff.'

'So you're a little big-ears, as well.'

'I'm sure I'll make a good witness.'

'Well, maybe I'll call on this solicitor and see what's on offer. But I'm not committing myself.'

'Call on him tomorrow morning and let Mum know by lunchtime. I wouldn't want to hide stuff from the police for longer than that.'

'You'd better get out of this car and hop it before I belt you one.'

'Goodnight, Mrs Kinch.'

Tess returned to the house and let herself in through the back door. Tomorrow morning she would go and see Kay and talk to her about the letter she had found by Malcolm's body. She was sure that there was something Kay could do for her in return for its disappearance.

Hanna had a headache next morning and resolved to stick to wine in future. But at least she heard that Malcolm's body was being released for burial. She could get on with the funeral arrangements, though the police and the doctor were still being uncommunicative about the cause of Malcolm's death. And just before lunch, Diana Kinch phoned, sweet as pie, having spoken to the solicitors and agreed to their proposals for her to take the boys. In a rush of gratitude, Hanna offered an immediate and large sum in cash to take them off on holiday for the ten days before term started. 'Give me a couple of days to organise something,' said Diana Kinch.

'You don't have to go to the funeral,' Hanna told Tess and Aurora. 'You can go to Mrs Elliott's for the day, if you'd rather.'

But Tess said that they wanted to go. 'With Joe and

Harry and Tom,' she said. 'We really want to say good-bye to Malcolm, don't we, Rory? He would have wanted it.'

It wasn't proper funeral weather, with squalls of rain and a blustery wind, but one of those balmy September days that caressed the skin and made you glad to be alive.

'It's not much of a service, is it?' Tess had said to her in the church. 'Not like one of ours.'

There were more people than Hanna had expected. Fox Hill turned up in decent black, and Hanna knew she hadn't a hope of remembering more than a handful of names. There were a number of Malcolm's staff: dark-suited, black-tied men who shook Hanna's hand and murmured condolences. And then Diana Kinch appeared in the chapel. There was little in Diana's looks to show to anyone that she was the boys' mother: they took so thoroughly after their father. But she did turn up, Hanna saw, looking like the chief mourner, in black suit and shoes, black tights and even a hat. The colour suited her, of course. The boys didn't recognise her with her dark hair hidden under the becoming felt and veiling, and she didn't make herself known to them. There would be time enough for all that getting-to-know-you rubbish, she had told Hanna, when she came to pick them up in a couple of days' time and took them on their cosy little holiday.

As she watched the coffin slide through the tasteful blue curtains, Hanna said her final farewell to Malcolm. He was a good man, really, she thought, firmly pushing to the back of her mind her knowledge of the unworldly old lady he had swindled to make his first killing in the

DEATHSPELL

property market. She had been quite surprised to see Kay Parker at the service: she must have been more grateful for all those bags of discarded bread than Hanna had imagined. She wasn't sure that Kay's outfit was entirely suitable for a funeral, though. Her suit was very close fitting around the bosom and waist, with a little frill that stuck out over her hips; it was in some sort of metallic scarlet and hyacinth-blue material, and with it she wore a tiny hat, the size and shape of a poached egg, perched over one eye, with a red and blue spotted veil hiding the top half of her face.

Tess hadn't told her mother that Gerard had been there at her shoulder all day. It was a funny thing, but since Malcolm died, Gerard seemed to be around most of the time.

Every day since Malcolm's death, when she sat up in her room, Gerard came and sat beside her and took her back to that afternoon when they walked through the fields and down to the river. And at other times he chatted to her about the people around them and her life today. He seemed to be up to date in all that was going on and he gave her sensible advice on how to cope with it. She was only surprised that no one else could see him.

You've been doing well, he said. *Once you got rid of that man, things started to fall into place, didn't they? The Kinch woman is taking the boys away and Kay Parker is keeping Steve Ratsaway out of the house. Soon, now, it will be just you and me, Hanna and Aurora, and we can all go back. I'll take you across the fields and down to the river. We're strong now, you and I, and we can do anything we want.*

★ ★ ★

After lunch on the day after the funeral, Tess and Aurora slipped away to the playroom. They couldn't hear the buzz of voices and scrape of knives on plates up there, and they couldn't see the pale, solemn faces of Joe, Harry and Tom, either. They could sprawl on the broken-down old sofa, which they shared with two of Aurora's dolls and a grey knitted rabbit, and allow their faces to relax into the smiles that they had known to be inappropriate in the company of the grown-ups.

'No Gryphons,' said Aurora.

'Back to St Fred's,' said Tess. 'I'm even looking forward to seeing Sister Patrick again.'

'Fatty ham and boiled cabbage for dinner.'

'Porridge and cocoa for breakfast.'

'Horrible chapel every morning.'

'Confession on Wednesday afternoons.'

'Boring old retreat before Christmas.'

Then, 'What will happen to the boys, now?' asked Aurora. 'Has Mum told you?'

'Their mother's picking them up this afternoon and taking them for a holiday. I suppose they'll be sent back to school when term starts, and then they'll have to live with their mother.'

'The one with the veil and the funny make-up, that you pointed out at the church? I don't like her, do you? I'm glad Mum isn't like that. And she didn't even say hello to Harry.'

'They deserve everything they get.' Tess picked up the grey rabbit, which belonged to Tom, and twisted its ears viciously before she threw it down on the floor among the jumble of other toys.

'But Harry's all right. Couldn't we keep Harry?'

Aurora rescued the rabbit, rubbed his ears and put him to sit in between the two dolls on the sofa.

'Yes, I suppose Harry is all right. OK, I'll talk to Mum and to . . . I'll talk to Mum about it and if she agrees, we'll have Harry here some of the time. The other two can go.'

She'd check with Gerard when Aurora wasn't around. Aurora might not understand about her conversations with Gerard, and she didn't feel like explaining it to her. Kay had been very helpful, when she had spoken to her, especially after she had mentioned the letter, and she had promised to keep Steve Ratsaway out of their hair. She quite understood that they wouldn't want him up at Martenswood, bothering Hanna.

They heard the boys come upstairs and call out to each other as they packed their bags ready to go away on holiday. Then they heard a car pull up on the gravel and went to the window to see if it was Diana Kinch.

Two dark-suited men and a uniformed woman got out of the car and came up to the front door. A moment later they heard them enter the house.

'Who was that?' asked Aurora.

'I expect it's the police,' said Tess, 'come to arrest Joe. And about time, too.'

Another, smaller, dustier car drew up beside the first. Diana Kinch got out, dressed now in a bright yellow skirt and a white polo-necked sweater.

'Good,' said Tess. 'Now the police needn't bother Mum any more.'

Some time later, the police left, with Joe in their car and Diana following in hers, accompanied by Harry and

Tom, with their pathetic bags and belongings. She and Hanna had to persuade Harry that he couldn't take all twelve of his teddy-bears with him. He seemed very nervous about leaving any of them behind. But in the end he just took Orly, Roundhouse and Gatwick.

When Tess and Aurora went downstairs, Hanna was pouring spoonfuls of sugar into a mug of tea and talking to herself.

'No,' she was saying. 'It isn't possible. I'm sure they've got it wrong. It was his heart. I knew he was overweight and overwrought and shouldn't be overdoing it the way he was. But not a skull fracture, or whatever that cervical thing they were talking about was. I thought it was something to do with wombs, anyway, though I suppose it couldn't be if Malcolm had one.'

'Why did they take Joe away?' asked Tess.

'They were asking him about the slug pellets they found in his anorak pocket and the plastic bag of rat poison he was hiding in his sock drawer and something about his fingernails. I don't understand any of it. What was he doing with rat poison? And why did they find those traces of poison in Malcolm's stomach? He couldn't have been eating slug pellets by mistake, could he? And then Joe lost his temper and shouted at the chief inspector about Malcolm not being poisoned, but how he was hit on the head with a block of wood. And the chief inspector looked at the sergeant and smiled and said how interesting, and Joe must tell them all about it, and what had happened to this block of wood after-wards, and Joe shouted about putting it on a bonfire.' She was curling her hair round her fingers again, Tess noticed. 'I do wish Joe hadn't kicked the policemen. I think it made things look worse for him. And they seem to have heard all about those fights he had had with Malcolm. Do you think the milkman can have said something? Surely he wouldn't. Or Verna Elliott?'

'Where've they taken him? Will they lock him up in prison now?'

'It's all quite complicated with a child of Joe's age, but I think they'll have to put him into the care of the local council.'

'Will there be a trial? Can we go and watch?'

'Eventually, I suppose, and no, you can't. But I still can't believe that he really did it.'

'It's best that he's gone,' said Tess. 'And for ever, now.'

But that night in bed Tess kept seeing Joe's face, white in the darkness of the police car, as they drove him away. He didn't look large and strong as he sat there with the policemen around him. In fact he looked small and frightened and unhappy. Just a kid, really.

Later, as she was falling asleep, Gerard came to fetch her and they went for a walk down to the river. She was wearing her red coat with the hood and her old jade-green pullover, which was odd because she thought that she'd grown out of them a couple of years ago. They walked through the copse and along the path to the five-barred gate. Gerard had lifted her up and they had sat on top of the gate until Aurora and Hanna had caught up with them. Then they went on through the field with the grazing sheep, and they told Aurora not to chase the sheep, and Aurora cried, because she wasn't going to chase them anyway. The sheep were very noisy, and they didn't say 'baa baa' like it said in books, but more like a sad, wailing 'mneea, mneea' sound, and they had faces like Harry's. And overhead the rooks were shouting angrily as they flew home to roost in the trees on the hill. The distant city was a misty blue lake, with floating concrete buildings turned to shining silver by the last rays of the sun.

Tess and Gerard strode away, leaving Hanna and Aurora behind again, as they made off down the hill towards the car. Gerard was wearing his small red backpack, where he carried a spare pullover and a lightweight mac, and a bar of chocolate with hazelnuts in that he kept just for Tess. When they got to the stile at the bottom of the hill he got out the chocolate and he and Tess shared the whole bar. She thought she saw Jeff walking through the trees towards them, waving to Hanna and Aurora, but Gerard frowned at him and he disappeared.

'There,' he said, as he left her safe in her white-covered bed, and climbed back into his silver frame, 'that's how it was supposed to be, now, wasn't it? Just you and me, and Hanna and Aurora. No boys, no Malcolm, no Jeff. And no going away to school. Remember that, Tess, and don't waste your time feeling sorry for any of them.'

Chapter Eighteen

Next morning, when Hanna went to put on a skirt, she found that the waistband was looser than it used to be. Still, she thought, sucking in her tummy and turning sideways to the mirror, it suited her, being just that little bit slimmer.

But later, when the two girls came into the kitchen while she was making herself her second pot of coffee and contemplating her first glass of wine, she saw that their expressions were disapproving. Aurora seemed to have brought a bundle of rags with her and they looked as though they were set for a long conversation. She wondered whether she had some aspirin somewhere.

Tess and Aurora sat down at the table and watched her as she dropped the kettle and failed to find a matching cup and saucer. 'Biscuits?' she asked them, generously finding the ones she had hidden away for Jean Rainbird and . . . but no, she must forget about him.

They helped themselves to milk chocolate digestives. Tess sat watching her as she poured out her coffee.

'Aurora's got something for you, Mum.'

'Oh, really, dear? How nice.'

'Something,' said Tess, 'that you'll be needing now

that Malcolm and the boys have gone.'

'Dead. I'd rather you didn't use euphemisms, Tess. Malcolm is dead. We don't use expressions like "gone" or "passed away" or "passed over". It really is better to face facts, darling, however hard it may seem at the moment. The boys have gone and Malcolm is dead.'

'I know Malcolm's dead,' said Tess. 'That's what I'm saying, Mum. Malcolm's dead and so now you'll be needing your old clothes. You can go back to being the way you were. The way Dad liked you to be.'

'But that's—'

Tess turned to her sister. 'Show her, Rory. She doesn't know what we're talking about.'

Aurora held out the bundle of rags. Only they weren't rags but one of her old cotton dresses that she'd put out for the jumble sale, oh, ages ago now. She'd felt a bit ashamed about it, the dresses were so shabby, but someone might have had a use for them. Well, she could see now that Aurora had.

'Darling,' she said carefully, taking in the expression of joyful anticipation on Aurora's face, 'it's very sweet indeed of you to have thought about keeping one of my dresses for me. But . . .'

'Yes?'

A very sharp challenge from Tess. She'd have to go carefully. 'I'm afraid that really it wouldn't fit me any more, you know. Look at how much fatter I was in those days.'

'You've got thin,' said Tess. 'But you can put the weight back on again, can't you? Have a chocolate biscuit.'

'No thanks. I don't want to get fatter again,' said

Hanna, thinking about this new attack on her identity. 'Aurora, darling, I'll wash and iron this dress and put it away in my wardrobe, OK? And then if ever I put back those pounds I've taken off, it'll be ready for me to wear. How's that?' And that'll make me watch what I eat if nothing else will, she thought to herself.

'I thought you'd be pleased about it,' said Aurora, lower lip trembling.

'Of course I am, darling. It was really very sweet of you to rescue my favourite dress from the jumble like that.'

Aurora looked puzzled, but she stopped arguing.

Tess started in on a new tack. 'Mum, can we go and get my new games skirt tomorrow?'

It was Hanna's turn to look bewildered. 'But you don't need one, do you. Tess? We bought all the games clothes and equipment you needed.'

'Yes I do, don't you remember you said you'd get me a new one because my old skirt was too short? And term starts next Monday.'

Light dawned on Hanna. 'But, Tess, you know you're not going back to St Fred's this term. You're going to Gryphons. Why do you think we bought all that uniform for you and Aurora?'

'But that was before! He's dead now, you just said he was! Not passed on or passed over or anything, you said. Dead, that's what you told us. So that means that we don't have to go to Gryphons, doesn't it?'

'Tess, darling, it's all arranged, you know it is. Malcolm fixed it before he died. They're not even expecting you at St Fred's. They've probably got two new girls by now to take your place.'

'Well, they can leave again! It's our school, not theirs, isn't it, Rory?'

'Look, darlings, you've got all your stuff, the uniform and the other things. I thought you were so pleased about it.'

'But I liked St Fred's! And I haven't even said anything about hating Sister Patrick this holidays, have I?'

'No. Just listen to me, now. St Fred's is very good for a local day school. But you're a clever child, Tess, and so is Aurora in her way, and you should have a chance to develop that intelligence by going away to a really good school. So let's hear no more of this nonsense. You're going to Gryphons on the seventeenth, and there's an end to it. You'll both be fine.'

'But suppose it *isn't* fine?' Aurora was whispering.

'You're to stop worrying. You know that if it really didn't turn out all right, we'd have to think again. But until you've been there for a term or two, and have given yourselves a chance to settle in, there's no argument. Understood? And no silly fussing.'

Two pairs of eyes stared at her out of two white faces. Tess's was set and stubborn. Aurora's mouth was drooping and she looked as though she was about to start crying. Hanna nearly weakened; then she thought about her future, and about the things she wanted to do. And she thought, too, about the superstitious nonsense that was filling up their heads. She wanted them to be bright, confident, *normal* children, not guilt-ridden little things who didn't know what they wanted in life. It wasn't only that having the children away at boarding school during the term time would make a big difference to her, she really had their welfare in mind. And was it so wrong to think about her own talents, and her own ambitions and her own life? Was that selfish of her? Was being selfish such a sin? What was sin? Who cared? The headache throbbed behind her eyes.

'Off you go, now. I've got some letters I must write. But I'll get you something really nice for lunch.'

Gerard was sitting in Tess's room. She had lit the candle in front of his photograph, but he had walked out of the frame and sat down on her bed, laughing at her when she grumbled about the way his shoes were marking the clean white bedspread.

Remember that afternoon in the fields, when we went for a walk?

'I remember. With the sun burning overhead, the sky a deep cobalt blue and the white clouds fluffing and trailing and breaking up into streaks and flakes.'

He frowned at her. *No, you've got it wrong there. There was a gusting, blustery wind. The sky was dark as night and the clouds were heavy and swollen with rain. We pulled our scarves over our heads and put up the collars of our raincoats as we ran for cover under the trees in the corner of the field. Elm trees, they were, huge old things, and their leaves dripped cold gouts of water on to our faces.*

'Yes, I remember it that way now.'

And in the next field one of the heifers started bellowing, God only knows why. She didn't like the rain, maybe, or she was suddenly missing her mother. But anyway, there she stood, with her head raised to the weeping skies and her great mouth stretched open and this God-awful noise blaring out.

'And what did I do?'

You were frightened, weren't you, now? And you hung on tight to my hand.

'Were you wearing your green gloves?'

I was.

'Tell me! Was Jeff there that time, too?'

I think I hear someone coming.

'Please, you've got to tell me before you go!'

Now, that time I didn't do anything much, did I, now? Just shouted and waved my arms until she stopped and looked at me in surprise.

'Did we go home after that?'

We still had something left to do.

'Tell me it didn't happen! Please don't go!'

I have to. But I'll be back.

Steve hadn't expected to be popular down at Sudden Cottage after the failure of his plan. But, oddly enough, Kay had been welcoming – clinging, even. It was odd, too, about Martenswood. He had kept away for a day or two, nervous that someone would ask him about his part in finding Malcolm and enquire what he had been doing in the woods at that time, and why he hadn't stayed with the body as he'd said he would. But after a couple of days he started dreaming about the house, and the dark glow of its elm floorboards, and the mahogany panelling around the bath, and the gleam of its brass taps and, with particular clarity, remembered the lovely little leaves and flowers that swirled around the ceiling rose in Hanna's spare bedroom.

He hadn't tried very hard to get rid of the mice in her house – they weren't that much of a problem, anyway, except to Malcolm, as far as he could see – and their continuing presence had provided him with a ready-made excuse to call whenever he wanted, to stand and scratch his head at more evidence of their destructiveness, and to wander around the house and garden whenever he liked, without anyone asking him what he was up to. He could check the bait he had put down, he could tap knowledgeably on the walls and skirting boards. He could keep reminding Hanna of his existence.

But when he thought fondly how she'd be needing a hand about the place, a woman like that who wasn't much cop at the practical things of life, and how she'd be looking for comfort and advice, somehow every time something stopped him from calling in there. Mostly it was Kay who prevented him, though he could have sworn that she knew nothing about his intentions. But she was quieter than usual and he found her a couple of times staring at her chickens with a faraway expression on her face. He thought it was probably time he moved on, but not quite yet: he still had unfinished business up on Fox Hill.

At eleven o'clock on Monday, Hanna asked Jean to join her for a coffee break. They were briefly alone in the great empty house, and she got out the posh coffee-maker with the metal mesh filter and the brass plunger. It should have made good coffee and Hanna never understood how somehow, when she used it, it turned out a pale, tasteless, mud-coloured sludge. At least she had a choice of four different sorts of biscuit for them and there was little she could do to ruin those. They drank their coffee out of blue and white flowered cups, overlooked by an enormous arrangement of twigs and seedheads and grasses and leaves that Hanna had placed in a wicker basket on the dresser behind them.

'I'm glad you're here,' said Hanna.

'I certainly don't want to let you down. Not this week . . .'

Words like 'murder' and 'arrest' hovered in the air and remained unspoken. Yet Jean must have driven her car through the knot of newspapermen at the front gate.

'I should have said how sorry I was about Mr Benson . . .'

Hanna sighed and poured her undrunk half-cup of coffee into the sink. 'This is horrible, isn't it? I can't think why I can never make decent coffee.' Then she went to the larder and returned with a bottle. 'Join me?' she asked, putting two glasses on the table and producing an efficient corkscrew.

'I shouldn't. But, well, in the circumstances . . .'

'Exactly,' said Hanna. 'I don't know how I'd have got through the past few days without it.' She poured the wine. 'Now don't get me wrong. It's not that I don't miss Malcolm, that I'm not devastated by his death, and by the things that have happened since. I'm not being heartless, you understand. But somehow, with all the gruesome details I have to get through, I do need a touch of anaesthesia from time to time.'

'Any news of Joe?'

'It looks as though he did do it, I'm afraid.'

'What will happen to him?'

'Apparently you can't be tried for murder in the juvenile court. Our solicitor is dealing with it all, but if Joe's found guilty then he can be sent away for a very long time.'

DEATHSPELL

They both stared into the depths of their glasses.

'When the girls are back at school, I'll pull myself together.'

'Perhaps what you need to do then is let yourself go.'

'What a very sensible woman you are,' said Hanna, filling her glass again and topping up Jean's, which was still three-quarters full.

'And there's the way Tess looks at me: as though she disapproves of the way I'm behaving, somehow. And I feel as though I'm under threat. No, that sounds silly, doesn't it? But it's as though she was planning something. I'd like to think that the worst is over, but I feel as though there's more to come.'

'You must be imagining it. You need to get things into perspective. Haven't you got any friends from before Malcolm . . . umm, from your old life?'

'I've moved around so much in the years since Gerard died, and it's difficult to keep up with old friends when you've got no home to invite them to. We had a few acquaintances, people that Gerard met at the pub and drank with and brought home for a bowl of spaghetti sometimes, but not what you'd call friends: lost souls, oddments of society, mostly. Not women friends that I could invite into the kitchen and let my hair down with. Like you and me.' She offered the biscuits to Jean and then helped herself to one. Jean took a Jaffa cake, and for a short moment Hanna remembered another occasion with biscuits and coffee and hot looks from a man with dark blue eyes. Was he a friend? She wondered. She had had so few in her life that she found it difficult to judge. She hoped he was. It seemed like years since she had entertained him at this table, and one more reason for feeling guilty.

'And why should I feel guilty?' she asked, following her own train of thought. 'I did my best to be a good wife to him, you know. It's just that I wasn't much good at running a house and keeping five children occupied and looking elegant all at the same time.'

'Who is?'

'Malcolm's fantasy woman was. The one who lived inside his imagination and that he hoped to meet when he got home from work each evening.' The wine bottle was half empty. Hanna peered at it in an unbelieving way before filling their glasses again.

'We both dreamed of bed, all evening,' she said. 'He hoped for something erotic and passionate, or at least moderately enthusiastic. I just wanted to go to sleep. For about twelve hours, usually. Do you realise that it takes at least as much energy – more, probably – to run a house badly as to run it efficiently? Like cooking. Not that I do like cooking, of course. But people who fling things into pots and produce wonderful, amusing little meals use much less effort than I do, with my chopping and sautéeing and fussing.'

'Well, you'll be able to sort out your life a bit now, won't you? Make your own decisions about what you do and don't want. Never cook again, if you like, at least while the girls are away at school.'

'When the children have all gone away to school. You're right. I just hang on to that thought like a lifebelt. I'll be as free as . . . Last week it seemed as though I knew at last. As though I could look in the mirror and see my real face. But it's gone again now. Do you think I'll manage to remember what it was that I wanted to do? I've spent so many years pushing it to the back of my mind, I don't think I'll ever be able to rake it out again.'

'You'll think of something, I expect.'

'You won't leave me now, will you, Jean? I really don't know what I'd do without you, you see.'

'Trust me.'

'Oh, I do. And the thought of sinking down below Level One again terrifies me.' She lifted up the bottle. 'More wine for you?'

Tess listened to her mother telling her not to worry for the twentieth time that day. Their suitcases were packed and the car was loaded. She and Aurora were wearing their stiff new uniforms.

'Don't worry,' Hanna was repeating. 'I'll be down to see how you're getting on in about three weeks' time. I'll take you out to tea and you can tell me all about it.'

'Look after Finnegan, won't you?' said Aurora.

'And you'll be back at half-term. You'll see, the time will just fly.'

'And you are sure you packed my teddy-bear?' said Aurora. 'You didn't forget it, did you, Mum? If you did, you'd have to drive all the way back to Gryphons to give it to me.'

'He'll be there, sitting waiting for you when you go to bed tonight,' said Hanna.

For a moment, Tess wondered whether Gerard would be waiting for her, too, like Aurora's teddy-bear, sitting by her bedside at Gryphons, or whether he would stay here and look after Hanna. Someone ought to keep an eye on her, she thought.

229

Chapter Nineteen

Steve didn't realise that it was the Gryphons' half-term when he at last came to call on Hanna, having first left his car down the lane out of sight. Kay didn't know where he was, and it was only because she had disappeared with what she described as 'a new friend of mine' in the direction of the city, that Steve had been able to get away to Martenswood. He noticed that the new friend drove a large quiet car and that Kay was wearing the red and blue number that she had worn to Malcolm's funeral and had spent the previous evening bleaching her roots.

Hanna was on her own in the kitchen, building another of her extraordinary bowery creations – for the sitting room this time, she told him. The table was heaped with what looked to Steve like the prunings from several large trees.

'Of course, I can't do it immediately, it wouldn't be right,' she told him. 'But I have an idea for running a small business. I'm going to start travelling around, looking for pieces I can use in my decorations. I'd like to use wire and silk and ... Sorry, Steve, I'm getting carried away. What do you think?'

231

He thought she was the most unlikely businesswoman he had ever met. 'Great, it's a great idea,' he said.

'Oh, is there anything you wanted, especially?'

He smiled down at her. Not the open-hearted, boyish smile that he used on older women generally, but the dependable, helpful, sympathetic smile that he had perfected on his mother when he was eight years old. It had got him anything he wanted then, and hadn't failed him often in the intervening twenty years. 'Look, Hanna, while I was checking to see that the mice had all gone, I came in to see whether there was anything I could do for you. Anything at all, you know? If you need a man about the house to fix a washer or a fuse or lift a heavy basket of logs or something, you just call on me, OK?'

'That is kind of you,' she said, pushing her hair back from her forehead and leaving a dusty smear in its place. 'I've got a bottle of wine open here somewhere, would you like a glass?'

She found the bottle in amongst the foliage, eventually. A hock, and well chambréed. She poured them each a glass. He was glad that at last she had given up trying to make coffee.

She was looking pretty good, considering everything, he thought. A bit paler than before, and maybe a pound or so lighter, but it suited her. She rambled on, oddly he thought, about silence and freedom and how you had to knit it up into a many-coloured carpet, and how it wasn't all in a piece but in knobbly strands that you had to keep grabbing hold of before they disappeared again. But maybe that was after her third glass of hock. She was obviously not used to drinking that much wine in the middle of the afternoon. When she'd opened a new bottle and downed her fourth glass, he suggested, very gently, that she might appreciate a bit of a lie-down. She was grateful for his supporting arm up the stairs and she didn't push him out of bed when he offered to join her under the bedcover. She was a little on the sleepy side to be very responsive to his lovemaking, or even appreciate its quality and inventiveness, and she had to leap up at four-fifteen and rush off to pick up the girls from somewhere on the other side of Fox Hill, but he was getting somewhere with her, he knew. And she left him to take a leisurely shower before letting himself out of the house.

'Just make sure you're out of the place before I get back with the girls, won't you?' she said.

Jean Rainbird had been on her way back to her flat from the Brackley Road job, and ready for a soak in a hot bath and a mindless evening in front of the television, when she realised that she hadn't got her Filofax. She felt bereft, as though her past had been stolen and her future was a wild, uncharted sea. How would she ever remember all the things she was supposed to be doing, the names and addresses, the phone numbers and idiosyncrasies of her clients – everything – without it? She drew into a lay-by and told herself to think about it calmly. Well, as calmly as she could.

Think logically, Jean, she told herself. Where did you last have it? For a time she thought she would never remember, but at last it came back to her: she took it out to mark in the two hours extra Hanna wanted while the children were at home, and then the phone rang, and by the time they'd sorted themselves out it was time for her to go, and Hanna had insisted that she should have some jam made by Tess from wild berries, and she must have gone away leaving the Filofax on the table in the kitchen. The jar of jam stood in the glove compartment, looking wholesome in a red gingham hat. Jean scowled at it, then turned the car round and made for Fox Hill.

The rain had started to come down in torrents so that it was as dark as evening when she drew up in front of Martenswood. The rain must have masked the sound of her tyres on the gravel, and drowned her called 'Hello' as she went through the open door and into the kitchen. The table was piled high with lumps of vegetation and there were a couple of empty wine bottles and two dirty glasses, but she couldn't see her familiar red binder. Perhaps Hanna had put it away somewhere safe.

There was a sound from upstairs: a clanking in the plumbing. Jean went up a couple of stairs and called out again. Maybe Hanna was resting.

When she got to the top of the stairs, she turned left towards the spare bedroom and the sound of gurgling wastepipes. The bedroom door was wide open. Its own adjoining bathroom was on the left. As she watched, the bathroom door swung open and a damp, naked figure emerged and walked across the bedroom carpet, only a few feet away, and then stood with its back to her, looking out across the garden towards Ruskin Wood. It was, she realised, an adult *male* figure. And it was, too, familiar. Particularly at that angle, naked, and looking out of the window. She would have recognised that long, suntanned back and that neat bum anywhere.

'What the hell are you doing here, Tracker?' Though of all the questions she could have asked him, that was probably the most superfluous.

Steve Tracker turned round, catching up a peach-coloured towel and wrapping it round himself in a strategic manner. Not for modesty, she realised, but for dignity's sake. It is difficult to have a really good row with someone if you're not wearing any clothes while they are fully dressed. Perhaps Tracker had had more experience of these scenes than she had, or perhaps he just understood it instinctively, as he understood so much else.

'You're not supposed to be here this afternoon,' he said.

'Don't be bloody stupid, Tracker. Do you think you're supposed to be here, in this bedroom, this afternoon or any other time?' She absorbed gradually, painfully, his wet, glossy hair and the sheen of well-being on his smooth brown face, the bed behind him with the bed-cover thrown to one side and the sheet wrinkled into hillocks and valleys.

'Rat,' she said.

'Do you think,' he said, 'we could meet downstairs, say in the kitchen, in a couple of minutes' time? I'd feel a lot more comfortable with a few clothes on.'

Jean sniffed at him. 'Tea Rose,' she said, 'Roget and Gallet. I should have guessed last time I smelled the stuff on you, but I was so tired that night that it didn't register properly.'

'Is it important?'

'And where's Hanna? I assume she's the one you've been screwing?'

'She's out collecting an infant or two. So we've only got about another ten minutes for our row. Unless you want to continue it at home.'

He had dressed while she was standing there, after all, and now they both went down to the kitchen. Jean found herself making them each a mug of strong tea and stirring in spoonfuls of sugar. They drank it scalding hot, aware of Hanna's imminent arrival.

'What makes you think my flat's still your home, Tracker?'

'Now you're just being bitchy.'

'I should have guessed, I suppose, when you started asking me all those questions about this place and about the Bensons. It's the money that's the big attraction, isn't it? That and the house and garden. You've always fancied this sort of place, Tracker, haven't you? Didn't you tell me some story about belonging up here?'

'Don't you think you could call me by my Christian name just for once?'

'Is that your excuse? Hanna called you Steve and I didn't!'

'Hanna treats me like I'm a real human being, Jean.'

'Hanna has just inherited a whole pile of money and a beautiful house, Tracker. That's her great attraction!'

'Well, no, Jean, it isn't all of it, as a matter of fact. Don't you know how you've got since you've taken up this Technicleen lark?'

'I've got to make money at it – and it pays for the roof over your head.'

'Yeah, but every time I try to get near you, you back off and either rush away in one of your green vans, or else you fall asleep.'

'Ten minutes you said we'd got. We'd better leave.'

'There you go again. Running away.'

'You can put these mugs in the dishwasher for darling Hanna. I'm leaving. If you haven't got your car with you, you'll just have to walk.'

'Hey, you can't do that. What about me?'

'The cry of every spoiled mother's boy. Ask Hanna, not me.'

'You might listen to my side of it.'

'I might. One day. But not now.'

And she left. She waited until she was in the van, out of the drive, down the hill and on the bypass before she let rip with all the rude words she knew.

Steve walked back down the lane towards Sudden Cottage. He would have to take seriously Jean's threat to throw him out of the flat. It was, after all, *her* flat. The sooner he found himself somewhere else to stay, the better. And would she let him leave his telephone answering machine at her place? He had a mate he could ask for a bed for the night, but he preferred a woman's touch when it came to home-making. Not that Jean had done much home-making for the past few months. She reckoned that if she spent her working day worrying about other people's housework, then the last thing she wanted to do when she got home was to care about her own. Oh, she wasn't a slut or anything, and she wasn't disorganised like Hanna, but she was a bit casual for his taste. If he wanted to see the cushions plumped up on the sofa, the fluff removed from under the bed and a real shine on the bath taps, then he just had to do it himself. And he didn't reckon that sort of thing was men's work.

A Volvo estate scraped past and sent him jumping for

the verge. From the back window two white faces with dark eyesockets looked back at him. He shivered. That Tess child gave you the creeps, and her little sister wasn't much better. That posh new school of theirs didn't seem to have improved them any.

This thought brought him to Kay's front door. It was a good thing he'd had the foresight to keep in with her. She was his best bet for a meal and a bed at the moment and it meant that he would be conveniently placed for moving in on Hanna when the opportunity arose. He didn't see Kay's new friend as a great threat, any more than he was giving up his hopes of Martenswood, not yet. Not after all he'd been through.

Kay was back. She opened the door, cigarette stuck to her lower lip, familiar green satin dressing-gown gaping slightly at mid-thigh level.

'Hello, Petal,' he said, with the number two smile. 'How about asking me in for a minute or two? I'm cold and wet and I've got an idea I'd like to share with you.'

'Oh yeah?'

'It's about making some money.'

She made a rude noise with her lips, but she let him in.

'What you after, then?' she asked.

'A hot meal and some sympathy, Petal, that's what I'm looking for.'

'You're a wicked bugger, Steve.'

'Any chance of a cup of tea?'

'Yeah. But afterwards.'

Back at her flat, Jean put the record player on, loud, and spent an hour on her accounts. Then she took a long time preparing herself a really nice meal, but it was still lonely in the place without Tracker. Unfaithful, unreliable, unnecessary Tracker.

Could she afford not to go back to Martenswood? No, and anyway she had promised Hanna, even if it was in the middle of a sentimental, alcohol-clouded scene. Hanna, after all, was unaware that her Rat Man was Jean's bloke. And there was something she'd seen or heard there that was making her feel uneasy. Now that Joe had been removed, the place ought to feel happier, but it didn't. Oh, come on, she told herself, it's because Tracker's mixed up in the place: that's why you feel on edge about it. Either that, or you're still mourning the loss of your bloody Filofax.

That had been Steve Ratsaway walking away from Martenswood, Tess knew. Things were going wrong and she had to do something about it quickly, or she and Aurora would be away at Gryphons with Harry and Tom for ever while Hanna grew less and less like her old self and Steve moved in to take Malcolm's place. And Gerard would be angry with her. She shivered at the thought. It was the Jeff thing all over again, only worse, because she and Aurora wouldn't be around to prevent it.

She took the folded paper from her treasure drawer.

She is a moth,
Pale, blind,
Tearing fragile wings against the light,
And the mermaid singing sailors to a blissful deep.
She is my rose, dusk pink and unfolding.

Gerard had been so angry when he read it, though Tess

couldn't see why. There was more of it, once, but the page was torn and the rest was lost.

What had happened to her magic? It had worked when Malcolm had died. It had worked when the police had taken Joe away and when Harry and Tom had gone off with Diana Kinch. It had worked at first to keep Steve away from the house. So why were things still wrong? However hard she worked to make things go her way, they were still outside her control. When she felt the magic in her hands she was powerful but somehow, afterwards, when it was over, she felt just like a child again, being told what to do by other people. Gerard would have to help her get rid of the Ratsaway man, then perhaps everything would be all right and they need never go back to Gryphons.

'Come on, Aurora, we're going out.'

'But it's raining.'

'No it isn't. Or it won't be in a minute or two. Wear your boots and anorak and stop making a fuss.'

'Oh, all right.'

She was in a grizzly mood. Tess would have to be firm with her.

They went out through the back gate and down the footpath, then turned left into the bridle way and up the hill towards Bennett's Farm. By the time they had climbed over the stile and were on the footpath, the rain had stopped and the sun was drying the puddles.

'What have you got there?' asked Aurora.

'Just one of my magic flowers.' It was one of the last small poppies, its petals faded to a soft pink and crumpled like an old handkerchief.

'What will it do?'

DEATHSPELL

'If I get the words right, this one will make us invisible.'

Aurora was silent with excitement. The footpath was overgrown, and the tall nettles kept people away. Thistles grew in the coarse grass, and marbled white butterflies drifted past like rags of lace.

Aurora capered in front of Tess, moving backwards so that she could watch everything she did. She had forgotten her bad mood.

'The words, Tess. Tell us the words.' Her curls were shining metal in the sun. Tess shook her head.

'No. They're still secret. They don't work if I tell people.' Aurora's mouth started to droop again. 'Here, hold on to this' – she handed her sister a poppy – 'and concentrate. You know, like we did when we found the way home to Mum.'

Aurora screwed up her eyes, furrowing her forehead and bunching up her shoulders with the effort. Gerard whispered swift magic phrases in Tess's ear, which swept her along in a flood as she held on tightly to her own limp flower.

'It's working. I know it's working,' she breathed.

'Can I open my eyes?' Aurora was dancing from foot to foot, ungainly in her Wellington boots. 'Will I really be invisible?'

'I'll still be able to see you. You'll still be able to see me. But no one else will until I say they can.' She held her breath for a second, then, 'Now!' she commanded. They opened their eyes.

Steve Tracker was leaning on the stile, smoking a cigarette, when they got back to the bridle-path. His car with its cursive Ratsaway name was parked in the entrance to the next field.

241

'Hello, you two,' he called out, smiling his friendly, fatherly smile at them and turning his forget-me-not gaze on Tess.

Tess and Aurora stopped and glared at him.

'I thought you said no one could see us,' said Aurora accusingly.

'They can't.'

'Well, he can. Why?'

'It's because,' said Tess, 'he's evil.'

'Hang about there,' said Steve. 'Evil, me?' and he laughed.

'Yes, that's it,' said Tess. 'He can only see us because he has been making magic too. Only his must be evil magic. I knew someone must be at it.'

Aurora looked relieved. 'You mean no one else can see us?'

'That's right. Just Steve Ratsaway. But don't worry, Rory, our magic's stronger than his, and I'll make him disappear soon.'

'Like Malcolm?'

'That's right.'

'Now look, you two, what are you on about? It's just one little fag, you know, and if you keep away from me you needn't even breathe in the smoke.'

'I know all about you,' said Tess. 'And I'm going to destroy you.'

'What do you want to do that for?' asked Steve, still laughing.

'Because I'm taking us back. All of us. We belong to Dad and he wants us back. He said, "You're mine, all of you, and don't you forget it. I'll never release you." And then he made Jeff go away. Then Malcolm went, too.

And Joe. And the boys. Now it's your turn.'

'Maybe, but I'm staying. You won't get rid of me so easily. In fact, you'd better get used to the idea that I'm going to be around, because your Mum and I are very close friends, and you may find that I'm here for good before too long.'

'I know you want to move in on us — I've seen the way you look at Mum — but I can work magic and I'll keep you out. I'll do everything I need to keep you away from us all.'

'That's the trouble with girls,' said Steve. 'You can never trust them. They're never straight, like men. And they never know what's good for them, either.'

'I want my Mum back. She never belonged to Malcolm, anyway, not properly. And she'll never belong to you, either.'

'You're mad, you are. People don't belong to each other. We're all free to choose, we're not slaves or something. And that's what Hanna wants, I'm telling you — freedom from Gerard and freedom from Malcolm. She likes me around because I'm different: I understand her. I make her happy and I don't want to own her.'

'You want to own Martenswood, but you never will.'

'Want to take a bet on it? And as for going back, you can't do it: the past is dead, like those elms over there. Go and take a look at that house where you used to live. Someone will have painted the door a different colour by now, cut the grass, dug new flowerbeds. Clinging to dead trees, that's what you're doing, Tess.'

'You're lying! It's still there, in Wootton Road, waiting for us. And my trees are all alive!'

'Make him go away, Tess,' shouted Aurora. 'Magic him away!'

Tess stood and stared at Tracker for a few moments. Then, 'He's gone,' she said, as he dropped his gaze, turned away and climbed back into his car. He and the dark blue estate disappeared up the bridle way.

'What did you mean, Tess? How did you destroy Malcolm? I thought it was Joe that did it.'

'Of course it was Joe. They said it was, didn't they? I used my magic on him, though. But if that fails with Steve Ratsaway, I know other ways, too. Dad tells me about them.'

'But it wasn't you really who got rid of him, was it, Tess? Not really and truly?'

Perhaps she should confess to it, then the great heavy bag of guilt would drop away from her shoulders and fly away with Gerard into the sky. But, 'Of course not,' she lied. 'Everyone knows that it was Joe, and he's been taken away so he can never do it again. Don't worry about it, Rory.' Now she had to do something about Steve.

When she came back into her bedroom she found that Jean Rainbird had moved the bed and was hoovering up the fluff from underneath it.

'You haven't touched it, have you?' Tess asked.

'What's that?'

'His picture and things.'

'Don't worry, they're all quite safe. I've just dusted round them very carefully. OK?'

'Thanks. That's all right.'

There was something different about Jean. She seemed less colourful today, somehow. Her face was pale and there were dark streaks under her eyes, and she hadn't made her hair stick up straight from her head. But she was friendly enough, and she knew how to look after Gerard.

'He's pretty special to you, isn't he?' asked Jean. The two of them were standing in front of the shrine to Gerard on top of Tess's chest of drawers. 'It's funny about faces, isn't it?' she said. 'People say that you can read a man's character in his eyes, but it isn't really so. It's in the mouth, I think. Look how it quirks up into a smile on this side, matching the creases round the eyes. But on the other side, he's really not smiling at all, is he?'

'He talks to me,' said Tess. 'Tells me things.'

'Does he now?' said Jean, as a cold finger traced its way down her spine. 'What sort of things?'

'He keeps me safe. He'd never let bad things happen to me. He told me that I had Mum to care for me and look after me, and him to protect me.'

'Did you need protecting?'

'He kept me safe from the cows and the bulls in the fields.'

'Quite right too. Terrifying things, cattle, I've always thought. And I don't care what people say about them not being dangerous, I reckon they're very big, don't you?' She checked that most of the fluff had gone from under the bed. There were never any mouldering socks or vests in Tess's room. She pushed the bed back into place.

'And Jeff, too.'

'Was he a friend of your parents?'

'I don't know if he was a friend, but Dad used to bring him home to supper sometimes and once he wrote a poem for Mum. I've still got it – well, some of it. But he shouldn't have done that. And he used to sit and look at her. And Dad didn't like it: he tore the page in half.'

'Oh yes? And what did your dad do to Jeff?' There was a prickle like a small electric charge working its way down her spine now.

'He hit him, I think.'

Jean dropped a plastic container of cream cleanser.

'Not too hard, I hope!'

'No.'

'Oh, good.' She had retrieved the cream cleanser and was squirting it into the hand basin. 'Did your father often hit people?'

'He used to talk about it a lot when he'd been down to the pub, but that was the only time he did it, I think.'

'Well, that's OK, then.' The taps had come up a treat.

'We used to sing that song.' And Tess lifted her voice:

'Wack fol the daddyo, there's whiskey in the jar.

Oh, and he showed me how to hit Malcolm too, of course.'

'You hit Malcolm?' Jean's voice sounded odd, as though her lips had gone suddenly stiff.

'Not exactly,' said Tess, remembering where she was and who she was talking to. 'But he shouldn't have changed our life like that.'

Jean stopped pretending that she was cleaning the basin and sat on the bed facing Tess.

'Dad didn't like that. We used to live in Wootton Road, and we went to the convent and Mum was always there when we got home, and everything was comfortable. But when we came here, Malcolm started changing everything.' She spoke in a perfectly normal voice, quite flat and down-to-earth, but her yellow eyes were focused on invisible, distant pictures. 'Mum doesn't look the same any more. She doesn't feel the same, either. She used to be all sort of soft and cushiony, but now she feels hard and smooth. And she smells of something different, too. But she ought to stay the way she was because she still belongs to Dad, really. He tells me so. He didn't like it when he thought she and—'

But at this point they were interrupted by Aurora who came to tell Tess that her mother wanted to see her about something. It was a pity that she couldn't finish telling Jean about the other things that made Gerard angry. If only she could remember clearly what had happened that day with Jeff, and what the knife had to do with it, she might start feeling better. Jean would have understood why he had to do it, though she might not understand about Steve and what she was going to have to do to him.

An hour or so after that, Tess left Aurora to open a fresh tin of cat food for Finnegan, and went upstairs into Joe's old room. Yes, he had left the book she needed. She thought that she would find it there, for the boys had taken so little stuff with them when they went away. She took the green cloth-covered book back to her own room. She also found and took with her several other useful bits and pieces that Joe had got together. For a moment she wished that Malcolm had given Joe the longed-for gun. It would have come in handy.

Back in her own room, she set about composing a

letter to Steve Tracker. She knew where to deliver it, because she had seen his car parked behind Kay Parker's chicken shed.

It was ten o'clock that night when Jean's phone rang.

'Hello, Jean?'

'What do you want, Tracker? You've already moved all your stuff out, haven't you?'

'Yes. It's nothing to do with that. Look—'

'I don't think there's anything else we have to talk about.'

'Jean! Will you just listen for a minute!'

He sounded desperate. She gave herself three seconds to calm down and then said, 'All right, I'm listening.'

'Look, it's those kids up at Martenswood. The girls. Well, the older one, Tess. The one with the peculiar eyes.'

'Yes, I know her.'

'She's odd.'

'Tracker, did you ring me up to tell me that? I know she's odd. But she's back to boarding school in a few days' time, and surely she isn't terrorising a big macho bloke like you, is she?'

'OK, you've had your joke. But listen now, will you? I'm serious. She says that she got rid of Malcolm, and now she's going to get rid of me. And then she looks at me.'

'Umm.' She knew what Tracker meant. She'd feel pretty scared herself if Tess said that to her. 'Did she tell you any more about how she got rid of Malcolm? I thought Joe did it.'

'No. And yes, he did.'

'Has she got something on you, Tracker? Is that why you're scared?'

'Nothing! For goodness' sake, Jean, what do you think she could have?'

'I thought I knew you, but I found I was wrong, so you tell me, Tracker.'

'Well, at the time Malcolm died, she did see me there in the woods.'

'Great. I'd gathered that bit, but tell me more. Did she see you beat him over the head, or what?'

'Look, we know Joe beat him over the head.'

'Sorry. Go on.'

'Well, that child must spent all her life listening at keyholes and creeping around watching people.'

'Yes, she is a bit spooky, I agree.'

'So her story is that Kay and I were trying to blackmail Malcolm. And then there's Kay's chickens.'

'You've lost me again, Tracker.'

'They fell sick and most of them died; Kay blames Tess.'

'It doesn't sound very likely to me. Anyone might die of food poisoning at Sudden Cottage. But has she got something to back this blackmail story up with?'

'She's got a letter and she wants to meet me and discuss it.'

'What did the two of you have on Malcolm?'

'Well, there was something going on between Kay and him, that he wouldn't have wanted Hanna to know about.'

'I'd be surprised if Hanna didn't know about it, if it's true. And how did Tess get hold of this unsavoury little story, then?'

'I'm afraid that she's got a note that Kay wrote to Malcolm, about how I was going to meet him in the woods to put her argument to him. She must have found it on the ground after he . . .'

'Does it mention you by name?'

'I don't think so, but I suppose they could jump to conclusions about it. If they misinterpreted it, that is.'

'I'm starting to get the picture. So what happens next?'

'She wants to meet me in the woods tomorrow afternoon at three thirty. Up at Haggett's Copse.'

'But that's where Malcolm's body was found.'

'Yes.'

'Are you going?'

'I'll have to go, even if it's only to talk to her.'

'You think she'll make you an offer you can't refuse?'

'Well, you can laugh if you like, Jean, but the kid scares me shitless.'

'No, Tracker. I'm not laughing. She scares me too.'

'So will you back me up?'

'Come with you, you mean?'

'If you like.'

'No, Tracker.'

Chapter Twenty

Gerard was shaking her awake. It was early, not even light yet, but his face was hanging over her with dark-shadowed features, eyes and teeth shining.

Get up, Tess. You have so much to do today.

'What? What is it?'

There isn't much time left, now. You have to get your mother back. Rescue her before she disappears for ever inside the skin of that glossy stranger. His fingers grasped her shoulder.

'What must I do? Where shall we go?' She wasn't properly awake.

We have to go back.

'Will you show me this time? Will you show me everything? Why can't I remember what happened?'

Everything, this time.

'The sun is shining . . .'

No. The sky is dark. The clouds hang low over the fields, pouring down rain, filling our ears with their roaring and spitting.

'Why are you so angry?' She was sitting up in bed now, looking into Gerard's long, thin face.

Haven't I told you I get like this when I've had a jar or

251

two? Must you always be nagging at me about it? And isn't a man entitled to get in a rage when someone is stealing his wife away from him?

'I don't want to come with you. Not this morning. Must I come, Dad?' She wished that her father would leave her alone. She couldn't bear it when he was angry with her. He showed her such ugly things.

'Don't hurt him! Don't hit him!'

Think over what I've said. When I get back, you must do what I tell you.

If Malcolm was resting quietly, back at the crematorium, why was it that Gerard couldn't stay in his grave and leave her in peace?

The Suttons were going to take Aurora out for the day. 'To take her mind off things,' as Mrs Sutton said. 'Stop the poor little thing from brooding.' There was a fat lazy pony to ride in the Suttons' field, and puppies to play with.

Tess said that she didn't want to go with them, but insisted on mooching about at home. Hanna wished that Tess would go too. She felt that her elder daughter could well profit from some unstressful and normal family life. The child was looking pale and tired, with terrible dark rings under her eyes. But maybe it was best to humour her for a short while.

'I'm going to the hairdresser's, Tess. I want to get my hair cut. Do you think it would suit me very short?'

'I dunno.' Tess was sitting on her favourite high stool in the kitchen, sharpening all Hanna's knives. Hanna found it irritating and slightly unnerving. 'I like it the way it used to be.'

'Oh, but it used to look a mess. It'll be much better when I've had it properly cut. And then I might look at some clothes. I don't want to buy anything just yet, but I'd like to see what people are wearing these days. Are you sure you wouldn't like to come with me? I don't like to think of you being here on your own.'

'I'll be fine here. I'm not alone. There's Kay down at Sudden Cottage, and Steve Ratsaway hangs around all the time. You go.'

'If you're sure you'll be all right.'

'Oh, there is just one thing I need . . .'

'What's that, dear?'

'Could you let me have a fiver?'

'Whatever for?' Tess had her pocket money and had always been very good at not asking for anything extra.

'There's something special that I want to get for Harry and Tom, to take back after half-term – just to show them that I'm sorry about their father and everything.'

She had never doubted her daughter's truthfulness up until this moment, but there was something so unblinking in the way Tess was looking at her that for a moment there she had the feeling that she was lying to her. She must have been mistaken. She reached into her handbag and got out a note.

'Here you go, then.'

It occurred to her later that if she hadn't been thinking about her new haircut and the clothes she was going to look at, she might well have asked Tess where she was going to spend her five pounds. There was only the small village shop, which didn't stock the sort of things that Tess, Harry or even Tom would be interested in. But the thought didn't strike her until much later and she got into the Volvo and drove off into the city. She might have wondered, too, about the extra knife that Tess had been sharpening particularly carefully, but she wasn't a very observant woman.

Tess finished with the knives and put away the fine grey stone. She put away in the kitchen drawer, too, all the knives that belonged to Hanna. The one that belonged to Gerard, however – the slim seven-inch blade with the black handle – she wrapped in a handkerchief and put in the pocket of her anorak.

She hadn't wanted to use violence. And, in particular, she didn't want to use the knife. There was something about knives, buried in the past, that she fought against remembering. She had believed that if she practised hard enough her magic would grow and work for her. It had all been going so well up to now. But it wasn't working on Steve Tracker. Nothing worked on Steve Tracker – only whatever it was that Kay and Hanna used that kept him hanging around, and that was something that she didn't understand properly yet. But she and Gerard had helped the magic get rid of Malcolm and Joe, so they would have to give it a helping hand in ridding them of Tracker.

What she did understand quite clearly now was that he was the one who had been conspiring against her all this time, that he was her real enemy – and Gerard's. It was Steve Tracker who had given her mother the idea about getting her hair cut and choosing new clothes. It was probably Steve Tracker who encouraged her mother to fill the house with all that wild and trailing greenery. And what was it Hanna was saying now about starting up a business? She mustn't do it. She mustn't change their lives like that. They couldn't stay here on Fox Hill any longer, it was time they were getting back to Wootton Road before someone really did paint the door a different colour. And her mother would never make a businesswoman, anyway. It was of course Steve Tracker who had persuaded her that they should still go to Gryphons, even after Malcolm's death. She knew that it was his fault because Gerard had told her so. He was all evil and the proof of it was that he had been able to see them when she and Aurora had been invisible to everyone else.

Gerard kept telling her that she had to get rid of him. *He means it when he says he's coming here to stay. Maybe he even dreams of marrying my Hanna. But you mustn't let him do it.* His voice hammered away inside her head. She tried to tell him to go away and leave her in peace, but he wouldn't. Perhaps he would leave her alone if she did this one last thing for him.

He reminded her about that day down by the river, three and a half years ago, picking the memory picture out of her head with his long thin fingers and holding it up. *Look*, he said, and she looked and she remembered.

The sky is dark, with thick rolling clouds pouring down rain and tears. The river is noisier than ever, its surface pitted and broken by the rain. On the towpath the bundle that was Jeff has stopped moving. Now they are running across the field, shouting. They are frightening the bullocks who gallop back into the corner by the hawthorn hedge. Gerard lifts her over the stile. The rain plasters her hair to her scalp and runs down her face. She puts out her tongue to lick it and finds it tastes as salty as tears. He only wrote her a poem, she wants to tell Gerard. Some of it was about me, too. What was so wrong with it? It was all about a moth and a mermaid and a rose, that's all. She never looked at him, not the way she looks at you. But Gerard wasn't listening. Gerard never listened to her again.

Since she had found that book of Joe's, she had been up in the woods, preparing her Trackertrap. It had taken her some time to work out how she could kill him. The first problem had been that he was so much taller and stronger than she was. But she had solved that now. Joe's book described how to construct a snare and catch a rabbit: she didn't think it would be hard to adapt it to make a snare to catch a Tracker. It was a question of getting him exactly where she wanted at a time when she was ready for him.

The book said that you first had to find where your quarry regularly walked. That was difficult, since she didn't think that Steve did come up here in the woods regularly, and she could hardly set a trap for him outside Kay's front door. So she sent him a note to make sure that he came up to Haggett's Copse to meet her at a definite time, and then she set the bait. She couldn't put the trap on the footpath, for someone else might get caught in it before Steve, so she watched him as he walked around Martenswood and the lane to Sudden Cottage and she estimated the length of his stride.

You had to set your snare in the middle of a pace, so that it caught the victim's foot as it lifted and moved forwards. And you had to calculate the height of the loop of wire. For a rabbit, this was reckoned to be the height of one fist placed upon another, but watching

Steve Tracker, Tess judged that she should set the lower edge of her wire loop just an inch or so higher than this, particularly as her fists were not very large. She was careful to make her loop in the shape of a tennis racket, not circular. Gerard had always impressed on her the importance of getting things right. If she did it properly, everything would be over, and she could get on with the rest of her life.

She cut a notch in the bender and set it so that the running ring rested on its tip, and fixed the other end of the wire securely to the ground with a tent peg.

She tested it a few times, matching her stride exactly to the way she remembered Tracker's to be, then made the loop a little larger, to accommodate his larger-sized foot. She set her snare at the place where she reckoned Tracker would be in mid-stride, and near enough to her chosen tree for him to be moving quickly after his momentary halt to inspect her bait from the path. When she had finished, she thought the snare was not particularly noticeable, especially if your attention was taken and caught by something at eye-level, but she disguised it with twigs and leaves, nevertheless. It was always best to be careful, Gerard said.

She returned home at lunchtime, just in case it was noticed that she was away in the woods, ate quickly and then disappeared again before anyone could see her and ask her where she was going. It was amazing the way any grown-up thought they had the right to question the movements of any child.

She wanted to be in position, ready, before there was any chance of Tracker turning up. She knew that he would turn up, because she wanted it so much. She had brought the green glove with her, though today it gave off the choking smell of freshly spilled blood.

Tracker nearly decided against going to his meeting with Tess. But then he thought that it wasn't worth chancing it. You never knew with that particular child. Maybe she would go to the police, at that, mincing and batting her eyelashes, and string them some plausible story. They'd come and talk to him and question him, and there were certain aspects of his life that he would rather not have examined too closely. But he thought that with the help of his best smile and a packet of Smarties he could probably win the child round. There was really nothing much to worry about. He wished he hadn't rung Jean up last night and whinged to her about it. He'd made himself look a right prat.

He left his car down by the sawmill and climbed up the path towards Haggett's Copse on foot, just as it was coming up to half-past three. He saw a large beech tree ahead of him and to the left of the path. It was so placed that at this time of day a beam of light seeped through the gap in the trees and struck its broad trunk, lighting up the green of the lichen and the grey of the bark. And there was something pinned to the trunk. Something like a small piece of paper. As he got closer, he saw to his surprise that it was a five-pound note. He walked across the short turf, with its covering of twigs and last year's mashed dead leaves, to see why anyone would have pinned a fiver to a tree in the middle of a wood.

When the wire snare caught his ankle and tightened, so that the impetus of his light-footed walk carried him forward and then sprawling on the ground, Tracker was

aware only of utter surprise. He let out one loud cry of
alarm, but before he could work out what had happened
to him and do something about it, a large, heavy and
sharp object hit him briskly on the head, just behind the
ear, so that for a long time he took no further interest in
the action.

Jean had two new girls working for her today. She sent
them out with an experienced worker as a partner, and
then settled down for an hour to catch up with her
paperwork. At eleven o'clock she had another prospec-
tive client on Fox Hill to see, and then she would drive
over to Franmore village to give Linda and Jenny a hand
clearing up after a break-in. If she was lucky, she could
fit in twenty minutes for a sandwich and a cup of coffee
after that. She ought to call in on the two new girls, too,
and make sure that they were happy and knew what they
were doing.

It was while she was driving home after this final visit,
and looking forward to the sandwich that she hadn't in
fact had time to eat, that she realised that she was
passing Ruskin Wood and that the time was twenty past
three.

Why should she worry about Tracker? He was a big
grown-up man and no ten-year-old was a match for him.
She should drive straight on and put him out of her
mind. It was bad enough going up to Martenswood
knowing that he had shared that double bed of Hanna's
without having to act as his nursemaid as well. But on
the long climb up the hill, the van slowed down and
threatened to stall its engine unless she accelerated away.
Ahead of her, the single-track tarmacked lane led down

to the sawmill. With a sigh of regret for her broken resolve, she signalled left and changed down to second gear so that the engine stopped protesting and purred happily along to the edge of the wood.

Tess stepped out from behind the broad trunk of the tree and stood over him, with the rock still in her right hand. She didn't think that anyone had heard that cry: there was no one within earshot and the bypass was on the other side of the copse and across a couple of fields.

'I thought,' she said, looking down at the motionless figure, 'that would bring you across. I went through all sorts of things to use as bait, a note or something like that, but in the end I decided that what you were most interested in was money.'

There was no reply from Steve Tracker. She dropped the rock on the ground and took out from the pocket of her anorak the seven-inch knife that she had sharpened to an edge like a razor. It had a wicked point, and she thought she could see it once again beaded with blood. Gerard was shouting in her ear that she must plunge it into Tracker – *Into his heart*, cried Gerard, *into his throat. There, below his ear, where the skin is soft and the bones are thin. Anywhere, girl! He won't stay quietly there on the ground waiting for you. You've hit him on the head and stunned him, like I showed you with the rabbit that time, but he'll be coming round soon and it won't take him long to get himself free from that snare. Go on, Tess! I can't do it for you this time. You remember now, don't you? I took the knife and I stuck it into Jeff, and he bled and he died. Go on, do it for me.*

On the palm of her left hand, where she had been

stroking the blade to test its edge, a thin line of scarlet appeared, then spread and blurred and formed into a drop. That was actual blood welling up from the thin cut and trickling down her hand. The blade grew warm with her handling, so that it quickened against her palm. How could she take this sharp steel and thrust it into that breathing, feeling body?

You've had your practice run, whispered Gerard. *You said it felt good when you punctured and stabbed. He's our enemy, Tess. Kill him! Do it now!*

She hadn't stopped and thought about it before picking up that block of wood and hitting Malcolm. She had thought very carefully about what she did afterwards, but that was different.

Steve Tracker moaned and shifted, but remained unconscious. As she looked at him lying there, she remembered his smile. She still didn't like him, but that was an ordinary, living, human smile he had turned on her.

She couldn't help it if Gerard did get angry, like he did when he'd been drinking a jar or two with the lads. She couldn't, after all, do what he asked her to. She raised her head and stared back at her father.

Chapter Twenty-One

'Give me the knife, Tess.'

Jean spoke calmly and firmly, though she was shaking inside and had to force the words out through dry lips.

She had taken in the scene as she came up the path. The child had seemed beyond any sort of normal awareness. She could have stamped up the path with the cavalry behind her and Tess wouldn't have heard them. But would she give her the knife? She looked as though she could inflict a lot of damage with it if she wanted. And why on earth was she wearing one peculiar green knitted woollen glove? It was far too big for her and the fingers stuck out beyond her own, long and thin and empty.

She walked up to her. 'The knife, Tess. Give it to me.' She sounded much braver than she felt. She sounded in control of the situation. Another illusion.

Tess turned her blank eyes on her. 'I can't do it, Dad. If you want him dead you'll have to do it yourself, like you did with Jeff.'

'That's right,' said Jean, soothingly. 'I'll look after Tracker, Tess. Just give me the knife.'

In the end, the child was unresisting and she took the

263

weapon away from her with no trouble. Then she bent down to look at Tracker.

There was a thin trickle of blood coming from a nasty-looking cut just behind and above his left ear. Oh well, if it was still bleeding, then the man must be alive. Her heart could stop pounding in her chest and she could stop feeling sorry for the two-timing bastard. It was odd how you could dislike someone and at the same time care about what happened to them.

Tess was speaking again. Jean hadn't been listening properly, but now she tuned in to what she was saying.

'I have to go now. Dad says we have to go. He says they'll find Steve Ratsaway the way they did Jeff, if we stay here. They'll ask questions this time, won't they?'

'Where is it you have to go?' This was a weird conversation they were having.

'Over there.' She pointed down the hill towards where the bypass hummed out of sight. 'There's a meadow over there. And the river. That's where we left Jeff. Dad says we have to go back there now. Steve wouldn't help bring Malcolm alive again, but maybe we could do something for Jeff. He must be cold and wet out there in the rain after all this time.'

It wasn't raining, Jean noticed in passing. Which meant that Tess was talking about another time and another place.

'We didn't mean him to be dead.'

And before Jean could make out what it was all about, or think of anything to say that would stop her, Tess had left and was running down the path, her pace increasing as she went.

Tess certainly had a surprising turn of speed. She was

away, nearly out of sight and turning right along the path through the beech trees before Jean realised that there was any danger and that someone ought to follow her. It dawned on her that Tess was making for the bypass and that, if the meadow she had in mind did exist, then it was on the further side of that lethal six-lane highway. Whatever the rendezvous that Tess had with whoever it was she had been talking to back there, it was unlikely that she would make it alive. So someone must catch her and stop her, and there weren't a lot of volunteers.

At her feet Tracker had started to moan.

'Oh, shit!' he was mumbling.

'Shut up, Tracker,' she said unsympathetically. 'Can you run?'

'Can I shit!' was the unpromising reply. It was definitely up to her.

The green overalls had been designed for movement, and she was wearing trainers, but once she was through the trees and pounding down the close-cropped grass of the pasture, she was longing for the thick cushioned soles of her Reeboks. Tess's white T-shirt with the amber hair swinging above it danced ahead of her. Under Jean's feet the ground was uneven and tussocky and she had to forget about falling over and hurl herself down the hill behind the small fast-moving figure. Sheep scattered away from them on either side, circling and bumping into each other, baa-ing in distress as the two of them hurtled down the hill towards the gate at the bottom.

Tess was over it as though she had been lifted by unseen hands, and she was already running across the next field as Jean reached the thick churned mud by the gate. Mud soaked her legs and splashed up to her knees, and clung in great clods and clumps to her trainers. There was no time to scrape it off, although it weighed down her feet by another couple of pounds, for she had to climb the gate, jump clear and set off again after Tess.

Her breath was coming in gasps and the muscles in her calves were hurting. Her knees ached from the pounding of the downhill run, while Tess, ahead of her, seemed to move as easily as a young deer. The terrifying roar of the bypass increased as they drew nearer.

Everything hurt now, legs and feet and chest and her shoulders where she had hunched them up with the effort. Her overalls were heavy and sticky with sweat, and her drenched hair clung to her forehead and neck. If ever this ordeal is over, she thought, if ever I catch that child and get back to my own peaceful flat, then I vow, solemnly, that I will get out there and get fit. How about that for a bargain, God? Just let me catch up with that child, and I'll get up an hour early every morning and start regular jogging instead of my half-hearted stumble round the block. Just, please, God dear, let me catch up with her before she reaches the bypass.

But she saw with despair that all that was left for Tess now was to make it across the field towards the stile, then to sprint across a couple of hundred yards of rough ground, and scramble up the embankment on to the six-lane highway. And no one would be expecting the sudden appearance of a small child as they thundered towards the Midlands at over seventy miles an hour. I can't catch her, Jean thought. There is nothing I can do to make my feet move any faster. There is concrete filling my legs, and my knees are made of cooked spaghetti.

Every time she breathed out, she groaned. If it didn't help her running, at least it relieved her feelings.

But perhaps someone was listening, after all. Or perhaps it was just that Tess hadn't realised that the route to her dream-meadow would take her through the field of bullocks. Perhaps it was that they weren't usually in this field, but in the one half a mile away. But on this day and at this time, however unexpectedly, there they were: large, black and white, gleaming with health and high spirits, and in the mood to play. As soon as they saw the small bobbing figure, making for the final stile, they turned and started moving in her direction. Then one of them frisked and bucked and started galloping, and the others, catching his mood, joined him. They seemed determined not to let anyone over the stile. One of them leaned against it, another raised his head to the sky and bellowed.

Jean couldn't see Tess. She had disappeared into this mass of shifting, heaving bodies. Then, as she got nearer, she could see that the child was crouched against the hawthorn hedge, scrabbling at the earth with her bare hands.

For a moment or two Jean could do nothing. Her breath was still coming in gasps, her heart was pounding and her legs were trembling with the unaccustomed effort. But then, after what seemed like an eternity, she got back enough wind to be able to shout at the bullocks, and wave her arms and push at the hundredweights of solid flesh until they tossed their heads and lost interest in their game, and wandered off to another corner of the field.

Jean turned to Tess and saw that the child was pushing

her green glove into the hole she had dug under the hedge.

'I have to get rid of it,' she said. 'We don't need it any more now.'

'Why did you need it before?'

'For remembering.'

'Come on,' said Jean. 'Leave it now. It's time to go home and start forgetting things.'

She took one of the small, cold hands and helped Tess to her feet. 'We'll have to walk back, though,' she said in as normal a voice as she could manage. 'I don't think I'm going to be fit to run for ages yet.'

Tess didn't say a word, but the hand that rested passively in hers trembled slightly as they went back across the field.

Chapter Twenty-Two

'You never told me,' said Jean, 'who Jeff was and how he died. That's the key to the whole thing, as far as I can make out.'

They were sitting in the kitchen at Martenswood, with coffee and whisky and the last of the chocolate biscuits. Hanna was just opening a bottle of Saint Emilion. She had returned from Oxford just as they got back to the house, with her hair short and spiked and blonder than before, and wearing new clothes. Tess was in bed upstairs, in a deep sleep.

Jean had told Tracker that he shouldn't be drinking whisky, not after a knock on the head like that, but he had said a rude word and gone right ahead and poured himself one. She had told him to pour another – large – one for Hanna while he was about it, as she thought she would need a drink before they were through with the explanations, but Hanna had said that she would stick with the claret.

Tracker said, 'OK, I'll play the part of the idiot, so that you two can tell me what all that was about. Who the hell was Jeff?'

'Jeff? What has he got to do with it?' asked Hanna.

'Everything. You told me, I think, that Gerard could be possessive and jealous. Well, it was Jeff he was jealous of,' said Jean.

'But I'm not even sure I know who you're talking about. The only Jeff we knew was that great gormless lad that Gerard brought back from the pub for a square meal a few times. He was the only person who ever looked enthusiastic about the food I produced. He used to sit and stare at me, but that was just his way, though it was a bit disconcerting.'

'And did he write a poem for you?'

'He fancied himself as a poet, I think. Look, I hardly remember him, Jean. How do I know?'

'It was something about a moth.'

'Oh, that. Yes, I think he did. Corny stuff, I thought.'

'What happened to it?'

Hanna ran a hand through the newly streaked hair and made it stand up on her head in ways that her hairdresser had not intended. 'Gerard got in a temper about it and tore it up. But it wasn't necessary. It didn't mean anything. He was only a kid with too much imagination.'

She was in danger of spilling red wine on her new cream trousers, Jean noticed. She should have chosen something in a more forgiving colour. It was just the haircut that was different, she realised, and the new clothes that Hanna had been unable to resist. Underneath there was the same puzzled woman who never quite grasped what was going on around her.

'I don't think that sort of jealousy needs a real reason, does it?' said Jean. 'And as far as I can make out, it was only when he had been drinking that Gerard felt like that. But he seems to have read a lot into this relationship between you and Jeff, and this poem thing he wrote.'

'Oh, come off it!' said Tracker. 'You're not telling me that all this load of aggro stems from some poem about a moth?'

'Shut up, Tracker. Just because you never read anything but *Exchange and Mart* doesn't mean there aren't people who take this poetry lark seriously. And there are men who care about relationships, too,' she added spitefully.

'I keep trying to tell you: there was no relationship,' said Hanna. She shook her head. 'I don't understand men. Do you?'

'I've had my experiences with them,' said Jean, giving Steve a sour look. 'Maybe I don't take them on trust the way you do.'

'I don't think I need them any more, though,' said Hanna. 'An accountant, maybe, but nothing more than that.'

'But about Jeff,' said Jean, who wanted to get to the bottom of it. 'I think he was saying that he was in love with you.'

'Silly sod,' said Tracker.

'Didn't you wonder what happened to him?' asked Jean, ignoring Tracker, but pouring another glass of wine for herself and Hanna. 'I mean, if Gerard really did have a fight with him, didn't the police come asking questions?'

'No one's explained why I got hit on the head and nearly killed.' Tracker sounded sorry for himself and bored with a conversation that wasn't about him any more. Jean gave him another small whisky to shut him up.

'You were a threat, Tracker. She thought you were taking her mother away from her. She wanted control over her life and this was the only way she could get it.'

'So she tried to kill me? Bit over the top, wasn't it?' Tracker wasn't buying Jean's amateur psychology.

'Well, she thought it was what Gerard wanted.'

'The kid should be in a nuthouse.'

'Let's get back to Jeff,' said Jean. 'Hanna? What happened to him?'

Hanna had started fiddling with a pot of ferns, arranging their silver-grey and dark green fronds into artistic patterns. She seemed hardly to be taking notice of what was being said.

'I don't know what happened to him. The last time I saw him must have been that weekend when Gerard died. We were staying in a bed and breakfast place for a couple of days, down in the West Country. And Jeff turned up, out of the blue.'

'Did he go off for a walk, maybe, with Gerard and Tess? Down by the river?'

'How should I know? The thing that I remember about that weekend is that Gerard took off in a filthy temper in the car and somewhere on the motorway he crossed the central reservation and came face to face with a container truck.'

'I'm sorry.' It seemed a feeble thing to say, but what more was there?

'I sat by his bed in that hospital for five days, but he didn't come to again. Me and a police constable, but

Gerard didn't say a word to either of us.' She looked up at them, the old puzzled Hanna looking out through blue-lined, silver-shadowed eyes.

'You think that Tess and Gerard killed him?' asked Steve. 'With that knife?'

'We'll never know now,' said Jean. 'I imagine the police closed the file a long time ago, unless his family are still pushing for an answer.'

'I don't know that he had any family of his own: he was a drifter, the sort of man that women feel protective and motherly about,' said Hanna.

Jean, who had never felt protective and motherly about a man (except for that brief moment when she had seen Tracker lying there bleeding into the lead-mould), nodded in agreement.

'And what about the kid?' put in Steve. 'I don't want her coming after me again when she thinks I'm blinking in her mother's direction.'

'She'll be all right, you'll see,' said Hanna. 'I've got money now and it solves a lot of problems. I'll make sure she sees the best people and gets herself sorted out.'

'I don't think I'll be hanging around to check,' said Tracker with feeling. 'And while we're on the subject, doesn't this put rather a large question mark over Malcolm's death? Are we all still quite sure that Joe did it?'

'Joe must have done it,' said Jean, 'and Tess picked up the violent vibrations in this house and that gave her the idea of stopping Tracker.'

'Stopping?' exclaimed Tracker. 'Killing, more like.'

'Don't over-dramatise,' said Jean impatiently. 'So?' Her green dungarees were clammy and cold from her unscheduled run and she had made herself a cup of instant coffee to warm herself up, added sugar, which she didn't normally take, and a large slug of whisky, which she occasionally did.

Hanna stopped rearranging leaves and came and sat at the table. She picked up a chocolate biscuit and started chewing it absent-mindedly. The last chocolate biscuit, Jean noticed.

'It was Jeff who first said I should get my hair cut short,' said Hanna. 'I'd forgotten about that.'

'He was right,' said Tracker. 'It does suit you short.'

'Shut up, Tracker,' said Jean. Tracker rubbed his ankle and shut up.

Hanna was picking nervously at her hair, trying to wind it round her fingers but failing because it was too short. 'It's coming back to me. Jeff's body was found down by the river, on the towpath. He'd been knocked down – his face was badly cut and bruised, they said – and then stabbed. But they never did find the knife.'

'I think I may have it here,' said Jean quietly. 'But didn't Tess ever say anything about it?'

'I don't think any of us could take any more. It was bad enough losing her father without adding that other nightmare.' She shredded a piece of fern. 'If any of it happened. There's no proof, is there? It's all just a story you're telling me.'

'How else do you explain it?'

'I've never had time for explanations. I had to get on with living. There was nothing in our bank account, just an overdraft.'

Tracker shifted in his chair, embarrassed, Jean could tell, by what Hanna was saying. 'Women have to be practical,' she said to him. 'It's part of the survival thing, isn't it? They can't waste energy on something that doesn't concern them and their children.'

Hanna went on, 'You may think it stupid of me, but no, I didn't need an explanation for Jeff's disappearance – and actually, I didn't even notice it. I haven't thought about him from that day to this. And I know Tess was silent, but what do you expect when a child's just lost her father? They were very close, you know. She never mentioned Jeff again. Not to me, anyhow.'

'Do you think he did it on purpose?' asked Jean. 'Gerard and the accident, I mean. Did he realise what he'd done and . . .'

'Ran away? Maybe. He couldn't have faced being locked up. But we're back with your imagination again, aren't we? And I don't know how much of it to believe.'

'What are you going to do about Tess now? You're sure you're going to get her that treatment you were talking about?' This was Tracker. He looked as though his head was hurting him again.

Hanna was as irresolute as in the old, Malcolm days. 'Perhaps she'll feel better when she wakes up,' she said hopefully.

'Poor little kid's been carrying round the memory of that day all these years,' said Jean. 'And she must have had the knife hidden away upstairs somewhere. You've got the money,' she said, practically. 'Tracker's right about buying her some expensive therapy.'

'Do the police have to be involved? Or the Social Services or someone? I feel as though I've had enough of them recently to last me a lifetime,' said Hanna.

'Not if Tracker keeps quiet about what happened

today.' Jean kicked Tracker, who was looking uneasy at the mention of the police.

'Yeah, OK. You can stop kicking me now, Jeannie. There isn't much I could tell the police, really, is there? And I'd look a bit of a fool if I said that a ten-year-old girl had nearly killed me.'

'Yes, that's right, Tracker. You'd look an idiot. Better remember that and keep your mouth shut.'

Tracker was determined on one thing, however. 'But that kid's mad, right? Barking. You've got to get her seen to, Hanna. Get her head fixed. Otherwise I'll tell people this story, even if I do look a prat.'

'And what about Gerard?' asked Hanna. 'And Jeff?'

'They're both dead now. I don't see that it will help anyone to resurrect that old story. I think you should let them rest.'

'Just one more thing,' said Tracker. 'You haven't convinced me about Malcolm. Are we still quite sure that Joe killed him? It seems a bit of a coincidence to me, having two homicidal juveniles under one roof.'

'But the police wouldn't have arrested him if they hadn't been sure he'd done it,' said Jean. 'They need evidence and a proper case.'

'Tess had nothing to do with Malcolm's death,' said Hanna. 'She couldn't have done. She'd grown too fond of him in the last few weeks of his life.'

'If you both say so,' said Tracker.

Upstairs, Tess was waking from her sleep.

'Are you there?' she called softly.

There was no reply.

Gerard looked down at her from the silver frame. His

eyes were blank. He was, she saw with relief, only a
photograph locked safely behind the glass in a frame.

She turned over and went back to sleep.

'I suppose I should thank you for saving my life.'

Jean was driving Tracker back to town in her green
van.

'Yes, you should. But think nothing of it, Tracker.' She
didn't tell him that Tess had already decided not to stick
her knife into him. He must have been unconscious
during that part of the drama, but it wouldn't do any
harm to have him unfairly grateful to her. It was time
someone or something made Tracker feel guilt and
gratitude.

'I don't suppose there's a bed going spare at your
place, is there?'

'No, Tracker.'

'Only I'm not sure where I'm going to sleep tonight.'

For a moment she weakened. Then she remembered
the sight of his naked figure crossing Hanna Benson's
spare bedroom. There was a limit to how much she could
ignore of the past, in spite of the afternoon's events. She
pushed out of her head the picture of Tracker lying on
the ground, bleeding and unconscious and vulnerable.
Don't start going soft, she reminded herself.

'No, Tracker. I can't help you.'

She had drawn up on the corner of Fridesley Road
and Waverley Lane: Tracker could walk to wherever he
was going from here. As she leaned across and opened
the passenger door, her eye was caught by a flash of red
in the glove compartment.

'But just to show I've forgiven you, I've got a farewell

present for you, Tracker,' she said. She placed something hard and sticky in his hands.

'What is it?'

'A jar of home-made wild-berry jam.' She closed the van door, depressed the clutch, shifted into first gear and took off the handbrake.

'Eat and enjoy!' she called through the open window as she moved away.